'Mr Devlin—'

'Alistair,' he whispered

'Mr Devlin,' Victoria
eyes. 'I beg you to listen to me—

'I don't want to listen,' he said, drawing close. 'I want…this.'

And then…he kissed her.

Victoria had been kissed before; once by a fumbling youth in a childhood game, and once by a friend in a Christmas theatrical. But she had never been kissed like this. Never been made to feel as though she was in danger of losing her mind. The searing heat of Alistair's mouth obliterated every rational thought, and for a moment she didn't care that she must tell him a potentially damaging truth.

All she knew was that she was falling in love with Alistair Devlin. Whatever happened tomorrow would have no bearing on that.

Slowly, reluctantly, they drew apart, their eyes holding each other's in the dim evening light. Victoria hadn't known it was possible to feel like this, but she did know that things would never be the same between them again. Soon she would have to tell him the truth. Soon she would have to explain why this secret life had been imposed on her. But in the aftermath of his kiss all she wanted to do was draw his head down to hers and kiss him again…

AUTHOR NOTE

The theatre has always been a popular form of entertainment, and it was well attended during the Georgian and Victorian periods. Jane Austen frequently went to performances at Drury Lane and Covent Garden when she was in town, and many a notable actor and actress rose to fame during this period. To others, however, it was a breeding ground for sin and corruption.

NO OCCUPATION FOR A LADY was born out of a single question. What might a gently bred lady do that was not entirely respectable and not widely approved of by society? The answer? Almost anything to do with the theatre—so naturally my heroine had to become deeply albeit secretly involved with the writing and production of plays.

This meant I needed an aristocratic hero who was not an avid theatregoer, who despised deception in all forms, and whose own interests were as far removed from the frivolous world of the theatre as possible. Throw in an eccentric uncle who owns a theatre, a mother who thinks it's the devil's playground and a brother who hates the spotlight and you have the makings of a family disaster—and, hopefully, of a compelling love story.

I hope you enjoy this light-hearted romp through the world of Regency theatre!

NO OCCUPATION
FOR A LADY

Gail Whitiker

MILLS & BOON

First published in Great Britain 2012
by Mills & Boon, an imprint of Harlequin (UK) Limited.
Harlequin (UK) Limited, Eton House, 18-24 Paradise Road,
Richmond, Surrey TW9 1SR

© Gail Whitiker 2012

ISBN: 978 0 263 89273 4

Harlequin (UK) policy is to use papers that are natural, renewable and recyclable products and made from wood grown in sustainable forests. The logging and manufacturing process conform to the legal environmental regulations of the country of origin.

Printed and bound in Spain
by Blackprint CPI, Barcelona

Gail Whitiker was born on the west coast of Wales and moved to Canada at an early age. Though she grew up reading everything from John Wyndham to Victoria Holt, frequent trips back to Wales inspired a fascination with castles and history, so it wasn't surprising that her first published book was set in Regency England. Now an award-winning author of both historical and contemporary novels, Gail lives on Vancouver Island, where she continues to indulge her fascination with the past as well as enjoying travel, music and spectacular scenery. Visit Gail at www.gailwhitiker.com

Previous novels by this author:

**Did you know that some of these novels
are also available as eBooks?
Visit www.millsandboon.co.uk**

Chapter One

It was important that one dressed appropriately for the theatre, if for no other reason than to spare oneself the embarrassment of being underdressed should someone of consequence happen to be seated in the box next to you. After all, one never knew when a marriageable viscount or an eligible earl might wander in for an evening's performance, and with so many single young women looking to find husbands, a girl couldn't afford to miss a single opportunity.

That, at least, was the justification Mrs Bretton had always given her two daughters for looking their best, and as Victoria Bretton studied her reflection in the cheval glass, she supposed it was not a bad way for an ambitious mother to think. The importance of presenting unwed daughters in the most favourable light possible could not be understated, whether it be at a musicale evening, a grand ball, or at the début of a new play at the elegant Gryphon Theatre, even if only Victoria thought the latter an occasion worthy of attending.

Fortunately, what she saw in the glass was enough to reassure her that it would not be her appearance that fell short of expectation that evening. Her gown of imported ivory silk was in the first state of fashion, and the exquisite pearl-and-ruby necklace lent to her by her aunt served as the perfect accessory. The flashing crimson stones nestled sweetly in the *décolletage* of her gown, which, as Aunt Tandy had pointed out, was neither too demure nor too daring, and her hair, once likened to the colour of clover honey, had been swept up and arranged in a most sophisticated style by the skilled hands of her aunt's French maid. She looked every inch the proper young lady society expected her to be.

What would they say, Victoria mused as she turned away from the glass, if they knew what this evening was really all about?

The house was quiet as she made her way down the long curving staircase to the black-and-white-tiled hall. Candles flickered brightly from wall sconces and chandeliers, casting a warm golden glow over the elegant furnishings, while portraits of long-dead aristocrats stared down at her, their critical expressions seeming to offer silent disapproval of her plans.

Victoria paid them no mind. Her concern was with the living, not with the dead.

Besides, they were not portraits of *her* ancestors. The paintings, like the house, belonged to her father's brother and wife, an eccentric pair of retired actors who owned a theatre as well as several houses in and around London. They had kindly allowed Victoria's parents the use of this house for the past two Seasons so that Victoria and her younger sister could make their entrance into society. Victoria had taken her bows last year, and with Winifred doing so this year Mrs Bretton was hopeful that at least one of her girls would end up married by the end of it.

The prospect of returning home to Kent with *two* unwed daughters in tow was simply too humiliating to be borne.

'Good evening, Miss Bretton.' The butler greeted her at the door. 'James has the carriage ready. Your brother has already gone out.'

'Thank you, Quince.' Victoria turned to allow the elderly gentleman to settle a velvet cape about her shoulders. 'Do you know where my parents and sister are dining this evening?'

'I believe with Sir Roger and Lady Fulton, miss.'

Ah, yes, the baronet and his wife—a promi-

nent society couple with two sons of marriageable age, the eldest of which Winifred was
hopeful of attracting. She certainly wouldn't
pass up an opportunity to spend time with him
for something as trivial as a night at the theatre.

After all, what was the opening night of Valentine Lawe's newest play when compared to
the prospect of batting eyelashes at Mr Henry
Fulton over the silver epergne?

'Thank you, Quince,' Victoria said, careful
not to betray even a twinge of disappointment.
'Goodnight.'

'Goodnight, miss. Oh, and your father asked
me to wish you…a very successful evening. He
said you would know what he meant.'

Victoria smiled. A few simple words, as enig-
matic as they were brief, and her spirits rose im-
measurably. Dearest Papa. Always her ally, even
in this. She thanked the butler and walked out
into the cool evening air. The late April day had
been unusually warm, but the evening tempera-
tures had begun to drop as soon as the sun went
down, making her grateful for the enveloping
warmth of the cape.

'Evening, Miss Bretton,' the coachman said
respectfully.

'Good evening, James.' Victoria smiled as the
under-coachman helped her into the carriage.
They didn't have an under-coachman at home in

Kent. There they functioned with only a cook, two maids, a kitchen helper and a good-natured fellow who served as both footman and groom. If they had to get anywhere, they either walked or used the gig. It was only since coming to London that Victoria had been exposed to such luxuries as personal maids and closed carriages, and the one into which she stepped now was sumptuous in the extreme. The interior was lit by the glow of two small lamps, the walls were lined with maroon silk festooned with gold tassels and the cushions were of plush maroon velvet.

Her brother was already seated inside reading a book. Laurence was a fine-looking fellow, or could have been if he made more of an effort. His jacket of dark-blue superfine over a plain white waistcoat didn't fit quite as well as it had last year and his thick, wavy hair was dishevelled, giving him an appearance of rumpled affability. Wire-rimmed spectacles perched on the end of a very handsome nose and he had a smudge of what looked like ink on his thumb.

'Let me guess,' Victoria said as she sat down across from him. 'White's *Observations on Certain Antiquities*, or Norden's *Travels in Egypt and Nubia*?'

'Neither,' Laurence said, dutifully setting the book aside. 'A recently acquired copy of Savary's *Letters on Egypt*. I thought it would make

for some light reading on the way to the theatre.'
He took off his spectacles and placed them on
top of the book. 'What about you? All ready for
what lies ahead?'

'I suppose, though I confess to being hid-
eously nervous,' Victoria confided. 'What if no
one comes?'

'Of course people will come. Uncle Theo expects the theatre to be sold out.'

'Uncle Theo is an optimist.'

'No, Uncle Theo is a man who knows his
business,' Laurence said calmly. 'He should,
given the number of years he's been at it. And
experience has shown that Valentine Lawe's
plays always do well.'

Victoria settled back against the velvet squabs
and wished she could feel as confident as her
brother. While it was true that all three of Lawe's
previous plays had met with critical acclaim, that
wasn't to say that any of his future works would
be guaranteed the same high level of success.
The theatre-going public was notoriously fickle.
What pleased them one day offended them the
next and, given the decidedly satirical nature of
Lawe's plays, it was quite possible some prom-
inently placed personage, believing himself to
be the butt of Lawe's wit, would take exception
to the humour and proclaim his disapproval to
anyone who would listen.

Still, there was nothing to be done about it now. In less than thirty minutes the curtain would rise and *A Lady's Choice* would make its début. The best anyone could hope for was that Laurence was right and that their uncle knew what he was talking about.

As usual, traffic in the city was dreadful—an endless stream of hackneys, barouches, tilburys and phaetons trundling over the cobblestones *en route* to their various evening pleasures. Victoria saw long line-ups of carriages outside several of the large houses in Mayfair and felt a moment's relief that her destination was not a grand house this evening, but the Gryphon, London's newest and most elegant theatre. Once a rundown warehouse, the old building had been extensively refurbished and was now filled with a small fortune in Italian marble, Venetian glass, and brocades and silks direct from the Far East. The seating was roomier and the boxes grander than at any other theatre in the city and the frescoes on the ceiling were said to have been painted by a descendant of Michelangelo himself.

As to the nature of entertainments provided, the Gryphon was not licensed to present legitimate drama, so had to settle for a variety of works ranging from comic operettas to the occasional burlesque. In the relatively short time it had been open, however, it had gained a reputation for providing quality entertainment and tonight promised more of that with the début of Valentine Lawe's newest play. Rumour had it that Sir Michael Loftus, theatre critic for the *Morning Chronicle*, was going to be in the audience, and Sir Michael's stamp of approval was as good as God's when it came to anything to do with the stage.

That, at least, was what her uncle had told her and, given his vast experience in the theatre, Victoria knew better than to doubt him.

Finally, the carriage rounded the last corner and the Gryphon came into view, a glorious, towering edifice that shone white against the darkening sky. Victoria caught her breath just looking at it. And what a crowd! Judging by the line up of barouches and landaus slowly making their way along the street, a goodly portion of society had come out for the opening.

'Almost there, Tory,' Laurence said as the carriage turned down the lane that ran alongside the theatre.

Victoria pressed a gloved hand to her chest and closed her eyes. 'I can't go in, Laurie.'

'Of course you can. Aunt Tandy and I will be waiting for you in the box and the play will be a smashing success. Uncle Theo said as much after the last rehearsal and you know he wouldn't lie.'

No, he wouldn't, because her uncle knew better than to offer false assurances when so much was at stake. Opening night was the first time eyes other than those of the cast and crew would be seeing the play and how the audience responded tonight would be a strong indicator of how long the play would run, how much money it would make, and what kind of effect it would have on the playwright's future.

A bad opening night could herald more than just an early end to a play's run. It could sound the death knell on a playwright's career.

'Give my regards to the cast,' Laurence said as the carriage drew to a halt. 'Tell Victor I expect a standing ovation, and Miss Chermonde that her performance had better warrant at least three curtain calls.'

'I'll tell them,' Victoria said as the door opened and James let down the stairs. 'Whether they heed you or not is another matter all together.'

And then she was alone. Standing in the street as the carriage pulled away, she took a few deep breaths to compose herself. No doubt the actors inside were doing the same. Stage fright was all part and parcel of opening-night madness, but hopefully by the time the curtain rose, the butterflies would have flown and the cast would have settled into giving the best performances of their lives. The audience would accept no less.

Neither, Victoria thought as she knocked lightly upon the unmarked door, would her uncle.

'Ah, good evening, Miss Bretton,' said the elderly gentleman who opened it. 'I wondered if I'd be seeing you tonight.'

'Good evening, Tommy. I thought to have a word with my uncle before the performance began. Is everything ready?'

'Aye, miss, as ready as it will ever be.' Thomas Belkins stepped back to let her enter. 'Had some trouble with the backdrop for the second act, but we got that straightened away, and Mrs Beckett was able to mend the tear in Mr Trumphani's costume neat as ninepence.'

'What about Mrs Roberts?' Victoria asked. 'Is she feeling better than she was at rehearsal?'

'Haven't heard her complain, but between you and me, she's a tough old bird who nothing short of death would keep from being on stage on opening night.'

The old man's cheerfulness did much to settle Victoria's nerves. Tommy Belkins had been in the theatre all of his life. Once an actor with a travelling Shakespearean troupe, he now worked behind the scenes at the Gryphon, overseeing the elaborate systems of lights, ropes, pulleys and reflectors that created the magic on stage. Both Drury Lane and Covent Garden had tried to lure him away, but Tommy had refused their offers, saying he'd rather work for pennies at the Gryphon than for a grand salary anywhere else.

Not that he did, of course. Her uncle paid a generous wage to all of the people who worked for him. It was one of the reasons the productions staged at the Gryphon were so good. He encouraged a spirit of co-operation and conviviality unusual in the theatrical world, and because Theodore Templeton was known for giving promising young actors a chance, he never found himself short of talent.

Still, in the end, it all came down to the quality of the play, and, knowing it was too late to do anything about that now, Victoria closed her eyes and whispered a silent prayer to St Genesius. It might just be superstition on her part, but she never ventured into a theatre without asking the patron saint of actors for his blessing.

Then, with both her brother's and Tommy Belkins's good wishes ringing in her ears, Victoria Bretton—alias Valentine Lawe—walked into the theatre and prepared to face whatever the Fates held in store for her.

The Honourable Alistair Devlin did not make a habit of going to the theatre. It was all right if no other more amusing pastime could be found, but given the choice between watching amateurish productions staged by men and women who suffered from the misguided notion that they could act, or spending the evening in the comfortably masculine ambiance of his club, he would always choose the latter. The only reason he *had* come tonight was to appease his good friend, Lord Collins, whose repeated requests that he come and see the nubile young actress he was intent on making his newest mistress had finally worn Alistair down.

'And I dare you to say she is not exquisite,' Collins said as they settled into their gilt-edged seats at the front of the box.

'I'm sure she will be all you have promised and more,' Alistair said, gazing with interest at his surroundings. 'You have always been an arbiter of female loveliness.' It was the first time Alistair had ventured inside the Gryphon, but not the first time he had heard about the celebrated theatre. Rumour had it that upwards of eighty thousand pounds had been lavished on the building's restoration and that a special company had been assembled to grace its stage.

According to Collins—who had already enjoyed an intimate liaison with another young actress from the company—it was not enough that an actor be able to recite his lines without stumbling. He must also be able to portray that character's feelings in such a way that the audience was moved to laughter or tears, without resorting to the facial contortions and physical gestures so often employed by under-talented performers.

Frankly, Alistair was sceptical. While he knew that some actors were talented enough to pull off such masterful performances, experience had shown him that most tended to fall back on the melodramatic posturings that left him entirely unmoved and prompted audiences to hurl both insults and orange peelings at the stage.

'By the by, did I mention that Signy has a friend?' Collins asked. 'Another actress in the company. You might do well to look her up, given that you're in the market for that sort of thing.'

'Thank you, Bertie, but I have absolutely no intention of looking for a new mistress,' Alistair replied, gazing at the magnificent frescoes overhead. 'The one with whom I just parted gave a new meaning to the word *vindictive.*'

Collins had the cheek to laugh. 'Yes, I did hear something about the glorious Celeste managing to knock over two rather expensive vases on her way out of your house.'

'Expensive? She wilfully destroyed a priceless Tang horse *and* a Sèvres vase that have been in my family for generations,' Alistair murmured. 'Grandmother Wilson still hasn't forgiven me for that lapse in judgement.'

Unfortunately, it wasn't only Celeste Fontaine's wanton destruction of family heirlooms that had prompted Alistair to end his relationship with her. It was the fact she had lied to him. She had told him to his face that he was the *only* man with whom she was keeping company, when in fact she had been spending as much time in Lord Lansing's bed as she had in his.

When Alistair had brought this trifling detail to her attention, Celeste had treated him to a performance that would have done the great Sarah Siddons proud. She had stormed out of the house, somehow managing to consign the two pieces of porcelain to their doom on the way, and the next day, had sent him a scathing letter in which she had told him exactly what she thought of his behaviour, adding that while he was an adequate lover, she believed his skills in bed to be highly overrated.

It was the contents of the letter that had hammered the last nail into her coffin. While not an arrogant man, Alistair took pride in his ability to please the opposite sex. As a callow youth, he had discovered that the sexual experience was heightened if both parties were able to enjoy it, and he had striven to learn the secrets of giving pleasure as well as taking it. So to have his skills in bed mocked by a woman who had never once left him in any doubt as to how much she enjoyed them seemed to him the height of hypocrisy.

Still, he'd managed to have the last word. Only last week, the celebrated courtesan had appeared at his door, saying with every appearance of contrition that she was genuinely sorry for the way she had behaved and that it was only in a moment of weakness she had succumbed to Lord Lansing's advances. At that point, she had batted her eyelashes and, with tears falling from her famous pansy-blue eyes, had begged him to take her back.

Alistair had not been moved. Giving her a handkerchief to dry her eyes, he had advised her to take herself back to Lord Lansing or whichever gentleman was keeping her and not to trouble him again. The one thing he would not tolerate from those closest to him was deceit. A woman who lied to him once would have no compunction about lying to him again and he had no reason to believe Celeste would not end up back in the arms of the man with whom she had already betrayed him.

Women like that always landed on their feet. Or on their backs, as the case might be.

It was then, as Alistair turned to ask Collins about the evening's performance, that his attention was caught by a movement in one of the boxes opposite. A young woman had stepped through the curtain and into view, emerging like a radiant butterfly into the sunlight. She was garbed in cream-coloured silk that shimmered with every movement and long, smooth-fitting gloves that covered slender arms from fingers to elbow. Her hair, a soft mist of golden curls, was arranged attractively around her head and, in the flickering light, Alistair saw flashes of crimson at her throat. She paused for a moment to watch the antics of the dandies and young bloods in the pit below, then turned to bestow a smile on the older woman and younger gentleman already seated in the box.

It was the smile that stopped him. As innocent as a child's, it tugged at something deep within Alistair's subconscious, reminding him of a time when life was simpler and pleasures more easily found. She looked as though there was nowhere she would rather be and nothing she would rather be doing than sitting in her box watching the performance taking place below.

Was that what drew him to her so strongly? he wondered. The pleasure she took in an activity he and the rest of society took so entirely for granted? Or was it the fact that she was, even to his experienced eye, an incredibly beautiful woman? Draped in silk and chiffon, she had the face of an angel, but a lush, sensual figure that made him think of hot nights between soft sheets and the sweet rush of intimacy as scented limbs wrapped around him and drew him close.

Unfortunately, given that the first thing the lady did was reach for the hand of the gentleman who rose to greet her, Alistair doubted it would be *his* body she ever wrapped them around. The two soon had their heads close together in conversation, and while it was clear the gentleman was no match for her in appearance or style, there was no denying the strength of the connection between them.

Lucky devil, whoever he was.

Then a ripple of anticipation as a tall and distinguished-looking gentleman walked out on to centre stage. He was dressed all in black, his long cape over breeches and boots giving him a decidedly swashbuckling appearance. Not a young man—his dark hair and beard were liberally threaded with silver and his lined face reflected the experiences of a lifetime. But he had a presence that could not be denied and when he held up one gloved hand, silence descended.

'Ladies and gentlemen, welcome to the Gryphon. My name is Theodore Templeton and tonight we present for your enjoyment two productions making their début on the London stage. *Mi Scuzi*, an operetta in Italian by Giuseppe Fratolini, and *A Lady's Choice*, a new work by the renowned playwright Valentine Lawe. The inimitable Signy Chermonde will play the role of Elizabeth Turcott opposite Mr Victor Trumphani in the part of Elliot Black. And now I invite you to sit back and prepare to be entertained.'

A polite round of applause greeted his words, as well as the expected whistles and jeers from the dandies in the pit. No sooner had he left the stage than the orchestra began to play and the curtain swept majestically upwards to reveal a setting reminiscent of a Mayfair drawing room, with a single actress, an elderly woman, seated in a wingback chair.

Alistair, who knew all too well that the build up to such productions was often the highlight of the performance, settled back and prepared to be bored.

He was not bored. He was mesmerized, the opening scenes of the play capturing his attention in a way no other stage performance ever had. The plot was intriguing, the dialogue witty and the cast gave such outstanding performances that, as the evening wore on, Alistair found himself growing more and more surprised.

This was not the type of performance he had come expecting to see. Knowing the play to be new and the company young, he had expected the production to reflect those shortcomings. But try as he might, he could find nothing to fault in either the play or in the actors' portrayals of their characters. Even the rowdies in the pit were silenced.

If this was an example of Valentine Lawe's talent, Alistair could well understand why the man was so popular. He was actually disappointed when the actors left the stage at the end of the first act.

'Well, what did you think?' Collins asked over the sound of enthusiastic applause.

'That it was far, far better than I expected,' Alistair said generously.

'Not the play! *Signy*! Is she not the most glorious creature you've ever seen?'

Alistair frowned. 'Signy?'

'The actress playing Elizabeth. Jupiter, don't tell me you didn't notice her?'

Alistair glanced down at the stage. Of course he'd noticed her, but as Elizabeth Turcott rather than Signy Chermonde. She was the glorious, titian-haired temptress who had made her first appearance on stage in the guise of an elderly woman sadly recounting the events of her long life, only to reappear in the next scene as a blushing bride on what was clearly the eve of her wedding. 'Yes, she was beautiful,' he agreed, 'but I was more impressed by her talent than I was by her appearance.'

'Then I can only hope she is as gifted in bed as she was on stage,' Collins drawled. 'Speaking of that, what did you think of Miss Lambert? And don't tell me you didn't notice *her*. Old Parker nearly fell out of his box the first time she walked on stage wearing that filmy white nightgown.'

Alistair laughed. 'Yes, I noticed her. She was very convincing in the part of Miss Tremayne.'

'Miss *Tremayne*?' Collins said. 'What's got into you tonight, Dev? The last time we went to the theatre, you couldn't even remember the title of the play, let alone the names of the characters.'

'That's because the play wasn't worth remembering and the actors were similarly forgettable,' Alistair remarked. 'This, however, is a first-class production.'

'Well, of course it is. Valentine Lawe is fast becoming one of England's foremost playwrights. Even a Philistine like you must have known that.'

The fact Alistair did *not* know failed to arouse any feelings of remorse or guilt within his breast. None of his family were ardent theatre goers. His parents refused to go as a result of the tragic events surrounding their eldest son's scandalous marriage to an actress, and his sister and brother-in-law, the Venerable Simon

Baltham, Archdeacon of Swithing, were of the belief that the theatre was a breeding ground for sin. It was their studied opinion that those who disported themselves upon the stage were vain and immoral creatures who sought aggrandisement through their occupations and were possessed of neither high moral fibre nor any discernible degree of integrity.

Ironically, it didn't stop them from attending the occasional operatic work, but seldom were they heard to praise a performance or to compliment any of the singers.

For his own part, Alistair didn't care. The only reason he had limited his exposure to the theatre was out of respect for his parents' sentiments and in an effort to maintain family harmony. A decision he hadn't come to regret… until tonight.

He let his gaze fall again on the occupants of the box opposite. The young lady was watching the antics of two young men rearranging props on stage, and looked, if possible, even more radiant than she had before the commencement of the first act. Her hand was again clasped in that of the gentleman sitting beside her, and when he leaned over to whisper something in her ear, she laughed and looked up—and, unexpectedly, locked eyes with Alistair across the theatre.

It was a fleeting glance, no more than a few

seconds in length, but for the brief space of that time, the noises around him seemed to subside and it was as though only the two of them sat in that crowded theatre. He watched her laughter fade until only the shadow of a smile remained, and though she didn't acknowledge his gaze, the soft colour blooming in her cheeks told him she was just as aware of him as he was of her.

As her glance slid away, Alistair leaned over to his friend and said, 'Collins, that woman in the box opposite…'

'Lady Lucy Prendergast?'

'No, the box above. Wearing the cream-coloured gown.'

Collins raised his opera glasses and trained them on the lady in question. 'Ah, yes, Miss Victoria Bretton. Eldest daughter of Mr and Mrs John Bretton.'

'How is it I haven't seen her before?'

'Because you don't move in the same circles, old boy,' Collins said, lowering the glasses. 'The family reside in Kent, but for the last two Seasons, have taken a house in Green Street for the purpose of introducing their daughters to society. Miss Victoria Bretton made her bows last year, and her younger sister, Miss Winifred Bretton, is doing so this Season.'

'Who's the man with her?' Alistair asked 'Dedicated husband? Devoted fiancé?'

'Good God, no, that's Laurence, her brother. Dry as a stick and completely lacking in fashion sense, but frightfully intelligent from what little I've heard. Apparently he speaks four languages and knows more about the classics than did most of his professors at Oxford. He and Victoria are said to be very close.'

'I'm surprised she isn't married,' Alistair commented. 'She is an exceptionally lovely young woman.'

'True, but she also has a penchant for speaking her mind and you can imagine how well *that* sits with the society matrons who believe young ladies should be seen and not heard. Also, do you see the rather flamboyant-looking woman seated in the box with her?'

Observing the lady's flame-coloured gown, her striking blue-black hair and the circle of diamonds flashing at her throat, Alistair said, 'It would be difficult not to.'

'Exactly. That is Mrs Anthea Templeton,' Collins said. 'Once a celebrated actress, now the second wife of Mr Theodore Templeton, owner of the theatre, and a man who just happens to be Miss Bretton's uncle.'

'Ah. So her family connections are not the best.'

'That's putting it mildly. Templeton left his first wife for the lovely Anthea—who was rumoured to be playing Juliet to his Romeo at the time—and the two set up housekeeping without the benefit of marriage. They continued to live and act in that blissfully unwed state for several more years before coming to London and setting up shop here. Needless to say, Mrs Templeton has not been embraced by society.'

'Hardly surprising,' Alistair said. 'She is no doubt accused of stealing Templeton from his wife and blamed for the demise of his marriage.'

'Of course, and the fact that Miss Bretton seems to enjoy her aunt's company naturally reflects badly on her. As does the fact that she has an unfortunate fondness for mingling with the cast.'

Alistair raised an eyebrow. 'She *fraternises* with the actors?'

'Oh, yes. Usually in the company of her brother, but she has been known to venture backstage alone,' Collins said. 'And while that is perfectly all right for him, it is *not* the thing for her.'

No, it wasn't, Alistair reflected as he watched the actors return to the stage for the start of the second act. It was all right for a young lady to go to the theatre and even to express enthusiasm for the performance she had seen, but it was not the thing to be spotted in the company of actors. While Alistair didn't agree with his brother-in-law's sweeping condemnation of all stage performers, he knew that many were possessed of questionable morals and that spending time with such people was frowned upon by those in good society. He was surprised Miss Bretton's parents would allow her to jeopardise her reputation by frequenting such a place, even if she did so in the company of her brother.

'By the by,' Collins said, 'is it true you've stopped seeing Lady Frances Shaftsbury? I thought the two of you were as good as engaged.'

'We were, until I found out Lady Frances was equally enamoured of the Marquess of Kopeham,' Alistair said distantly. 'If I cannot trust a woman to tell me the truth before we're married, what hope is there for honesty after the vows are taken?'

'All women lie, Dev. Harkens back to the Garden of Eden,' Collins said. 'Eve probably told Adam nothing would happen if he bit into the apple, and we all know how wrong that went.'

'Fortunately, there are more women in the garden now and a man isn't compelled to marry the first one that comes along.'

'Perhaps, but attractive daughters of wealthy earls don't come along every day either.'

'No, but I *will* not suffer the company of a woman who lies. Secrets may abound in society, but they have no place in the relationship between a husband and his wife,' Alistair said. 'If I cannot trust the woman to whom I would give my name, I would rather not give it at all.' For a moment, his gaze returned and lingered, somewhat regretfully, on Victoria Bretton. 'Life is unpredictable enough. No point making it worse by starting everything off on the wrong foot.'

Chapter Two

A Lady's Choice was an amusing satire about the foibles of married life. It was clever without being condescending, moralistic without being straitlaced, and funny without being ribald. Alistair actually found himself chuckling at the subtle innuendos flying back and forth and was moved to think that Valentine Lawe was a man who understood the ups and downs of marital relationships.

As such, when the actors delivered their final lines and Mr Templeton walked back on to the stage, Alistair rose to his feet along with the rest of the audience to pay the cast a long and well-deserved tribute.

'Thank you, ladies and gentlemen,' Templeton said. 'I am gratified by your response and delighted that *A Lady's Choice* has lived up to your expectations.'

'Where's Valentine Lawe?' shouted a voice from the audience.

The cry was picked up and echoed throughout the theatre, but Templeton only shook his head. 'I regret to inform you that Mr Lawe is not with us this evening, but I thank you on his behalf and will be sure to communicate your pleasure to him. And now, I am pleased to introduce the talented members of the cast.'

'Here we go,' Collins whispered in Alistair's ear. 'Pay attention. You're looking for Signy and Miss Lambert.'

The performers came out two by two, with the lesser members of the cast leading the way. A young actress whose performance had greatly impressed Alistair turned out to be a Miss Catherine Jones, who took her bows with the portly gentleman who had played the vicar. Miss Lambert, a buxom blonde with a voluptuous figure, came out with the older woman who had played the part of Elizabeth's mother.

Collins nudged Alistair in the ribs. 'There. Take note so you can find Miss Lambert later on.'

Alistair smiled, but saw no point in telling his friend he would have been far more inclined to approach the sylph-like Miss Jones than the overblown Miss Lambert.

Then Signy Chermonde and Victor Trumphani made their entrance to a thunderous round of applause. Signy was truly a beautiful woman and Alistair had no doubt she would enjoy an illustrious career both on and off the stage. Trumphani, too, possessed the kind of polished masculine appeal that would appeal to débutantes or duchesses, and after taking their final bows, the pair stepped back to let Mr Templeton reclaim centre stage.

'Thank you, ladies and gentlemen. I know I speak for Valentine Lawe when I say how pleased I am by your response to *A Lady's Choice*. I hope you will come back and enjoy it again. Now, after a brief musicale interlude, we present *Mi Scuzi!*'

Not surprisingly, a good portion of the audience stayed on its feet to get a better look at the people around them, but, having fulfilled his obligation, Alistair decided it was time to leave. Collins would no doubt abandon him to seek out his hoped-for new ladybird, and given that the occupants of the box opposite had already left, Alistair saw no point in staying for the operetta. His grasp of Italian was such that he could follow the lyrics if they were sung with any degree of proficiency, but he feared an English soprano with no ear for the language would mangle it beyond all hope of recognition. Better he leave now while he could still take away a favourable impression of the evening.

He was almost at the door when he saw her. Victoria Bretton was standing alone in the vestibule, her head down, her attention focused on the evening cape in her hands. She seemed to be attempting to undo a knot in one of the ribbons, but her efforts were hampered by the weight of the garment and by the constant brushing of people as they passed.

Clearly, the lady was in need of assistance.

Alistair slowly made his way through the throng and stopped a few feet away from her. She truly was a pleasure to behold. Her face was a perfect oval set upon a slender neck that rose from smooth shoulders seductively displayed by the low bodice of the gown. As he moved closer, his gaze dropped to the rubies nestled in the shadowy cleft between her breasts, aware that the stones were almost as magnificent as what they were nestled in…

'Can I help you, sir?'

The tone, completely at odds with the colour blossoming in her cheeks, caused Alistair to smile. 'Forgive me, Miss Bretton. I was lost in admiration of your necklace.' His gaze rose to a pair of bright blue eyes framed by long lashes under an artful sweep of honey-gold brows. 'It is…a striking piece.'

'It is a replica of one given to an Egyptian princess by a devoted swain. My aunt was kind enough to lend it to me for the evening.' Her chin rose, but her colour remained high. 'May I ask how you know my name?'

'I noticed you when you walked into your box,' Alistair said, seeing no reason to dissemble. 'When I asked my companion who you were, he kindly vouchsafed your name. May I?' he asked, indicating the cloak. 'Undoing knots is a speciality of mine.'

She glanced down at the twisted ribbons and, after a moment, said 'thank you' and handed the cloak to him, adding, 'Was there a reason you wanted to know who I was?'

'Curiosity.' Alistair tucked the garment under his arm and set to work. 'Most people prefer to observe the antics going on around them than the ones taking place on the stage. You were clearly more interested in the play.'

'It is the reason I come to the theatre,' she said simply. 'If I wished to observe society at play, I would go to one of the many soirées held for that purpose.' There was a brief pause before she said, 'Why did *you* come to the Gryphon tonight? To see the play or to watch the other entertainments taking place?'

Alistair smiled. It seemed Collins hadn't been mistaken when he'd said that Miss Bretton was fond of plain speaking. 'I came to see the play.'

'And what did you think of it?'

'That it was humorous, well plotted and skilfully enacted.'

'Then you enjoyed it?'

'I did.'

'Do you come often to the theatre, Mr—?'

'Devlin. And, no, I do not.' The knots untied, he shook out the cloak. 'On the few occasions I have, I've found the farces ridiculous, the historical adaptations weak and the melodramas pathetically overacted.'

'But you did not feel that way about *this* play?'

'No. I was caught up in the story from beginning to end,' Alistair said, placing the velvet cloak around her shoulders. 'Something rather rare for me and I admit to being pleasantly surprised.'

Then she did smile. Gloriously. Without reservation. The way she had smiled at her brother earlier—and the words were out of Alistair's mouth before he even realised he was thinking them. 'Miss Bretton, I wonder if I might call upon you tomorrow morning.'

Her eyes widened, but she did not blush. 'It

is very kind of you to ask, Mr Devlin, but I'm afraid I have a prior engagement.'

'Of course. Tomorrow afternoon?'

'I'm not sure what time I shall be home.'

'The following day, then?'

This time, a hint of colour did rise to her cheeks. 'Mr Devlin, pray do not think me rude or unkind, but there really is no point in you calling. You have told me all I wanted to hear.'

'About the play, perhaps, but there is so much more—'

'Actually, there is nothing more,' she interrupted. 'I appreciate the trouble you went to in finding me, but it would be best if you did not pursue this. It is evident we would not suit.'

'Not suit?' He gazed at her in confusion. 'How can you say that when you know absolutely nothing about me?'

'Ah, but I *do* know something about you, Mr Devlin, and it is that which compels me to demur. Good evening.'

With that, she walked towards the double doors where her brother was waiting for her and, slipping her hand into the crook of his arm, left the theatre with him.

Too bemused to offer a reply, Alistair watched them go, aware that for the first time in his life he was actually at a loss for words. *The lady had put him off!* He had gone to the trouble of

tracking her down and of making his interest
known—and she had put him off. Not because
she hadn't known who he was—but because she
had!

'What, still here, Dev?' Collins said, saunter-
ing across the floor to join him. 'I thought you
left half an hour ago.'

'I did, but I ran into Miss Bretton and stopped
to have a word.'

'How providential,' Collins drawled. 'Well,
what did you think? Was she as tactless and unpredictable as I led you to believe?'

The question recalled Alistair to the lady's
parting words. '*I appreciate the trouble you went
to in finding me, but it would be best if you did
not pursue this. It is evident we would not suit.*'

'She was far from tactless, but I am not convinced that meeting me was the highlight of her
evening,' Alistair said drily.

'Nonsense! Any girl would be delighted at
being singled out for attention by a nonpareil
like you.'

Alistair didn't bother telling his friend that
Miss Bretton hadn't seemed at all delighted by
her so-called good fortune. On the contrary, she
seemed genuinely convinced they had nothing
in common—and, irrationally, that irked him.
While it was true they *might* not have anything
in common, how could she know until they'd

had an opportunity to spend some time together? A man deserved a chance to fall from grace before a lady cast him out. Surely it was only fair he be given that chance before being dismissed out of hand.

Victoria had not spent many hours in sleep that night. How could she have slept when everything within her was shouting with joy! She had wanted to dance across the rooftops, to shout her happiness from the top of St Paul's.

A Lady's Choice had been a success! The cast had recited their lines to perfection, the scene changes had gone without a hitch and the musicians had timed their crescendos and pianissimos exquisitely. If she died this very instant, she would go to heaven with the most contented smile on her face.

The fact she had spent time talking to one of London's most eligible bachelors really had nothing to do with it. It had been pleasant to bandy words with the gentleman and flattering to know that he was interested in calling upon her, but at the moment, there was no room for romance in Victoria's life. And certainly not with a man like that!

'*Alors*, you are finally awake!' her maid said, appearing at Victoria's bedside with a cup of warm chocolate. 'And looking very 'appy.'

'That's because I am happy, Angelique.' Victoria sat up and stretched her arms over her head. 'It was a very good night.'

'Zey liked your play?'

'They *loved* my play! The applause went on for ever and the cast was called back three times to take their bows!'

'*Bon*! Did I not tell you it would be so?'

'Oh, yes, you can say that now when you know everything turned out well. That isn't what we were saying this time yesterday. At least,' Victoria added with a frown, 'it wasn't what I was saying.'

'Zat is because you do not 'ave enough confidence in yourself.'

'That's not true! I do have confidence in myself, but I write plays that suit me. I don't always know if they will suit my audience.'

'Of course zey will suit your audience,' the feisty little maid said. 'You are very good at what you do! Your uncle tells you so all ze time.'

Yes, because Uncle Theo had always been one of her most staunch supporters, Victoria reflected. He was the one who had encouraged her to write, impressing upon her the importance of allowing her artistic side to flourish, no matter what her mother or the rest of society thought.

Speaking of her mother... 'I don't suppose

you've seen Mama yet this morning?' Victoria enquired.

When Angelique didn't answer, Victoria turned her head—and saw the answer written all over the maid's face. 'Ah. I see that you have.'

'Do not take it to 'eart, mademoiselle,' Angelique said quickly. 'Madame Bretton does not love *le théâtre* as you do. She would prefer zat you find a nice man and get married.'

'Yes, I know, but a nice man won't let me write plays,' Victoria pointed out. 'He will expect me to sit at home and knit tea cosies.'

'Tea…cosies?'

'Hats for teapots.'

'Your teapots wear 'ats?' Angelique frowned. 'You English are very strange.'

Victoria just laughed and sent the maid on her way. She sometimes forgot that while Angelique knew everything there was to know about taking care of a lady, she was far less adept when it came to making conversation with one. Still, it came as no surprise to Victoria that her mother wasn't pleased about her success at the theatre last night. Having been raised in a rigidly moralistic house where the only occupations deemed acceptable for a woman were those of wife and mother, Mrs Bretton decried the idea of her eldest daughter doing anything else.

A *lady* did not involve herself with the world

of the theatre. A *lady* did not write plays that poked fun at members of society. And a lady did *not* discourage gentlemen who came up to them and made polite conversation, the way the dashing Mr Alistair Devlin had last night.

Oh, yes, she'd known who he was. Between her mother pointing him out to her at society events and listening to Winifred go on about him until she was tired of hearing his name, Victoria knew all about Alistair Devlin. The man owned a string of high-priced race horses, kept a mistress in Kensington and a hunting box in Berkshire, and was equally skilled in the use of pistol or foil. He patronized Weston's for his finery, Hobbs's for his boots and Rundell and Bridge for his trinkets.

He was also a viscount's son—a man who moved in elevated circles and who possessed the type of wealth and breeding that would naturally preclude her from being viewed as a potential marriage partner. Her mother had been right in that regard. Refined ladies did not direct plays or go backstage to mingle with actors and actresses. And no one but a refined lady would do for Lord Kempton's heir. As it was, Devlin's sister was married to an archdeacon, and for all Victoria's being the granddaughter of a minister, it would not be good enough for Devlin's family, so why bother to pretend the two of them stood *any* chance of finding happiness together?

Victoria was almost at the bottom of the stairs when she heard raised voices coming from the drawing room. But when she recognised two of them as belonging to her Aunt and Uncle Templeton, she quickly changed course and headed in that direction. Given the lack of warmth between her mother and her father's brother and wife, Victoria had to wonder what had brought them to the house so early in the day. She opened the drawing-room door to see her mother standing ramrod straight by the window and her father, looking far from relaxed, sitting in his favourite chair. Her uncle stood in the middle of the room and her aunt, flamboyant as ever in an emerald-green gown and a glorious bonnet crowned with a sweeping peacock feather, lounged on the red velvet *chaise*.

It looked for all the world like a convivial family gathering—until Victoria realised that no one was smiling and that the tension was thick enough to cut with a knife. 'What's wrong?' she asked, looking to her father for an explanation.

It was her uncle who answered. 'Victoria, my dear, I have just informed your parents of your stunning success at the Gryphon last night.'

'And I have been trying to tell your uncle it

is *not* a success!' Mrs Bretton snapped. 'It is an abomination.'

'Come now, my dear,' her husband said. 'I think *abomination* is doing it up a little strong.'

'Do you, Mr Bretton? Well, let me tell you what *I* think is doing it up a little strong. Your brother, trying to make us believe that Victoria has done something wonderful when anyone in their right mind would tell you she is making a fool of herself!'

'Oh, Susan, you are completely overreacting,' Aunt Tandy said with a long-suffering sigh. 'Victoria did not make a fool of herself last night. Her work was applauded long and loud by every person in that theatre. Your daughter is a brilliant playwright—'

'My daughter is a lady! And ladies do *not* write plays!' Mrs Bretton said, enunciating every word. 'They do *not* produce plays. And they certainly do not tell other people how to act in plays. Ladies embroider linens. They paint pictures. And they get married and have children. They do *not* spend their days at theatres with the most disreputable people imaginable!'

'Here now, sister-in-law, I'll have you know that not all actors are disreputable!' Uncle Theo objected.

'Indeed, I had a sterling reputation when I met

Theo,' Aunt Tandy said. 'And contrary to popular opinion, I *was* a virgin at the time.'

'Oh, dear Lord, must we be subjected to this?' Mrs Bretton complained. 'Will you not say *something*, Mr Bretton?'

Victoria looked at her father and wished with all her heart that she could have spared him this inquisition. He was a gentle man who disliked confrontation and who had spent most of his life trying to avoid it. Pity that his only brother and sister-in-law, both of whom he adored, should be the two people his wife resented more than anyone else in the world.

'I'm not sure there is anything to be said, my dear,' he said. 'I cannot help but be proud of what Victoria has accomplished—'

'Proud? You are proud that our eldest daughter has to pretend to be a man because if anyone found out what she really did, we would be cut by good society?' Mrs Bretton demanded. 'You are proud that she spends her days with actors and actresses and avoids the company of fine, upstanding people?'

'I do not avoid their company, Mama,' Victoria said. 'In truth, they have become the source of some of my most amusing and successful characters. Nor do I think my conduct is putting anyone in this family at risk. I have been very careful, both about what I say and about how I behave when in society because I know there is Winifred's future to consider and I *am* very cognisant of that. But to suggest we would be cut is, I think, going a little far. Other ladies write plays—'

'I do not care what *other* ladies do!' her mother snapped. 'I care about what *you* do and how it affects *your* future. Something you seem not to care about at all! Spending all that time at the theatre and consorting with people like that is not good for your reputation.'

'I am well aware that certain people think Laurie and I spend too much time at the theatre,' Victoria allowed, 'but surely the fact that Uncle Theo *owns* the Gryphon excuses us to some degree.'

'It does not excuse you, and in truth, I blame *him* for everything that's happened!' Mrs Bretton said coldly. 'If he had not encouraged you when you first went to him with your stories, we would not be having this conversation now. You would be doing the kinds of things a lady of good birth *should* be doing.'

'What, like taking a lover thirteen months after she married and produced the requisite heir?' Uncle Theo said laconically.

Mrs Bretton's face flushed crimson. 'I *beg* your pardon?'

'Haven't you heard? Lady Tavistocke went

to Venice and took up with a gondolier,' Uncle Theo said. 'Shocking scandal. Poor old Reggie Tavistocke doesn't know what to make of it.'

'Mind, you can't blame the poor girl, darling,' Aunt Tandy said. 'Reggie is getting on for sixty, after all, and you know how dashing Italian men can be. And gondolas are very comfortable. I've always thought the movement of the water very conducive to—'

'Enough!' Mrs Bretton shrieked. 'Get out of my house! Both of you!'

'In point of fact, this *is* my house, Susan,' Uncle Theo said amiably. 'And one I am very pleased to have you and my brother staying in. However, perhaps it is best we leave you to your discussions. Just don't be too hard on Victoria. She is not in the least deserving of it. Speaking of which, there is something I would like to say to her before we go.'

'Something *we* wish to say,' Aunt Tandy corrected him with a smile.

'Of course, my darling, something *we* wish to say. And that is, how very proud we were of you last night, Victoria. After you left, I had a visit from Sir Michael Loftus—'

Victoria gasped. 'Sir Michael!'

'Yes, and he was very impressed with your latest play. Or rather, with Valentine Lawe's latest play. He thought it was…now, how did he phrase it exactly? "A comedy of stunning brilliance exquisitely characterised and plotted with a deft hand."'

Victoria gazed at him in wonder. 'Sir Michael Loftus said I had a deft hand?'

'Those were his very words.'

She was floating on air. Euphoric. To have received such praise from one of the foremost critics in the theatre. She must surely be dreaming...

'And you looked absolutely beautiful,' Aunt Tandy said, giving Victoria an affectionate hug. 'I noticed several gentlemen watching you throughout the evening, Lord Vale and Mr Chesterton amongst them, and I hear even the top-lofty Mr Devlin stopped to speak to you.'

'Mr *Devlin*?' Mrs Bretton said with a gasp. 'Lord Kempton's heir *spoke* to you and you did not think to *tell* me?'

Victoria blushed, uncomfortably aware that her mother was staring at her with a mixture of astonishment and reproach. 'There really wasn't any point, Mama. We were not formally introduced and spoke only about the play.'

'But he *engaged* you in conversation,' Mrs Bretton persisted. 'Without benefit of introduction. He *must* have had a reason for doing so.'

'He thought I was in need of assistance,' Victoria said, her cheeks warming at the memory of his long, slender fingers undoing the knots in her ribbons…*and* of her turning down his request that he be allowed to call upon her. 'I'm sure it was nothing more than that.'

'Unfortunately, I tend to agree with Victoria,' Uncle Theo said, starting for the door. 'Women have been chasing Devlin since he was a boy, but no one's been able to catch him. I thought Lady Frances Shaftsbury was close to doing so earlier in the year, but even that appears to have cooled. And given Lord Kempton's resentment towards the theatrical world, I'd venture to say there's absolutely no chance of him allowing his eldest son and heir to pursue a relationship with Victoria.'

'But you just said no one knows Victoria *is* Valentine Lawe,' Mrs Bretton remarked. 'Why should that have any bearing on Mr Devlin's interest in her?'

'Because he *will* find out in the end, and I don't want to see Victoria left with a broken heart because the man cannot return her love,' Theo said. 'And I know that's how it will end. But come, Tandy, my dear, we must be getting back. Rehearsals start in less than two hours.'

'Yes, of course,' Aunt Tandy said. 'Will you be coming tonight, Victoria?'

'No, she will *not* be coming!' Mrs Bretton snapped in vexation. 'We are expected at Lord and Lady Holcombe's musicale this evening. *All* of us.'

'Pity,' Uncle Theo said. 'As it happens, we're sold out again. But then I expect we'll be sold out most nights from now on and I don't suppose you will be able to attend every performance.'

'She most certainly will not.'

'But I will be there as often as I can,' Victoria said firmly. Her sister might have come to London to find a husband, but her main purpose in being here was to see her play, and as many times as she could! 'Thank you both for coming. I can't imagine a nicer way to begin my day.'

'Our pleasure, my dear.'

They departed noisily, shouting goodbyes and congratulations as the drawing-room door closed behind them. Left alone with her parents, Victoria didn't know what to say. The joy she'd felt earlier was gone, trampled into the dust by her mother's patent displeasure.

Unfortunately, silence was not a problem from which her mother suffered. 'Really, Mr Bretton, if it weren't for the fact that you and your brother are so close, I would not allow him or that *woman* in my house,' she said huffily.

'That woman happens to be your sister-in-law,' her husband reminded her. 'And denying them entrance would be difficult given that, as

Theo pointed out, he does own this lovely house and several others in the area.'

'A fact he throws at us at every opportunity,' Mrs Bretton said bitterly. 'Oh, how I *wish* we had the wherewithal to do without him.'

'But we do not, so there is no point in wishing it true. Personally, I am very grateful to my brother for all he's done for us. You might find it in your heart to show him a little more gratitude.'

'Gratitude? You expect me to show gratitude to a man who earns his living from the stage and who left his first wife to marry that wretched actress?'

'As a matter of fact, I do. You may not approve of Theo and Tandy, but I will not hear you denigrate them,' her husband said quietly. 'If you cannot bring yourself to say anything kind, I suggest you say nothing at all.'

The gentle reprimand was clearly too much for Victoria's mother. Stamping her foot, she turned and flounced out of the room, prompting Victoria to offer her father a sad smile. 'I'm so sorry, Papa. I never meant to bring all of this down on your head.'

'You've not brought anything down on my head, Victoria, so don't even think to malign yourself in such a way. Though I know it is best not to say so in your mother's hearing, I am very proud of you. Writing a play is no small feat, and to have written four that have received such critical acclaim is worthy of commendation. I certainly couldn't have done it, but I'm as proud as punch that you have.'

'Oh, Papa, you are so good.' Victoria put her arms around his neck and hugged him. 'I don't know what I would do if both you *and* Mama despised the theatre.'

'I dare say it would be an impossible situation for all of us,' her father agreed. 'But, like it or not, your aunt and uncle's success in the theatre is what allows us to stay in this fine house. They have certainly been good to you, reading your work and producing your plays while making sure no one finds out who Valentine Lawe really is. We owe them a great deal, yet they ask for nothing in return and seem willing to turn a deaf ear to your mother's criticisms.'

'Indeed, they are exceedingly generous and forgiving,' Victoria agreed. 'I like to think my adding to the success of the Gryphon is in some small way a repayment for everything they've done for me. I only wish Mama could find it in her heart to be kinder to them…and to be happier about my own success. I don't like knowing I am the cause of so much grief within the family.'

'I know that, child, but your mother will be

fine. She is just afraid you will be found out. You cannot disagree that the nature of what you write would make you unpopular in certain drawing rooms if your identity were to become known,' her father said. 'And given that a large part of the reason for coming to London was to try to settle you and your sister in marriage, we must do whatever we can to present you in the best light possible. Personally, I think you've done an admirable job of keeping the identity of Valentine Lawe a secret.'

'I gave Mama my promise I would.'

'Just so. As to your spending more time at the theatre than other young ladies, I suppose it isn't a good idea, but Laurence is with you and no one could ever accuse him of moral misconduct.'

'No, though I wish he would make more of an effort socially,' Victoria said with a sigh. 'He is so quiet and reserved most women tend to overlook him.'

'He is a scholar, my dear, and scholars are not, by nature, outgoing fellows. But I have no doubt that when the right woman comes along, Laurence will sit up and take notice. And I fully expect to see a very different side to your brother when that happens.'

'Well, all I can say is that I hope she loves the theatre as much as he does. I've often wondered if he didn't have a secret longing to tread the boards himself.'

'Perish the thought! That *would* put your poor mother into Bedlam,' her father said drily. 'Now, off you go and talk to her about this evening's event.'

'Yes, I suppose I must.' Victoria's face twisted. 'I don't mind the Holcombes so much, but they really do invite the stuffiest people to their soi-rées.'

'I know, but it will be good for you to be seen in society for a change. It's time you gave some thought to settling down. Lord knows it's all your mother thinks about, and now that Win-ifred is out, it behoves you to marry well in order that she can do the same. I believe Henry Fulton was rather taken with her last night.'

'And why would he not be taken with her? Winifred is beautiful and accomplished and she will make some man an excellent wife,' Victoria said generously. 'But what man is going to want *me*, Papa? A woman who writes plays and even takes a hand in producing them? I am destined to become an ape-leader.'

Her father chuckled. 'Nevertheless, you must make an effort. Marriage will give you a home and children of your own, and who knows? If you have enough, you might be able to form your own troupe!'

Victoria burst out laughing. Only her father would say something like that—and only when her mother wasn't in the room. 'Dearest Papa. I hate to think what Mama would say if she heard you trying to persuade me in such a manner.'

'No more than I, Victoria,' her father replied with a smile. 'No more than I.'

Chapter Three

Lord and Lady Holcombe lived in a magnificent house filled with more exquisite artwork than many of London's finest museums. The walls were covered with paintings by every famous painter, living and dead, and entire rooms had been given over to showcase the hundreds of sculptures and historical relics Holcombe had collected during his travels around the world.

Meandering through one such room filled with ancient Roman artefacts, Alistair stopped to admire a jewel-encrusted dagger and wondered if anyone would notice if he slipped out through the French doors. As much as he liked the marquess and his wife, they really did invite the most boring people to their gatherings. If he heard one more lurid tale about Lady Tavistocke taking up with a gondolier, he would go mad!

Surely there were more interesting topics to discuss? The deplorable conditions in the East End. The bodies found floating in the Thames. Riots and child labour and conditions in the mills. Anything but this mindless prattle...

'—think Shakespeare was intent on pointing out the frailty of the human mind,' he heard a woman say. 'Lady Macbeth was clearly mad, but was it due to the guilt she felt over the murder she convinced her husband to commit, or as a result of her own unending quest for power?'

Alistair frowned. A bluestocking at the Holcombes'?

He turned to see who was speaking—and promptly bumped into another young lady who had clearly been waiting to speak to him. 'I beg your pardon—'

'No, that's all right, Mr Devlin,' the lady said, blushing furiously. 'It would be difficult not to bump into someone with so many people crammed together in one place.'

She smiled up at him in a manner that led Alistair to believe they had previously been introduced, but while her face was familiar, her name escaped him entirely. 'Are you having a good time, Miss...?'

'Bretton.' She pouted prettily. 'We met two weeks ago at the Roehamptons' reception. I was hoping you might remember me.'

He didn't remember her. He remembered her name. 'You're Victoria Bretton's sister?'

Her smile faltered, as though he had said something distasteful. 'Yes. Do you know my sister?'

'We met last night at the Gryphon.'

'You *spoke* to Victoria?'

'Indeed. I had the pleasure of conversing with her at the conclusion of the play.'

'A play, which, as I recall, you enjoyed very much.'

Alistair smiled. Oh yes, he knew *that* voice. Lower pitched and decidedly less breathless, it was not in the least anxious or in any way eager to please. 'Good evening, Miss Bretton.' He turned to find the elder Miss Bretton looking up at him. 'What a pleasure to see you again.'

'How nice of you to say so. Mr...Devlin, wasn't it?'

Her deliberate hesitation made him smile. 'I'm flattered you would remember.'

'Why would I not? It *was* only last night.'

'Yet how long the night seems to one kept awake by pain.'

She raised an eyebrow in surprise. 'I doubt you were in pain, Mr Devlin. Unlike Saurin's *Guiscard*.'

'Ah, but you do not know how I suffered in being so cruelly dismissed.'

The effect of this rejoinder was to make her laugh. 'You were not dismissed. And even if you were, it was not with any degree of cruelty.'

'Victoria, how nice of you to join us,' her sister interrupted in a chilly voice. 'When last I saw you, you were enjoying the pleasure of Mr Compton's company.'

Alistair frowned. 'Mr *George* Compton?'

'Yes. Victoria was partaking in a most lively conversation with him.'

'It was not a lively conversation, nor did I particularly enjoy it,' Victoria said. 'I made the effort because Mama asked me to, but having now fulfilled my social obligation, I am ready to go home. She sent me to ask if you would like to leave as well.'

'I would rather not.' Winifred sent Alistair a coquettish glance. 'I am enjoying a conversation with Mr Devlin.'

'So I see. Unfortunately, Mama said that if you were not ready to leave, she would like you to keep her company for a while. Papa is playing cards and you know she doesn't like to be left alone at these large gatherings.'

'But surely *you* can keep her company,' Winifred said. 'You don't *have* to go home right away.'

'In fact, I do. I promised Laurence I would help him with a project and I know he would like to work on it this evening. I *am* sorry, Winnie,' Victoria said gently, 'but I really do have to leave.'

Alistair wisely remained silent. It was obvious the younger Miss Bretton wasn't happy at being summoned back to her mother's side, but equally obvious that she knew better than to make a scene in front of an eligible gentleman.

'Oh, very well.' Winifred glared at her sister, then turned to offer Alistair an apologetic smile. 'I'm sorry we are unable to finish our conversation, Mr Devlin. I hope we will have an opportunity to do so the next time we meet.'

'I look forward to it, Miss Winifred.'

It was the polite thing to say, and when Alistair saw the sparkle return to the girl's lovely green eyes, he knew it had been the right thing. But he waited until she was safely out of range before saying to the lady who remained, 'Is your sister always so brusque, Miss Bretton?'

'Only with me.' Her smile appeared, but Alistair thought it vaguely preoccupied. 'She can be exceedingly pleasant to people whose company she enjoys.'

'She doesn't enjoy yours?'

'My sister does not entirely approve of me. She believes I am too opinionated and that I speak my mind when I would do better to keep silent. She also thinks I spend too much time at the theatre associating with people who are not worthy of my regard. An opinion shared by my mother and a number of others in society, I suspect.'

'They are not wrong,' Alistair pointed out bluntly.

'No, but I would be lying if I said it bothered me enough to make me stop,' she told him. 'I enjoy spending time at the theatre. I appreciate the beauty of the language, the intricacies of the plays and the diverse talent of the actors and actresses. Had circumstances been different, I wonder if I might not have enjoyed *being* an actress.' She gazed up at him without apology. 'Does that shock you?'

'You must know that it does. Most ladies take pleasure in more traditional pastimes such as reading and needlework. Activities that do not put their reputations at risk.'

'Yet you believe what I do jeopardises mine?'

'You've just said that it does, yet you do not seem to care.'

'Why pretend concern where none exists?'

'For appearances' sake?'

She laughed, a low, throaty sound that did the strangest things to his equilibrium. 'I am past doing things for the sake of appearances, Mr Devlin. Though you cannot be expected to know, I come from a rather unusual family. We are the equivalent of Lady Tavistocke and her gondolier…without Venice and its canals. And before you find yourself tarred by the same brush, I suggest you make good your escape.'

'My escape?'

'From my company. I did warn you last night.'

It took Alistair a moment to tie the two together. 'Is that what you meant when you said we should not suit?'

'In part. Look around if you don't believe me,' she advised. 'But be subtle, if you can.'

Alistair casually turned his head—and saw a group of dowagers quickly avert their eyes. Standing just behind them, an earl and his countess abruptly resumed their conversation, and as he secured two glasses of champagne from a passing waiter, he observed the top-lofty Mrs Howard draw her daughter away. 'Good Lord, is it always like this?'

'No. Sometimes it's worse.'

'Then why do you come?'

'Because Mama insists upon it. She is anxious for me to marry so that my sister can do the same. Hence the required conversation with Mr Compton.'

Alistair snorted. 'The man has four unmarried sisters at home. What kind of welcome do you think you would receive in an establishment like that?'

'None, but the fact I would *have* my own establishment is reason enough for my sister to believe I should make the effort.'

'Nothing would be reason enough to encourage George Compton,' Alistair said. 'As for your reception here, surely there are places you could go where you would be made to feel more welcome.'

'Actually, I don't do so badly. My uncle and Lord Holcombe did some business together last year and ever since, Lord and Lady Holcombe have been very welcoming towards us.'

Alistair watched Victoria raise the glass to her lips, his gaze lingering on the tempting curve of her bottom lip. 'So your uncle owns the Gryphon Theatre?'

'Yes. Does that surprise you?'

'Only in that if your mother is unhappy with the amount of time *you* spend at the theatre, I cannot imagine how she reconciles herself to the fact that her brother *owns* one.'

'With great difficultly, but as it happens, Uncle Theo is Papa's brother.'

'But his name is Templeton.'

'My uncle did that out of kindness to Mama,' Victoria explained. 'He was performing with a small repertory company when my parents met. Naturally, being the daughter of a minister, Mama was horrified that her future brother-in-law was on the stage, so hoping to make relations between them easier, my uncle assumed the surname of the first character he ever played. It made matters better at the time, though once he started buying up large chunks of property in London, I don't think anyone cared.'

'So your uncle is an actor.'

'*Was* an actor. He gave up performing not long after he married my aunt.'

'Who, I believe, is also an actress?'

'Yes, but she seldom appears on stage any more,' Victoria said. 'They are both more involved in the production end of things now. Pity, really, since they were both exceptional performers.'

Alistair stared at her in bemusement. A stunning young woman, eldest daughter of a gentleman, speaking not only without embarrassment about the black sheep of her family, but with admiration…?

'Devlin, where on earth have you…oh, I beg your pardon.' Lord Collins came to an abrupt halt. 'I wasn't aware that you and the lady were engaged in a conversation.'

'Then you're the only one in the room who isn't,' Alistair drawled. 'Miss Bretton, I believe you are acquainted with Lord Collins?'

'Indeed, I've seen him at the Gryphon quite

often of late,' Victoria said with a smile. 'I believe he has a fondness for Miss Chermonde.'

To Alistair's delight, Collins actually blushed. 'The lady and I are...acquainted, yes.'

'Then a word of advice, my lord,' Victoria said. 'As my uncle is aware of your...acquaintance with Miss Chermonde, I feel it only fair to warn you that, if you do anything to adversely affect the quality of her performance, he *will* take you to task. My uncle demands a great deal from the members of his troupe and if an actor or actress delivers a substandard performance, he will be looking to know the reasons why. And I should tell you that in his younger days, he had quite a reputation as a pugilist.'

Collins's blush receded, leaving his face starkly white. 'I appreciate the warning, Miss Bretton, but I can assure you I would never treat Miss Chermonde with anything but the utmost respect and I intend to shower her with gifts that will keep her very happy indeed.'

'Good. Just *please* do not feed her oysters,' Victoria said with a sigh. 'She *will* ask for them, but they make her sneeze and that ruins her voice for a good day and a half.'

'Then there will definitely be no oysters,' Collins said stiffly.

'Thank you. Well, I had best take my leave. Good evening, Lord Collins. Mr Devlin.'

Alistair bowed. 'Miss Bretton.'

Collins gave just a brief nod and waited until she was safely out of range before saying, 'Trumped-up little baggage! Imagine telling me what I should and shouldn't do with my own mistress. I should have told her it was none of her business!'

'But you did not,' Alistair said with a broad smile. 'In fact, your response was uncommonly meek for you, Bertie.'

The other man flushed. 'It was not meek! I was merely being polite. But you see what I mean about her being outspoken. And about how people treat her.'

'I saw a few old tabbies turn up their nose, but if she was that unacceptable, she wouldn't be here. They don't get much stuffier than the Holcombes.'

Collins sighed. 'You know Theo Templeton's her uncle, right? Well, he's also reputed to be worth a bloody fortune. No one knows where the money came from. Some say it's his wife's, others say he won it at cards. Either way, he's as rich as Croesus and doesn't give a damn what society thinks about him.'

'What has any of that to do with Miss Bretton?'

'Last year, when Holcombe ran into financial difficulties, Templeton bailed him out, no questions asked,' Collins said. 'Everyone's dying to know why, of course, but Holcombe isn't talking and neither is Templeton. But it's the reason Holcombe won't hear a bad word spoken about Templeton *or* about any member of his family, if you know what I mean.'

Alistair did. 'You're saying Templeton's kindness to Holcombe is the reason Victoria Bretton is accepted in society.'

'In part. Her immediate family are mindful of the proprieties, but her aunt and uncle are not and neither is she. She has gained a reputation for being blunt and there are those who predict she will suffer for it. In which case, having Holcombe on her side is a definite advantage. There's not many who'll gainsay a marquess.'

Alistair stared into his empty glass. No, there weren't. He'd dealt with his fair share of toad-eaters in his life and *his* father was only a viscount. There was even more grovelling the higher one climbed on the social ladder.

But Victoria's uncle wasn't even *on* the social ladder. He and his wife had both acted upon the stage, and the fact he was rich or that he had bailed out a peer of the realm would make no difference. He would still be viewed as a mushroom at best and an actor at worst; both of which would serve as strikes against him *and* against members of his family. 'Does Templeton move much in society?' Alistair asked now.

'To the extent he wishes. Beyond that, he doesn't seem to care.'

'What *does* he care about?'

'His wife, his theatre, his brother and his niece. Everything else can go to hell as far as he's concerned. At least, that's what I've been told.'

And Collins would know, Alistair reflected, given his current association with Signy Chermonde. 'An interesting man.'

'Eccentric, if you ask me,' Collins said with a sniff. 'But, when you're that rich, you can afford to do as you please. Victoria Bretton, however, is another matter. The lady falls somewhere between the devil and the deep blue sea. Even her own sister keeps her at a distance.'

Yes, Alistair had seen first-hand evidence of that. The lovely Winifred had all but curled her pretty little lip during her conversation with her sister, and if her mother was pushing her in George Compton's direction, it was evident the family was determined to marry Victoria off to any man who expressed an interest.

And yet the lady didn't seem to care. She had walked around that room with her head held high, blissfully serene in the face of all those hostile stares. She was the one who had drawn his attention to the way people were looking at her and to the effect it could have on his reputation. What did that mean? That the lady truly was impervious to the snubs and the remarks people were making about her? Or that she was simply a better actress than the celebrated Signy Chermonde could ever hope to be?

It was Victoria's habit to write early in the morning, usually long before the rest of the family were out of bed. Her mind was clearest at that time of day, and it was during those pre-dawn hours that she did her best work. But when on the morning following the Holcombe's soirée, the words did not flow freely, Victoria did not immediately put it down to anything that had taken place at the soirée.

While it was true the memory of her conversation with Alistair Devlin had kept her awake long into the night, she couldn't believe it was the reason she was feeling creatively stifled this morning. That kind of reaction usually came about as a result of her emotions being tied up in knots, and given that she and Alistair had spoken on only two prior occasions, the chance of having developed any kind of feelings for him was highly unlikely.

Yes, he was charming, and there was no question he was intelligent, but while those were qualities she would always admire in a man, Victoria wasn't looking for them in Alistair Devlin. She shouldn't even be *thinking* about the man. Her uncle had made it very plain that she would end up nursing a broken heart for her trouble because Alistair's position in society, and his father's antipathy towards the theatre, would always preclude them from having a relationship.

Then why *did* she keep thinking about him? And why, if he wasn't interested in her, had he sought her out and spoken to her at the theatre?

That was the question plaguing Victoria as she trotted her mare along Rotten Row an hour later. She had given up on the idea of writing and had asked for her mare to be saddled and brought round, hoping that a change of scenery would be good for her. But even though her groom rode far enough behind so as not to disturb her concentration, her mind remained stubbornly and most disappointingly blank. No clever ideas leapt to mind, and while she was reluctant to put a name to the cause, Victoria had a sinking feeling it was all because of—

'Miss Bretton,' came an all-too-familiar voice. 'What a surprise. I'd not thought to see you out so early in the day.'

Victoria looked up—and instinctively her hands tightened on the reins. 'Mr Devlin.' The *last* person she'd needed—or wanted—to see. 'I cannot think why. I did not stay late at the Holcombes' soirée.'

'No, but most ladies do not care to ride in the Park at a time of day when society is not around to admire them.'

'Ah, but I ride for pleasure. Not to be stared at by those who opinions matter not in the least.'

'Yet, anyone who sees you cannot help but be impressed by your beauty.'

Unexpectedly, his boldness made her laugh. 'It is a little early in the day for such excessive flattery, Mr Devlin,' she said, flicking a glance at the lady at his side, who wore a striking burgundy habit and was riding a pretty dapple-grey mare. 'Are you not going to introduce me to your companion?'

'But of course. Miss Victoria Bretton, may I present my cousin, Miss Isabelle Wright.'

Victoria started. His *cousin*?

'How do you do, Miss Bretton,' the lady said in a bright, youthful voice. 'What a pleasure to finally meet you. I was introduced to your sister at the Roehamptons' reception a few weeks ago and thought her ever so nice. Your aunt and uncle were there as well.'

Not having been at the reception, Victoria assumed Miss Wright was referring to her mother's brother and wife who lived in Edinburgh.

'I wasn't aware Aunt and Uncle Taitley were in London.'

'Oh, no, not *that* aunt and uncle. I meant the ones involved with the Gryphon Theatre. They are related to you, aren't they?' Miss Wright said. 'Mr and Mrs Templeton?'

Astonished that a cousin of Alistair Devlin's would be familiar with the owner of *any* theatre, let alone the Gryphon, Victoria said carefully, 'Yes, they are.'

'I thought so. I was terribly pleased to meet them. I truly believe your uncle stages some of the finest productions in London.'

'Why don't you tell Miss Bretton the name of your favourite play, Isabelle?' Alistair said with a smile.

The girl laughed. 'I don't suppose it's all that surprising. *A Lady's Choice*, by Valentine Lawe. Cousin Alistair tells me you've seen it too, Miss Bretton.'

'Yes, I have.'

'Did you not think it brilliant?'

'Well, I'm really not sure—'

'Oh, but you must, because Valentine Lawe *is* the most talented playwright in all London. Surely we can agree on that?'

Somewhat nonplussed, Victoria took a moment to straighten her mare's reins. How bizarre. She had never been asked a question about Valentine Lawe before, so really had no idea how to answer it. 'I suppose I would have to say that he is…quite good.'

'Quite good? My dear Miss Bretton, he is exceptional!' Miss Wright exclaimed. 'I've seen all of his plays: *A Winter's Escapade*, *Genevieve*, *Penelope's Swain*. But I think *A Lady's Choice* is definitely his finest. Have you met him? Cousin Alistair said you must have, given that your uncle produces all of his plays.'

'That would seem logical, but as it happens, Mr Lawe tends to keep…a very low profile,' Victoria said, sticking as close to the truth as possible. 'My uncle says he's never met a more reclusive playwright in his life.'

'Is that so?' Miss Wright's face was, briefly, a study in disappointment. 'I wonder why?'

'Perhaps he is afraid of being mobbed in the streets,' Alistair drawled, 'by overly enthusiastic fans like you.'

To Victoria's amusement, the girl actually blushed. 'It isn't nice of you to make fun of me, Cousin Alistair. I know you don't think much of Mr Lawe's plays, or of anyone else's for that matter—'

'On the contrary, I think Lawe's work is head and shoulders above *everyone* else's. I may only have seen *A Lady's Choice*, but based on that I am more than willing to acknowledge the man's talent. Just because I don't go to the theatre often doesn't mean I can't appreciate excellence when I see it.'

For a few heady moments, Victoria allowed herself the pleasure of basking in the warm glow of his praise. That was the worst part of not being able to acknowledge who she really was: being unable to express gratitude to people who enjoyed and appreciated her work. Especially a man like Alistair Devlin...

'Is he very handsome?' Miss Wright asked suddenly.

Guiltily, Victoria started. 'Who?'

'Valentine Lawe. Your aunt must have made some comment as to his appearance.'

'Oh. Well, I'm really...not sure. I've never asked her what she thought of him...in that regard.'

'I have a picture of him in my mind,' Miss Wright admitted. 'He's as tall as Cousin Alistair and his hair is just as dark, but he has the most amazing blue eyes you've ever seen. When he looks at you, you feel as though he's gazing right down into your soul.'

'Really?' Victoria hardly knew what to say. She'd never given a moment's thought to her alter ego's appearance. 'How...interesting.'

'And he's brooding, just like a romantic hero should be,' Miss Wright went on. 'But as brilliant as he is on paper, he's very quiet and withdrawn in person. And he dresses well, but only in black and white. And he wears a single red rose in his lapel and—'

'A diamond stud in his ear?' Alistair enquired. 'Or a gold hoop?'

'He is not a pirate, Cousin Alistair,' Miss Wright said, rolling her eyes. 'He is a playwright. And I'm not the only one who fantasises about his appearance. Ellen Standish thinks he's fair, Jenny Hartlett is convinced he has red hair and Mrs Johnston is of the opinion he hasn't any hair at all. But she is partial to balding men, so I suppose that is her idea of attractive.'

Victoria just stared, aware that the conversation was getting more bizarre by the minute. 'Well, if I am ever fortunate enough to meet… Mr Lawe I will be sure to communicate the details of his appearance to you.'

'You would do that for me?' the girl said, looking as though she had been given the secret to eternal youth.

'Happily. But I should warn you that I have no expectation of seeing the gentleman any time soon.'

'I don't care!' Miss Wright cried. 'It is enough to know that when you *do* see him, you will tell me what he looks like and I shall know whether

I have been right or wrong. Thank you so very much, Miss Bretton!'

Victoria inclined her head, grateful for having emerged unscathed from what could have been a very embarrassing situation. She didn't like telling lies, but what was she to do with Alistair Devlin sitting right there? She could hardly admit to being Valentine Lawe now when she had not told him the truth during any of their previous conversations.

She glanced at him sitting relaxed and at ease in the saddle and wished with all her heart that she might feel as calm. But her pulse was racing and when he smiled at her, it only grew worse, so much so that Victoria feared he must surely be able to *see* her heart beating beneath her jacket. Because his was a smile that was at once beguiling and disturbing, a smile that hinted at things she knew nothing about and had never experienced.

A smile that lingered far longer in her mind than it had any right to, and that would not be shaken, no matter how hard she tried.

Chapter Four

That evening found Victoria alone in the drawing room with a pencil and piece of parchment in her hand. The rest of the family had gone out, and though her parents had asked if she might like to join them, Victoria had excused herself by pleading a megrim. In truth, she was desperate to start writing again and while the evening wasn't usually a creative time for her, she needed to get past this wretched block and come up with some new ideas.

Unfortunately, the longer she stared at the blank page, the emptier her mind grew. Surely her burgeoning career as a playwright wasn't already over?

Needing reassurance, Victoria set the paper aside and reached into the pocket of her gown. She had managed to find a copy of Sir Michael

Loftus's review in the newspaper that morning
and had torn it out, basking in a warm glow of
satisfaction every time she read it…which she'd
done so many times she had actually committed
the piece to memory…

> …yet another piece of brilliance from the
> inimitable Valentine Lawe, *A Lady's Choice*
> is easily his best work yet. Lawe's deft
> handling of an intricate plot is exceeded
> only by his skilful use of characterisation,
> and, in typical Lawe style, he has
> lampooned members of society and the
> church in a way that one can only admire.
>   Performed at the Gryphon Theatre by
> that establishment's exceptional company,
> *A Lady's Choice* is a lively and thoroughly
> entertaining romp. I take my hat off to
> Signy Chermonde as Elizabeth Turcott
> and Victor Trumphani as Elliot Black,
> and once again, profess myself in awe of
> Lawe's talent. I look forward to seeing
> many more of his plays…

'"In awe of Lawe's talent,"' Victoria murmured, breathing a sigh of pure pleasure. It
wasn't every day Sir Michael Loftus delivered
such a flattering review. She knew that as a result of having read several of his less compli-

mentary critiques. The man could destroy a playwright's career in a single column. Or, as in the case of Valentine Lawe's, he could make it.

'What, not locked up in your room writing?' Laurence asked, strolling into the room with a book in his hand.

'I can't think of anything to say.' Victoria slipped the review back into her pocket. 'I'm having a devil of a time coming up with *any* ideas for my next play.'

'I shouldn't worry about it. You expended a great deal of time and effort on *A Lady's Choice*. It's really not surprising that the creative well has temporarily run dry.'

'But I've written three other plays and never had this problem before.'

'No, because as good as your other plays were, they didn't draw on the same level of emotional intensity,' Laurence said. 'You explored both the light and the dark side of love in your last play, Tory, and writing like that takes a toll. As Uncle Theo says, art demands passion and passion demands intensity…and intensity can be very tiring.'

'I hope that's all it is,' Victoria said, refusing to let her mind drift off in other directions…or to one other person in particular…

'So where is everyone tonight?' Laurence asked, settling into the chair across from her.

'The Hungerfords are hosting a card party.'

'Oh, Lord, that should be interesting.' Laurence opened his book. 'Mother and Father usually play together. I hope they're on better terms now than they were earlier.'

'You mean, has she forgiven him for standing up for his brother and sister-in-law when she thought he should have sided with her?' Victoria shook her head. 'I doubt it. You know how she likes to hold a grudge. But I suppose it's not her fault. She just wants me to find a nice man and get married.'

'Then why don't you?'

'Because I want to write plays and a husband won't let me do that. He will expect me to pay calls and arrange dinner parties, and to sit at home with no opinions of my own. He certainly wouldn't approve of my going to the theatre as often as I do now.'

'You don't know that,' Laurence said.

'Yes, I do. He can say what he likes before we're married, but once he puts a ring on my finger, he will expect me to be mindful of my responsibilities.'

'I think you're using the writing as a smoke-screen,' Laurence said bluntly. 'I think you don't want to get too close to a man because you're afraid of falling too deeply in love. I remember how devastated you were when Phillip Chesham left England without asking you to marry him.'

Victoria blushed, painfully reminded of a childish crush she was just as happy to forget. 'I wasn't devastated. I was just…surprised. I thought Phillip cared for me.'

'He did, but he was young, Tory, and he wanted to see the world. You just wanted to get married and settle down. It wasn't the right time for either of you.'

No, it wasn't, Victoria admitted, but while her heart and her pride had been wounded, it was her writing that had suffered the most. Emotionally crippled, she had gone for months without even feeling the *desire* to write. She wasn't willing to let that happen again. 'I agree that falling in love can be destructive to a creative mind,' she said. 'But I'm older and wiser now, and I've established myself in a career. I want to see how far I can take this and I know a husband would try to restrict my activities.'

'I wouldn't care if my wife wrote plays,' Laurie said conversationally. 'As long as she was happy, I wouldn't care what she did.'

'Even if she was an actress?'

Laurence blushed to the roots of his hair. 'What's that supposed to mean?'

'Oh, Laurie, I've seen the way you look at

Signy Chermonde and how you blush when she speaks to you.'

'I do not blush!'

'I'm afraid you do, dearest. You've gone quite pink even now.'

'Oh, God!' Laurence said on a groan. 'And here I thought I was being so good at concealing my feelings.'

'You forget, I'm your sister. I know you better than most. But you must know that nothing can come of it.'

'I'm well aware of that,' Laurence said, more than a little put out. 'She's taken up with that lecher Lord Collins.'

'That is entirely beside the point. Mama would *never* allow you to marry an actress,' Victoria said. 'You know how she feels about poor Aunt Tandy.'

'All too well,' Laurence murmured. 'Speaking of ineligible suitors, Winnie tells me you were monopolising Mr Devlin at the Holcombes' musicale last night.'

Victoria could feel the heat rising in her cheeks. 'I was not monopolising him,' she retorted. 'Winnie's nose is out of joint because I interrupted her conversation with the gentleman and then sent her back to Mama's side. I dare say she would be even more annoyed if she found out I'd met up with him in the Park this morning.'

'You never did. Was he alone?'

'No. He was with his very pretty and much younger cousin.'

'Are you sure she was his cousin?'

'I did briefly wonder if she might be his mistress,' Victoria allowed, 'but once I heard them talking, I realised there was nothing of a lover-like nature between them. She is terribly smitten, however, with Valentine Lawe.'

'She *told* you that?'

'Oh, yes, and I must admit, I found it very strange to talk about him as though he were a real person. I was informed that he wears a red rose in his lapel, which would only ever be black, and that he has dark hair and quite the most amazing blue eyes anyone has ever seen. If I didn't know better, I'd swear she was describing *you*!'

'Unfortunately, I lack the talent and flair necessary to fit the bill,' Laurence said drily. 'I take it you did not encourage Miss Wright to seek out an introduction?'

'As best I could without coming out and saying the man is pure fiction. But I did feel guilty about having to deceive her.'

'What else could you do? Mother would be furious if you'd told Miss Wright the truth, es-

pecially in front of Devlin. She hasn't stopped
talking about him since Aunt Tandy let slip
that you'd met him at the Gryphon.' Laurence
grinned. 'He must have been surprised to see
you at that time of the morning. Did you ex-
change pleasantries?'

'A few, but in truth, I spent most of the time
listening to Miss Wright go on about Valentine
Lawe. I believe Mr Devlin was as amused by
her fascination with him as I was.'

'A point of similarity, then.'

'The only one.' In spite of herself, Victoria
felt her cheeks grow even warmer. 'Mr Devlin
and I really have nothing else in common, Laurie. He has no fondness for the theatre, and that
would have to make matters difficult for me.'

'Not necessarily. Not all husbands and wives
enjoy the same things,' Laurence said. 'Our parents don't have many similar interests, yet they
manage to rub along fairly well.'

'Only because Papa is not concerned with
his position in life. Mr Devlin has to be and it's
quite likely I would be a terrible embarrassment
to him,' Victoria said. 'Besides, I'm sure he has
his clubs and his politics, and lives as indulgent
a life as most other gentlemen in his circle. And
he will be Lord Kempton one day and so has to
bear in mind the responsibilities and obligations
owed to the name. What could he possibly want

with a woman who has no desire to be married and who does exactly the opposite of what society expects her to?'

At half past two the following afternoon, Alistair Devlin snapped his pocket watch closed in frustration. He had instructed the estate agent to meet him at Gunninghill House at precisely two o'clock and it was now half an hour beyond that. If the man did not wish to sell the building, he should have just said so.

'Mr Devlin!' A rotund little man clutching a satchel under his arm came hurrying up the lane towards him. 'Hedley Brown. Apologies for my tardiness. I was delayed by my last client. Quite forgot he was coming.'

'Never mind, you're here now. I take it you have brought a key?'

'Yes, indeed, I have it here.' Mr Brown reached into the satchel and withdrew a key, which he proceeded to insert into the lock. 'Took me a while to find it. We haven't had much interest in this old place.' When the key wouldn't turn, he pulled it out, brushed off a few flecks of rust and reinserted it. 'I suspect it will need a bit of work to make it comfortable. Ah, there we are.' He pushed the door open to reveal a large, empty hall. 'However, it is a fine house and the price makes it quite attractive for...whatever purposes you have in mind.'

Alistair stepped across the threshold and gazed around the shadowy hall. No doubt Mr Hedley thought he intended to house his mistress here, though why he would establish a night-time lover at such a distance was anyone's guess. 'Lead on, Mr Brown. I am anxious to see more.'

The agent began the tour on the ground floor, which boasted a dark and rather dingy dining room, a breakfast parlour and what might once have been a library. Climbing the stairs to the first floor, Alistair was shown several good-sized rooms, some with windows that faced the road while others looked out over the badly overgrown gardens. Climbing yet another flight brought them to the bedrooms, each with its own dressing room, any one of which was large enough to accommodate several small beds. Above that were the servants' rooms and the attics. The kitchen, located below ground, was surprisingly large and well laid out.

It took fifteen minutes to view the house, less for Alistair to come to the conclusion that it was exactly what he needed. The space was commodious and, while there weren't sufficient windows, the ceilings were high enough that the space did not feel cramped. Outside, there was plenty of room for vegetable gardens and the fields could be used for play areas. There was even a small pond. Mrs Hutchins would have to keep an eye on the younger children around that, but the older ones could help out. 'I'll take it,' he said.

Mr Brown stared at him. 'But we haven't discussed the price.'

'There is no need. I told you how much I was willing to spend and instructed you to find a house that fell within that range. I assumed when I received your note that you had found such a place.'

'Well, yes, but—'

'Then there is nothing to discuss,' Alistair said, 'except when I can take possession.'

'Well, I suppose if everything meets with your approval, there is no reason why you may not do so as soon as you wish.'

'Excellent. Have you brought the papers with you?'

'Er…no.' Mr Brown's cheeks coloured. 'I had no idea our business would be concluded so swiftly.'

'Then I shall meet you at your office in precisely two hours. Pray have the papers ready for me at that time.'

Without waiting for the estate agent's reply, Alistair headed back in the direction of his phaeton. It always amazed him how some people could make an entire afternoon's work out of what should have been a simple transaction.

Still, the main thing was that the house was perfect for what he had in mind. It would take work to make it into what he wanted, but he had accounted for the cost of renovations in his calculations. It was unlikely he would have found anything better. If he had, the price would have been that much higher, or it would have been too far out of London to make it viable.

No, Gunninghill House would do nicely, Alistair decided, glancing up at the old stone building one last time. It had everything the children needed. For that, he could forgive the less-than-efficient Mr Brown his numerous shortcomings.

Although Victoria preferred dramatic works, she occasionally went to the King's Theatre for operatic performances. She had been fortunate enough to hear the great Italian soprano, Angelica Catalani, perform some years earlier and remembered it as being one of the few performances where the audience had actually been well behaved. Even the dandies who typically made the evening performances into something of a spectacle had been content to sit and listen to the diva sing.

Tonight, she and Laurence were to see a production of *Tancredi* by Rossini before going on to a card party at the home of one of Laurence's friends. Victoria had heard great things about Fanny Corri, who had been cast in the lead role, and expected it would make for a pleasant change.

What she had not expected was to see Alistair Devlin and Miss Wright seated in the company of another well-dressed couple in one of the best boxes in the house.

'If I didn't know better, I'd swear the man was following you,' Laurence murmured.

'Good thing you know better, then, isn't it?' Victoria quickly looked down at the stage. She had no wish to be caught staring at Alistair, but it was hard not to let her eyes drift in that direction. He was like fire on a winter's night—a source of heat that could burn if one ventured too close.

The performance began shortly thereafter and was a delight from beginning to end. Miss Corri was exceptional in the role of the heroine, Amenaide, and the mezzo-soprano singing the part of Tancredi had a marvellous voice. Only the gentleman playing Orbazzano fell short of expectation.

'I think he might have been the understudy,' Laurence said as they made their way out of the box at the end. 'He certainly wasn't up to the calibre of the other singers. But Miss Corri was well worth hearing. I suspect there will be a line up outside her door this evening. I wonder if Devlin will be one of them. Rumour has it he's looking for a new mistress.'

If either of them thought the nature of the conversation unusual, neither of them said so, perhaps because they had each been exposed to the theatrical world for most of their lives—a place where morals were lax and love and sex interchangeable.

Yet another reason, Victoria reflected, for men like Alistair Devlin to avoid her.

Still, the thought of him vying for the favours of an opera singer left her with a distinctly unsettled feeling. She preferred not to think of him as a man who took advantage of such women, yet everyone knew that well-born gentlemen chose mistresses from within the acting profession. She'd heard stories about his liaison with Celeste Fontaine and of their tumultuous parting, but she couldn't recall there being whispers about any other woman having taken her place.

Not that she cared, Victoria assured herself. What Alistair Devlin did with his personal life was certainly no interest to her.

Pity, then, that he should be the first person she encountered upon entering the lobby.

'Good evening, Mr Bretton,' Alistair said. 'Miss Bretton.'

'Mr Devlin,' Victoria said, striving for a casual tone. 'Did you enjoy the performance?'

'Mildly. I am not a great fan of opera, but I was persuaded to come by my sister and brother-in-law and prevailed upon to bring Cousin Isabelle as well.' He turned to introduce the couple standing behind him.

'A mediocre performance at best, wouldn't you agree, Miss Bretton?' the Archdeacon enquired.

'The tenor's performance, perhaps, but I thought Miss Corri was exceptional,' Victoria said, grateful not for the first time for the anonymity of her name. In her last play, she had poked fun at the character of an archdeacon, and while she hadn't had any particular archdeacon in mind, she suspected if Alistair's brother-in-law had seen the play, he would have taken offence. 'While she is not in the same league as Catalani, her voice is very fluid and her range is astonishing. I venture to say she has a promising future ahead of her.'

Mrs Baltham's left eyebrow rose a fraction of an inch. 'You seem to know a great deal about such things, Miss Bretton. You are an aficionado, perhaps?'

'Of course she is!' Miss Wright said with all

the naïveté of youth. 'Miss Bretton's uncle owns the Gryphon Theatre. I'm sure she knows everything there is to know about opera and the stage.'

It was not a recommendation. Victoria knew it from the way Mrs Baltham's nostrils suddenly dilated, as though finding herself in the presence of a vaguely unpleasant smell. 'Really? I was not aware of the connection.'

'It is not generally well known,' Laurence remarked.

'And I am sure you are happy it remain that way,' the Archdeacon replied stiffly. 'Come along, Isabelle.'

The dismissal could not have been more obvious. The Archdeacon and his wife moved away, leaving poor Miss Wright to follow numbly in their wake.

Victoria didn't say a word. Quietly fuming, she kept her eyes on the floor, painfully aware of the snub she and her brother had just been dealt.

'Well, I'll just go and find the carriage,' Laurence said, obviously feeling the awkwardness of the situation. 'Coming, Victoria?'

'A moment, Miss Bretton,' Alistair said quietly. 'Please.'

Victoria glanced at her brother and nodded. 'I'll be along directly.'

Laurence bowed and left them. As soon as they were alone, Alistair looked at Victoria with an expression she could only call pained and said, 'I am truly sorry for what just happened. They had no right to speak to you like that.'

'It is not for you to apologise, Mr Devlin,' Victoria said, anger lending sharpness to her tone. 'Clearly, your sister and brother-in-law are not as impressed with my connection to the theatre as Miss Wright so obviously is.'

'I fear they share my father's opinion in that regard.'

'Then why did they come?' Victoria was stung into replying. 'Is opera not a form of theatre?'

'I've always thought so, but the Archdeacon is of the opinion that the talent required to sing opera well puts those performers ahead of commonplace actors. It doesn't make any sense, but it is beyond my power or interest to try to change his mind. But I am sorry that you and your brother had to suffer for his prejudices.'

Victoria managed a thin smile. She hadn't been sorry to see the Archdeacon leave. She hadn't liked him any more than he had liked her. But she did regret that Alistair had been there to witness his disapproval, knowing it only served to reinforce what she had told him the night they had met. 'It isn't your fault, Mr Devlin. It is not the first time I have been criticised for my associations and I doubt it will be the last. With both an aunt and an uncle so heavily involved in the theatre, such snubs are hard to avoid.'

'Nevertheless, you are not an actress, nor have you anything to do with the profession. You simply enjoy going to the theatre, as so many do, and there is nothing wrong with that.'

Victoria glanced away, uncomfortable with the concern she saw in Alistair's eyes. Every time she saw him now, the pretence of innocence grew harder to maintain. When Miss Wright had expressed admiration for Valentine Lawe, Victoria had been able to assuage her guilt by telling herself how disappointed Miss Wright would be if she were to learn that the object of her affection was actually a figment of Victoria's imagination rather than a flesh-and-blood man. But standing here now, wilfully deceiving Alistair, left her with a decidedly hollow feeling, as though she was keeping secrets of a most immoral kind. 'It is not for me to criticise your sister and brother-in-law's beliefs, Mr Devlin,' she said in a low voice. 'But I hope you will not allow their prejudices to adversely affect Miss Wright's enjoyment of the theatre. She should be allowed to form her own opinions.'

'She will, but as long as she is a guest in my father's house, she will be exposed to his beliefs,' Alistair said slowly. 'And I must tell you, they are not favourable.'

'Yet she still goes to the theatre.'

'Her parents indulge her and they have instructed that she be allowed to do as she wishes. My father doesn't like it, but given that the final say is not his, he tends to ignore her. He finds her headstrong and opinionated.'

'Yes.' Victoria began to smile. 'I liked that about her from the start. But I am grateful for the explanation. And for the apology.'

'I would not wish you to think the Archdeacon's feelings are in any way a reflection of my own,' he said quietly. 'Because they are not. I look at you…quite differently.' He offered her a bow, then went to join the rest of his family.

Seeing Laurence waiting for her at the door, Victoria started in that direction, but the memory of Alistair's words lingered. '*I look at you quite differently.*'

'As I do you, Mr Devlin,' Victoria whispered under her breath. What a pity the gulf between them suddenly seemed wider than ever.

Chapter Five

There were only two cast members on stage when Victoria arrived at the Gryphon to speak to her uncle the following morning. Miss Catherine Jones, the young lady who had been engaged in the role of understudy to Signy Chermonde, and the actress playing Elizabeth Turcott's mother. Why the great actress herself wasn't on stage was anyone's guess, though Victoria suspected it probably had something to do with Lord Collins.

Fortunately, Miss Jones was giving a marvellous performance as Elizabeth, communicating the character's emotional suffering in a quiet and thoroughly believable manner.

'She has the makings of a fine actress,' Uncle Theo said as he came and sat down next to Victoria. 'I predict she will do very well.'

'Where did you find her?'

'At a small theatre outside Cardiff. She was playing Ophelia and caught my eye at once. After the performance, we talked for a while and I said if she was ever interested in coming to London, she should contact me. Much to my surprise, a year later, she sent me a letter, asking if the offer was still open.'

'How fortunate for you,' Victoria said. 'She hasn't Signy's exotic looks or her flair for the dramatic, but there is an innocence about her that is highly engaging.'

'I thought the same thing the first time I saw her. I'll likely cast her in *ingénue* roles and ensemble pieces until I've had a chance to work with her. She's already learned a lot from watching Signy.'

'Dare I ask where the great lady is this morning?'

'Still in bed, I suspect.' Her uncle kept his eyes on the stage below. 'The question is, whose?'

Victoria knew she shouldn't have laughed. Had she been more like her mother or sister, she would have been deeply embarrassed by the decidedly *risqué* comment. But her association with the theatre had long since stripped away those blinds of false modesty, allowing her to appreciate the humour in her uncle's remark. 'I did warn Lord Collins about the risks involved in doing anything that might adversely affect Signy's performance,' she said now.

'So far, other than make her late for rehearsal, he has heeded your advice. If anything, Signy's performances have become even richer and more compelling since she became his mistress. God knows what will happen when he discards her.'

'Do you believe he will?'

Her uncle shrugged. 'He did it to Sarah Littlewood last year. Completely devastated the poor girl. Couldn't remember any of her lines and spent most of her time crying. It was the reason I had to let her go.'

'But Signy is far more beautiful.'

'Yes, but men like Collins don't take relationships like that seriously. Once they tire of their mistresses, they move on. When that happens, I predict an emotional storm of such staggering proportions it will leave Signy incapable of performing in any but the most pathetic of tragedies. I shall have to have a play in hand for just such an occasion.' Her uncle grinned. 'In the meantime, I am well pleased with Miss Jones. She makes a very appealing Elizabeth.'

'She does indeed,' Victoria said. Then she sighed—and her uncle picked up on it at once.

'What's wrong?'

'Nothing.'

'Yes, there is. You only sigh like that when you've something on your mind. Has your mother been complaining about us again?'

Victoria managed a weak smile. 'No. This has nothing to do with you or Aunt Tandy.'

'Then what?'

Victoria stared down at the stage, listening to Miss Jones recite the lines she had written. Lines that had come so easily to her in the past, but that didn't any more. Not since Alistair Devlin had walked into her life. 'You said something the morning after the play, about there being… very little chance of Mr Devlin pursuing a relationship with me,' Victoria said slowly. 'Why did you say that?'

'Are you asking because you like Mr Devlin and have some hopes in that direction?'

'No,' Victoria said, feeling her face burn. How ironic that where talk of mistresses didn't make her uncomfortable, the mention of a romantic association with Alistair did. 'I am well aware that he is far above my touch. But he is… an interesting man. Witty, clever. Exceedingly charming.'

'Charm runs in the family. His grandfather was one of the most charming men I ever met,' Uncle Theo said, 'though he was also one of the most boring. His son follows in his footsteps.' He leaned back in his seat and rested his arm along the back of the chair next to him. 'Have you seen much of Devlin since the night the two of you met?'

'Not really. I spoke to him at the Holcombes' soirée, then again whilst riding in the Park. The last time I saw him was at the King's Theatre. Laurence and I had gone to see a performance of *Tancredi*. Mr Devlin was there with his sister and brother-in-law, who, I must say, were not in the *least* charming.'

'Ah, yes, the Archdeacon and his wife,' her uncle said with a sigh. 'I've run into them more than once and it's never been a pleasure. You would think the Archdeacon's position in life would make him more tolerant, yet I find he condemns rather than commends, and as far as he is concerned, the theatre is a virtual pit of human frailty.'

'Yes, he made that quite clear the night I spoke to him,' Victoria said. 'I made the mistake of expressing an opinion as to the calibre of the performers, whereupon Miss Wright told him I knew everything there was to know about opera and the theatre because I was related to you. Once the Archdeacon heard that, neither he nor his wife had any particular interest in furthering the acquaintance.'

'I'm not surprised. The theatrical world isn't well thought of by anyone in that family.' Her uncle hesitated before saying, 'Has anyone told you the story about Devlin's older brother, Hugh?'

Victoria didn't have to pretend surprise. 'I wasn't even aware he *had* an older brother.'

'He doesn't any more. Hugh died some years ago. Tragic set of circumstances,' her uncle said. 'Hugh Devlin was a fine man. Handsome, charismatic, even more charming than his father and brother. But he fell passionately in love with an actress and when his father refused to let them marry, they eloped to Scotland and married there.'

'Gracious! Who was she?'

'Her name was Sally Tamblin. I doubt you would have heard of her. She wasn't in the theatre long. But she was an extremely beautiful young woman who more than one young buck fancied himself in love with. But there was only ever one man for Sally.'

'Hugh Devlin,' Victoria whispered.

Her uncle nodded. 'The pair were madly in love. And they did run away and get married, but it didn't turn out well. Within a few years, Hugh contracted a fever and died, leaving Sally to raise their daughter alone. And though he wrote a letter to his father asking him to take care of his wife and daughter, Kempton refused, saying he wanted nothing to do with either of them.'

'How cruel!'

'Kempton's a proud man,' her uncle said. 'He disowned Hugh the day he ran off, and when Sally and her daughter turned up at his door asking for his help, Kempton turned them away, saying they were no relations of his. He blamed Sally for the disgrace his son had brought upon the family, and, not surprisingly, his anger grew to encompass the entire acting profession. It's the reason he won't set foot in a theatre to this day.' Her uncle sighed. 'It is also the reason he would never condone a relationship between his son and a woman known to have close ties to the theatre.'

'Close ties,' Victoria said softly. 'Like mine to you and Aunt Tandy.'

'I'm afraid so.'

Victoria stared at the edge of the box where a loop of golden braid had come undone. Absently, she reached out and tied the pieces together. 'I had no idea.'

'There's no reason why you would. No one talks about it any more. But because you asked, I thought it best to tell you the truth. I would hate to see you get hurt.'

'I doubt it would have come to that,' Victoria said, trying for a convincing smile. 'Even without his father's sentiments, I knew there was very little chance of anything developing between Mr Devlin and myself. He is a man who demands honesty above all, and I have told him nothing but lies since the night we met.'

Her uncle's dark brows drew together. 'Why would you say that?'

'Because he doesn't know I'm Valentine Lawe. And I can't tell him because I gave Mama my promise I would not.' Victoria stared down at the stage, though it was Alistair's face she saw. 'I don't need anyone to tell me there is no future for a woman like me, with a man like that.'

There were few enough reasons for a gentleman to be in the vicinity of the Gryphon Theatre at half past ten on a Tuesday morning. There were even less for a lady, and Alistair had to admit to a moment of surprise when he saw Victoria Bretton emerge from the building unaccompanied by either her brother or a maid. 'Miss Bretton,' he said, drawing his phaeton to a halt. 'Good morning.'

She had been looking to the left, but turned upon hearing his voice. 'Mr Devlin!' Her dismay, momentarily obvious, was quickly concealed. 'This is a surprise.'

'It is indeed,' Alistair said, aware that while her appearance was as correct as that of any lady strolling on Bond Street, the fact that they were nowhere near Bond Street was bound to raise questions. 'Might I ask where you are bound?'

'Home. I was about to hail a hackney.'

'Then perhaps you would allow me to convey you in that direction.'

'I would not wish to inconvenience you.'

'It is no inconvenience,' Alistair said truthfully. 'I have a stop to make on the way, but if you do not mind waiting, I would be happy to see you home immediately thereafter.'

She hesitated for a moment, but obviously seeing no reason to hire a public carriage when a private one was offered, walked down the steps towards him. 'Thank you. That would be most kind.'

He climbed down to assist her and within moments they set off again. Alistair kept his attention on the road, though he was conscious of the warmth of her thigh brushing against his, and the scent of her perfume sweetening the air around him. Something innocent, yet unknowingly provocative. 'I was surprised to see you coming out of the Gryphon at this time of the day,' he said, forcing his mind to more practical matters. 'Have you been to see your uncle?'

'Yes. I needed to speak to him.' She glanced down at her hands. 'About…a costume.'

'A costume?'

'Yes. For Lord and Lady Drake's masquerade.' Her eyes finally lifted to his. 'You must have been invited.'

'Of course. As was the rest of my family.'

'You sound as though you would rather not go.'

'In all honesty, I don't enjoy dressing up and pretending to be someone else,' Alistair admitted. 'I have none of the actor's spirit in me. However, as it is Isabelle's first masked ball, I have agreed to take her along. More to the point, I have been asked to effect an introduction to Lord Drake's youngest son, Lord Robert.'

'I've heard Winifred speak of him,' Victoria said, remembering her sister's one-time hopes in that direction. 'Do you think Miss Wright will like him?'

'I have no idea. I don't usually get involved in matchmaking, but I believe they have much in common and Isabelle could certainly do worse.'

'She is a delightful young woman,' Victoria said.

'She is lively and spontaneous and my family doesn't know what to make of her,' Alistair said baldly. 'They find her lacking in decorum when it comes to talking about the things she doesn't like, and far too open in her enthusiasm of the things she does.'

'Like Valentine Lawe?'

He slanted her a sidelong glance. 'Indeed. Why women swoon over men like that is completely beyond me. Look what it did for Lady Caroline Lamb,' he murmured. Then, breathing deeply, said, 'What *is* that fragrance you're wearing?'

He saw colour bloom in her cheeks. 'It is…a special blend from a perfumer on Clifford Street. My aunt took me there when I first arrived in London.'

'If it is the store with which I am familiar, the proprietor charges a hefty fee for his custom blends.'

'Yes, but he also guarantees that no other woman in London will ever wear that same fragrance,' Victoria said. 'The exclusivity of the product appealed to my aunt.'

Her sudden burst of defiance made Alistair smile. 'Your aunt is, I believe, something of an original.'

'I have always admired her flair for the dramatic and her gift for plain speaking.'

'Qualities shared by her niece, I am discovering.'

He didn't turn his head, but he felt the weight of her gaze on him. 'How is it, Mr Devlin,' she said, 'that on such short acquaintance, you feel you know me well enough to offer such opinions?'

'There are certain women whose manners make them easy to identify, Miss Bretton. You and I have not spent a great deal of time in conversation, but what time we have has allowed me to form an opinion of your character. You spoke plainly at the Holcombes' musicale and, by doing so, revealed much of yourself.'

'Then I must remember to guard my tongue when I am around you.'

'I'm glad to hear you say that.' Finally, Alistair did turn to look at her. 'At least you have given me hope that I *am* likely to see you again.'

He watched colour run hot and quick over her face, but he also saw a flicker of pain darken the brilliance of her gaze. 'I told you the night we met that you would do well to avoid me, Mr Devlin,' she said, 'and nothing that's happened since has induced me to change my mind. You were given proof of that at the Holcombes' musicale, just as you were by your sister and brother-in-law's reception of me at the King's Theatre.'

'Fortunately, I care little for my brother-in-law's opinions and I am used to the pettiness of society,' Alistair said. 'Assumptions about other people's characters are all too often made without the information necessary for such opinions. People see a beggar in the street and believing him to be without, see no reason to ask him what manner of man he is. He might be able to quote Plato and Aristotle, but he is assumed to be ignorant because of his appearance. The Archdeacon suffers from the same misconceptions. For all his being a man of the cloth, he is quick to dismiss based on what his eyes tell him. Your uncle owns a theatre and both he and your aunt have spent time upon the stage, but that doesn't make *you* an actress or entitle people to treat you like one.'

'No, but I am despaired of for reasons other than just my family connections, Mr Devlin.' Victoria's smile appeared briefly, but he saw what looked like resignation in her eyes. 'I speak too plainly for most people's liking and while I do some of the things I am expected to, for the most part, I derive little pleasure from them. I suspect many of the ladies with whom I socialise would be horrified to know that their behaviour only gives me more fodder for—' She broke off abruptly, her blush deepening. 'That is…they would not like to think I was being cynical of what they said, or of how they said it. Their goal is to be married and they see nothing more important than that.'

'And you do.'

'My goal is to lead a happy and fulfilled life.'

'You do not think marriage would give you that?'

'I believe marriage to the right man might

make me happy,' Victoria said carefully, 'but there are things that would give me greater pleasure and I fear they are not the type of things any man would willingly smile upon.'

'Like what?'

'Independence. The freedom to pursue the activities I wish, as I wish to pursue them.'

'You intrigue me, Miss Bretton,' Alistair said quietly. 'You have from the moment we met.'

'Only because I am not like the ladies with whom you normally associate. It is human nature to be curious about that with which we are not familiar.' Her smile appeared, but there was a pensive shimmer in her eyes. 'But I think we have spoken quite enough about me for one day, Mr Devlin. I should like to know something of you and how a gentleman like you passes his time.'

Alistair shrugged, reluctant to talk about himself when he was so much more interested in her. 'I am heir to my father's title and am, therefore, involved in the business of the estate.'

'Does your father not employ his own man of business?'

'He did, but they parted company last year. When my father discovered my skills in that area, he encouraged me to make use of them and to develop them further.'

'Still, you cannot spend all of your time poring over account books and journals,' Victoria said. 'You must have time to enjoy the kind of activities so often indulged in by young men of your class.'

'My class,' he repeated in amusement. 'What does that mean exactly? That I while away my hours in idleness and debauchery?'

Alistair made the remark in a light-hearted manner. He was surprised when she did not respond in kind. 'I cannot speak to the latter, Mr Devlin, but my knowledge of the type of men with whom you associate would lead me to believe the former.'

'The type of men with whom I associate?'

'Mr Bentley-Hyde and Lord Shufton. Your good friend, Lord Collins.'

'You do not like Lord Collins?'

'I neither like nor dislike him,' Victoria said, though the tone in which she said it led Alistair to believe she was not being entirely truthful with him. 'From what I understand, he is not engaged in any worthwhile activity and wastes much of his time in hells and brothels.'

'And in the company of women like Signy Chermonde,' Alistair said, wondering if Collins's association with the actress had anything to do with Victoria's sudden reserve.

'At present. No doubt he will have a different mistress by the end of the Season. I've heard that he is fickle.'

'And you see me as being no different?'

'I do not know you well enough to say.'

'But based on what little you *do* know of me, you are willing to say that I am no better than Collins, whom you acknowledge to be a rake and a wastrel.'

'I did not say that,' Victoria said quickly. 'Pray do not put words in my mouth, Mr Devlin. It is simply that I have seen you on several occasions with nothing more pressing to do than to enjoy every minute of your life.'

'I see,' Alistair said. 'So apart from minding my father's books and occasionally checking in on the welfare of his estates, I have little else of value to occupy my time, is that what you're saying?'

'If you have, I would be happy to hear about it.'

If you have… Alistair's mouth tightened. So, that was what she thought of him. That he was an indolent gentleman with nothing better to do than while away his spare time in brothels and hells. How lowering to see himself through her eyes. To think he had been about to tell her about Mrs Hutchins and the children. Perhaps even to take her there and explain what he hoped to do with the new orphanage. To try to make her understand how important the work was to him. He could only think now how fortunate was the timing of her remarks. He had no intention of proving himself to her—or to anyone else. 'I regret, Miss Bretton, that your opinion of me is so low,' he said at length. 'Clearly I am no different to you than the beggar in the street.'

'That's not true!'

'Isn't it? You see me as being rich and indolent, with nothing more important to do than while away my time in idle pursuits. But you know nothing of my life or of the type of man I am,' he said, turning the carriage left at the next street. 'Which is your house?'

He saw her look around in surprise, as if only now becoming aware of where they were. 'I thought you had a call to make first.'

'I did, but the nature of my business would have prevented me from including you in it and I had no wish to leave you standing in the street.'

Alistair knew he was being vague, just as he knew from the expression on Victoria's face that she had absolutely no idea what he was talking about. Even so, he was totally unprepared for her next remark. 'Is it a gambling hell or a brothel from which I have kept you, Mr Devlin?'

The question stung; the casual assumption that he must be bound for one or the other an unexpected blow to his pride and his self-esteem.

But he would not let her see how hard the blow had landed. 'In my experience, there is little difference between the two. Both offer pleasure without obligation. The type a gentleman like myself enjoys above all.'

He heard a soft exhalation of air. 'Then you do not deny that you were *en route* to one or the other?' she whispered.

'You have obviously made up your mind about who and what I am,' Alistair said with a feigned lack of concern. 'Far be it from me to disappoint you.'

'Stop the carriage here,' she said tersely. 'I will walk the rest of the way. I only hope I did not keep you too long from your…intended purpose.'

'You did not. The lady will wait all day for me if she has to.'

He saw her stiffen and knew she had taken his statement exactly as he'd intended.

'How fortunate for you. No, thank you, I can get down myself.'

'Don't be silly,' Alistair said, jumping down and holding his hand out to her. 'A lady is not meant to disembark a phaeton without assistance.'

It was true, she did need his help, but the moment her feet touched the ground, she pulled away. 'Thank you, Mr Devlin. It has been a most enlightening morning.'

'In more ways than you know, Miss Bretton,' Alistair said, touching the brim of his hat. 'In more ways than you know.'

Alistair was not in a good mood by the time he reached his second stop of the morning, one located in a far more humble part of town than the one he had just left. There were no fancy wrought-iron railings here. No brass number plates affixed to freshly painted doors. Just grey stone houses that fronted on to narrow streets populated by people whose priority it was simply to get by.

He drew the carriage to a halt in front of one such house and glanced at the boy of sixteen leaning negligently against the wall. 'Mr Tanner,' he called, 'be so good as to make sure no harm comes to my property.' He tossed a shiny silver coin in the boy's direction. 'You may have this for your trouble.'

The lad snatched it out of the air. 'I'll pay it good mind, Mr Devlin.'

Alistair jumped down and headed for the front door. He was glad now that he had not brought Victoria here. Though he had toyed with the idea of showing her what he was involved with, it was clear to him now that her opinion of him was already formed. If she wished to think him a hell-born babe, so be it. It was no concern of his.

As expected, Mrs Hutchins was waiting for him. A compassionate woman of middling years, she had a round face and rosy cheeks, a generous figure and the energy of six. She still wore a plain-gold wedding band, even though she had been a widow these last five years, and the room into which she welcomed him was bright and cheerful—a reflection of the woman and all she brought to the job. 'Morning, Mr Devlin. If you'll give me a minute, I'll put on some fresh tea. I wasn't sure what time to expect you.'

'Thank you, Mrs Hutchins, but that won't be necessary. You have more than enough to do. How fare the twins this morning?'

The housekeeper's smile faded. 'Not as well as I'd hoped, sir. I had the doctor in as you instructed, but I don't know that he holds out much hope. It's their lungs, sir, and they're not going to get better.'

No, Alistair reflected grimly, they weren't. Too many years spent working in the mills for that. Barely eleven, the girls had gone in at six years of age and had toiled alongside their parents and their older brother until the mill had burned down and taken both parents and brother with it. After the funeral, they had been brought to London by a well-meaning uncle, only to be turned out by an aunt who wanted nothing to do with them. They had ended up on the streets until their ill health had brought them to the attention of the people Alistair paid to make sure such things were noticed.

Sadly, for girls like Margaret and Molly, there was only so much money and care could do.

'What about Teddy?' Alistair said, hoping for better news.

'I don't think he's in as much pain, but he's a brave little soul and doesn't say much,' Mrs Hutchins said. 'The doctor left some salve for his burns.'

Alistair nodded. Teddy Erskine was a climbing boy. Not the worst he'd seen, but bad enough. The lad had been skin and bones when he'd come to Mrs Hutchins, with a fear of almost everyone he met. Not only had he been forced up narrow chimneys alive with rats, he had been beaten by a cruel master. A sorry state for a boy of eight, Alistair thought grimly.

He stood up, tempted to pace, but the confines of the office gave him precious little room to do so. 'How many are left?'

'Ten,' Mrs Hutchins said. 'I sent twelve away with Mr Scott, as you instructed.'

'And you made sure families were kept together.'

'I did, sir. I hope you don't mind, but I sent young Edward White along with the Dawkins pair. I thought it would be easier for the three of them to stay together, being as they came in that way.'

Her concern moved Alistair to a smile. 'You know the children better than anyone, Mrs Hutchins. I have every confidence you would have done what was best for them.' His smile faded. 'How's Jenny?'

The matron's face clouded over with concern. 'I do worry about her, sir. She hasn't said a word since she arrived and she still cries every night. I try to spend as much time with her as I can, but I don't know how much good it's doing.'

'If nothing else, it's making her feel safe,' Alistair said. 'A trauma like that doesn't clear up overnight. Have they caught the man who did it?'

'Aye.' Alistair saw despair darken the woman's eyes. 'Her father turned himself in two days ago.'

'Dear God! Her *father*?'

'He'd been drinking hard, like he did most nights. But apparently, this night he was much worse. One of the fellows saw him stagger out of the tavern. When he got home, he took it out on his wife. Jenny's mother probably told her to run, fearing he'd go after her next.'

It was a harsh story, but one Alistair had heard many times over. Poverty brought out the worst in some men. Men who were decent when they were sober, but whose personalities changed under the influence of drink. The best thing that could have happened to Jenny was to escape such an environment, even though it might be years before she realised the extent of her good fortune.

'As soon as the new house is habitable, we'll move them all over,' Alistair said. 'Hopefully the fresh air and sunshine will help.'

'Fresh air will help Molly and Margaret's spirits,' Mrs Hutchins said, 'but it won't do much for their lungs. And Jenny's recovery is going to take time. But at least it will be better than being here. For all this being a safe haven, we're bursting at the seams. Do you have any idea when we'll be moving, sir?'

'The arrangements to purchase are finalised and I expect renovations to get underway soon, but there is still much that needs to be done,' Alistair said. 'I'll let you know more as we proceed.'

'Am I to tell the children anything?'

Alistair thought about that for a moment, then shook his head. 'Best not to just yet. While I'd like them to have something to look forward to, every day stretches long when you're waiting for something good to happen, and you're the one they'll keep coming to with questions.'

'Aye, but I'll never tire of telling them their lives are going to get better.' She managed a smile. 'You're a good man, Mr Devlin. I've met none better!'

Alistair smiled as he walked up the narrow staircase to visit the children. Now that the house in the country had been purchased, he couldn't wait to get the ten remaining orphans out of this building and into their new home. Children needed room to run and fields in which to play. As a boy, he'd craved such things. And though he had grown up in a mansion and Teddy Erskine a hovel, their basic needs were no different. The circumstances of Teddy's birth had simply denied him that right.

Fortunately, the circumstances of Alistair's would make sure Teddy and the others benefited from it.

As for Victoria Bretton, she could believe what she liked. He knew he was nothing like Collins or Shufton or Bentley-Hyde. He wasn't concerned solely with his own pleasures and he didn't spend his time getting drunk in the hells or whoring his nights away in high-priced brothels. He had the wherewithal to do something about the lives of those less fortunate than himself and he wasn't afraid to get involved.

He had his brother, Hugh, to thank for that.

The hardest part was choosing which children he helped and which he did not. The need was so great; the number of children orphaned or abandoned so high he could have spent his entire fortune and still not saved them all. But with Mrs Hutchins's help, and that of the two men who worked for him, he did the best he could. He intervened in the lives of those he could make better, or, in the case of Molly and Margaret, in those whose remaining years could be lived out with some degree of comfort.

As much as it irked him, Victoria Bretton could think what she liked, Alistair decided as he walked into the children's playroom. He knew how he spent his days and that was good enough for him.

Chapter Six

It was Mrs Bretton's habit to pay calls between the hours of eleven and one, so it came as no surprise to Victoria that it would be the time of day Uncle Theo stopped by to pay a call.

'I thought the house might be quieter,' he said as Victoria welcomed him into her writing room. 'I don't like to disturb the routine.'

Aware that it was her mother and not the routine he had no wish to disturb, Victoria just smiled. She wasn't about to tell him that his timing couldn't have been better, that she needed an escape from the gloominess of her thoughts because the memory of the harsh words she had exchanged with Alistair was making her miserable. 'I've just rung for tea. Will you join me?'

'Delighted, my dear.' He sat down in the chair across from the desk and crossed one elegantly clad leg over the other. 'So, how goes the battle of words?'

'Not well. I have been tossing around a few ideas, but when I sit down to write, my mind goes blank, which leads me to believe the ideas were not all that compelling to begin with.'

'Well, perhaps this will help stir your creative juices,' Uncle Theo said. 'I've had a letter from Sir Michael Loftus.'

Victoria's breath caught. 'A letter?'

'It was delivered this morning.' He reached into his jacket and withdrew the letter. 'I thought you might like to read it for yourself.'

Victoria's hands were shaking as she unfolded the heavy sheet of parchment.

Templeton,
It will likely not have escaped your notice that I am a great fan of Valentine Lawe's work. However, given the gentleman's penchant for privacy and his strange preference for your company, the opportunity to speak with him in person is difficult at best, so I write to you with my offer.
I have been approached by a certain Esteemed Gentleman who has much to do with the running of Drury Lane, and he has expressed an interest in talking to Mr Lawe

about his next work. I realise you have served in the capacity of producer for each of his four plays and perhaps you are both happy to continue with that arrangement. But the brilliance of the man cannot be denied and it would give me great pleasure to see one of his works staged at a theatre licensed for the production of more serious works. I do not know if Mr Lawe has any interest in writing plays of that nature, but I thought it worth the time and trouble to ask.

It will, of course, be necessary that you, Mr Lawe, and myself meet in person to discuss how best to proceed, but I believe Mr Lawe will find much in this offer to interest him. I trust you will communicate my desires to him. In anticipation of a response, I remain,

Yours most sincerely...

'"Sir Michael Loftus,"' Victoria finished aloud, her voice barely above a whisper. 'He wishes to see one of my plays staged at Drury Lane?'

'That seems to be the gist of the message,' Uncle Theo said with a smile. 'The question is, how do *you* feel about it?'

'I'm not sure.' Victoria sank down into the

nearest chair. 'To be accorded such an honour…
to have caught the eye of a man like that, and
possibly of Mr Elliston…how *can* one feel but
overwhelmed?'

'But with joy or trepidation? You know what
this means, of course.'

Victoria did. It meant she was to be granted
a face-to-face interview with one of the most
influential men in the theatre. A man who believed Valentine Lawe was a man.

It could be the beginning of a whole new
stage in her career…or the end of everything.

A light knock signalled the arrival of the maid
with tea and, being closest to the door, her uncle
opened it and took the tray from the girl's hands.
Only after he set it down and closed the door
again did Victoria say, 'I am cognisant of the difficulties, Uncle, but I cannot help but be gratified by the intent.'

'As you should be. If you were to write a play
for Drury Lane, you would be able to do the kind
of work you have been longing to do: a work of
serious drama. I'm sure the ideas would begin
to flow again. And Sir Michael's enthusiasm
is nothing to be made light of. Any playwright
would give his right arm to be so honoured.'

Victoria nodded as she picked up the teapot.
What her uncle said was true, but while the opportunity was enormous, the consequences were

equally staggering. 'What do you think he will say when he finds out that Valentine Lawe is really a woman?'

'I honestly don't know. Loftus and I have never been close so I've no idea how his mind works. But if he believes, as I do, that the play is the most important thing, it likely won't matter. Here, let me pour,' Uncle Theo said when he saw how badly her hand was shaking. 'You're going to end up with more tea in the saucer and that is a tragic waste of a good bohea.'

Aware that her uncle was right, Victoria switched chairs and let him pour. But it did not slow down the workings of her mind. 'What if he doesn't care about giving me away, Uncle? If he is willing to acknowledge me as the playwright and to work with me in the production of my next play, he may not be as inclined to keep my secret as you and Aunt Tandy have. Indeed, as my entire family has.'

'We could appeal to him to keep silent,' Uncle Theo said thoughtfully, 'but he may have no wish to do so. He may see nothing wrong with revealing the true identity of Valentine Lawe. Women have been writing for the stage for years, many without the need of a false identity.'

'But I have invited a certain amount of criticism of my plays by mocking those in society I feel deserving of it, and while I sometimes chafe at Mama's insistence upon keeping my real name concealed, there have been times when I have been glad of it,' Victoria admitted. 'If it was discovered that *I* am the author of those plays, I would be looked upon differently.'

'By some people, yes,' her uncle agreed. 'But it will be your decision whether or not you wish to face them. As I said, you would not be the first woman to be revealed as a writer of material for the stage.'

'No, but I would be the first of my *mother's* children to be so revealed,' Victoria said wryly. 'And we both know how she would react if that were to happen. She lives in fear now of the truth being made known, especially given Mr Fulton's ongoing interest in Winifred.'

'Well, these are all things that must be considered prior to your accepting Sir Michael's offer,' Uncle Theo said. 'While there is much to be gained, there is also a downside, and if you feel the negatives outweigh the positives, you must refuse.'

'But if I do, what might he have to say about any future plays I write?' Victoria asked. 'He may feel like a lover spurned, his praise turning to condemnation because I refused to work with him. He may feel I have slighted him professionally when there was never any intention of doing so, or that I have offended him personally when that was the furthest thing from my mind.'

'Or, he may accept that you are content to let me continue producing your plays at the Gryphon and that will be an end of it. Beyond that, I cannot speak to the direction of his response.'

Victoria sat back in her chair. Why did life have to keep taking these troubling turns? First her friendship with Alistair had gone awry, and now what seemed wonderful a moment ago had suddenly become an unwelcome weight hanging over her head. If she agreed to Sir Michael's offer, she risked exposing herself and her family for the deception they had played. If she refused, she might hopelessly damage her career.

And then there was Alistair. What would he say if the truth about her was revealed in such a manner? What would he think if he found out she had been lying to him all along? She knew that if her lies were exposed it would be the end of any semblance of a friendship with him. 'I don't know what to say.'

'Then for the moment, say nothing,' her uncle advised. 'I shall write back to Sir Michael and tell him I have no answer to give because Valentine Lawe is travelling on the Continent.'

'Will he not find that strange given that my newest play has just opened?'

'I think not. You are a creative soul. Why should he not believe that, having seen at least one performance of your play and knowing it to be a success, you would wish to escape for some much-needed rest? That is what I shall put to him and that your return is, at present, uncertain.'

'Will he expect you to forward the letter on to me?'

'He may, but I shall inform him that in my studied opinion, being away from everything to do with the theatre will be far more beneficial to your creative well-being than having to worry about coming up with a new play to satisfy him.' Her uncle finished his tea and stood up. 'I shall tell him that a mind as imaginative as yours needs time to restore itself. And I think I shall tell him in person. You know how persuasive I can be when I set my mind to it.'

'You were not acknowledged as one of the finest actors of your time for nothing.' Victoria likewise rose and put her arms around him. 'Thank you. Uncle Theo. I don't know what I would do if you were not looking out for my best interests.'

'My dear girl, do not forget that your best interests are also *my* best interests. If Valentine Lawe stops writing, I shall be forced to look

for a new source of material, and if you think
good writers are easy to come by, think again!'

Victoria laughed, as her uncle intended she
should, and when she sat down at her desk after
he'd left, she found her gaze not going to her
work but to the bust of Shakespeare that stood
on a pedestal by the window—a Christmas present from her aunt and uncle. 'How much simpler
it would have been had I been born a man,' she
whispered to the chiselled face. 'Then I would
not have to pretend to be Valentine Lawe. I could
proclaim to all the world that I *am* him!'

But in doing so, she would also never be anything more than a friend to Alistair Devlin and
that troubled Victoria a great deal more than not
being able to tell the world who she was. She
hated the thought of losing whatever good opinion he might still have of her. He had already indicated that she risked damaging her reputation
by spending too much time at the theatre, but
her involvement did not stop at the printed page.

Sitting unnoticed in the back of her uncle's
box during rehearsals for *A Lady's Choice*, Victoria had watched each of the actors perform,
after which she had given her uncle her opinion
of their portrayal of the part. Her uncle had then
approached the actor in question and suggested
any changes that were necessary. Not once had
he led anyone to believe that the opinions ex-

pressed were any but his own, and, apart from
the few occasions where Victoria had appeared
at rehearsals, no one knew she was there. If, by
chance, someone did happen to see her, her presence was accepted by the cast because she was
Theo Templeton's niece.

But Alistair Devlin was not related to her,
nor was he a member of the cast. Would he be
as willing to accept the role she had played as
she was to rationalise her need for playing it?

It was a few days before Victoria saw Alistair
again, though he was never far from her thoughts.
The memory of their last encounter, combined
with the knowledge that she might have to tell
him the truth, served to keep him uppermost in
her mind. As such, it was hardly surprising that
she would have little inclination to attend a garden party to which she was quite sure he would
have been invited.

'Is this not the most beautiful place, Victoria?'
her sister asked as they strolled through the picturesque grounds of Lord and Lady Hincham's magnificent estate. Winifred, radiant in a pale-blue
gown with a lacy white shawl arranged attractively over her shoulders, all but purred with pleasure. 'I would have loved to call this my home.'

'I'm sure you would,' Victoria said, 'but,

given that Lord and Lady Hincham no longer have an eligible son, the possibility is remote.'

'Impossible, more like.' Winifred's pretty mouth turned down at the corners. 'Had I come out a year earlier, I might have been able to catch Lord Clarkson's eye, but by the time I did, he had already announced his engagement to Miss Shutters.'

'Never mind, there are plenty of other eligible gentlemen out there,' Victoria said, of a mood to be conciliatory. 'Mama said Mr Fulton is quite taken with you, and there are bound to be other gentlemen anxious to secure your favour.'

'I wish Mr Devlin was one of them.' Winifred gazed longingly in the direction of that gentleman, who was strolling with his cousin on the lawn close to the house. 'Unfortunately, he seems more interested in you than he ever was in me.'

Victoria felt her cheeks burn. 'That might have been the case at one time, but I doubt it is now.'

'Why not?'

'Because I told him he would do better to look elsewhere.'

'Look *elsewhere*?' Winifred gasped in disbelief. 'Why on earth would you say something so foolish?'

'Because it is the truth. Neither he nor his family would ever approve of my outspoken nature,' Victoria said. 'Or of what I do.'

'Then stop doing it,' Winifred said, as though the solution was just that simple. 'What woman in her right mind would not wish to marry a man like that? He is handsome and charming and—'

'Heir to his father's title, yes, I know,' Victoria said, pausing to admire the picturesque scene of a stone bridge crossing a meandering stream. 'But that doesn't mean he is the right man for me.'

'Well, all I know is that if I were in your position, I would be doing all I could to encourage him. Mama would be thrilled to see you married to a man like that. She might even forgive you your involvement with theatre.'

Victoria kept her eyes on the path ahead. There didn't seem to be much point in telling her sister that even if her mother forgave her, Alistair's father never would.

'Oh, look, I think he's seen us,' Winifred said suddenly. 'The young lady seems to be pulling him in this direction.' She frowned as she squinted into the sun. 'Isn't that Miss Wright?'

'I think so.'

'He seems to be spending a great deal of time in her company. Do you think they are romantically involved?'

Victoria laughed. 'Not at all. I chanced to meet them in the Park the other morning and I can assure you, their relationship is purely platonic.'

Winifred sighed. 'How is it you keep running into Mr Devlin, whereas I, who diligently attend society events, have encountered him only twice?'

'There is far more to London than ballrooms and breakfasts, Winnie,' Victoria said. 'I've told you more than once to brush up on your equestrian skills. Gentlemen like Mr Devlin enjoy riding.'

'But I don't like horses.' Winifred made a moue of distaste. 'They're large and smelly and they bite.'

'It was a pony that nipped you and they are notorious for being short tempered. But a sweet little mare would be just the thing,' Victoria said. 'You would look lovely in a dark-blue riding habit. Quite striking with your hair and complexion. You should give it some thought.' She turned towards Isabelle. 'Good afternoon, Miss Wright.'

'Miss Bretton, hallo! I thought it was you. Haven't we a perfect day for an alfresco gathering?'

'We have indeed,' Victoria replied. Reluctantly, she glanced at the man standing beside Isabelle. 'Mr Devlin.'

'Good afternoon, Miss Bretton. Miss Winifred. How nice to see you both again.'

The words were polite, but Victoria heard an

edge of restraint and wondered if he was finding this as difficult as she was. Fortunately, Miss Wright was her usual ebullient self. 'Miss Bretton, I simply had to come across and tell you the exciting news. Alistair has agreed to take me to see *A Lady's Choice* tomorrow evening.'

'But you've already seen it.'

'I know, but this is to be the seventh performance and my friends and I believe Valentine Lawe will be in attendance.'

'Really?' Victoria hoped she didn't look too surprised. 'What makes you think so?'

'We believe the number seven to be significant. Mr Lawe makes reference to it several times in the opening scenes. Elliot Black tells Elizabeth Turcott he will wait seven days for her answer, and that he will call at the seventh hour of the seventh day.'

'So you believe it to be…a code of sorts,' Victoria said. 'To let people know he would be there at the seventh performance.'

'Exactly! And Alistair has agreed to take me, even though I know he is less than thrilled by the idea. But I cannot go alone, and since we are making up a party, I suggested that you should come as well,' Miss Wright said. 'Surely if there is a chance Valentine Lawe is going to be present, you would wish to meet him. Perhaps you would like to come too, Miss Winifred?'

Winifred blanched. 'Thank you. That would be…most delightful, of course,' she stammered, 'but I am already committed to dinner at the Roarkes' tomorrow evening.'

'Oh, what a shame.'

'Yes, isn't it?' Winifred said, surprising Victoria with a credible appearance of regret. 'But I'm sure Victoria and Laurence would be happy to join you.'

It was an exceedingly awkward moment for Victoria. Though she understood Miss Wright's excitement, how could she spend an evening in the company of a man to whom she was barely speaking? Surely he would wish to have nothing more to do with her?

'Thank you. It is very kind of you to offer,' she said, 'but under the circumstances, I think it best I refuse. I hate to think that word of our association might get back to your cousin and her husband.'

'Oh, but you mustn't worry about them!' Miss Wright said. 'I don't care what they think and neither does Cousin Alistair. He told them as much in the carriage after we saw you at the opera.'

Victoria blinked. 'He did?'

'Isabelle,' Alistair cautioned, but Miss Wright ignored him.

'He certainly did. He told them they had no business saying what they did about you and that he would speak to whomever he pleased—'

'Isabelle, you really do talk too much,' Alistair said with a weighted sigh. 'Remind me to take your former governess to task over the matter. But I think you probably should come with us, Miss Bretton. As Cousin Isabelle said, if there is any chance of meeting the esteemed Mr Lawe, surely it is an occasion not to be missed.'

Victoria hardly knew what to say. She could detect no echo of resentment in his voice, and she doubted Miss Wright's words had been provoking enough to incite any feelings of guilt on his part. But even if the invitation had been motivated by guilt, was she willing to walk away without making any effort to apologise? 'Thank you, Mr Devlin,' she said. 'I shall ask my brother if he is free, and, if so, we would be pleased to join you. Perhaps you would allow me to offer you seats in my uncle's box.'

'That would be most kind. But I hope you will come even if your brother does not.'

His eyes were shuttered and there was nothing in his voice to suggest intimacy, yet Victoria felt it keenly and her pulse accelerated. Before she had a chance to reply, however, Winifred interjected, 'Excuse me, Mr Devlin, but I do believe that gentleman is trying to catch your eye.'

Victoria looked up and saw a man staring in their direction. He was standing on the terrace and, when they all turned to look, he raised his arm to wave.

Alistair just smiled. 'Excellent. I was hoping he would come.'

'Do you know the gentleman?' Victoria asked.

'Oh, yes. Lord Valbourg and I went to Oxford together, but he's been in America these past six years, amassing a small fortune,' Alistair told them. 'We chanced to meet up at my club last week, after which I asked Lady Hincham to invite him to today's event.'

'Poor Lord Valbourg,' Miss Wright said. 'His mother, Lady Alderbury, hasn't been at all well. Mrs Shepherd mentioned it over cards last week. She said it was the reason he came back to England. And to find a wife, of course.'

'He's not married?' Winifred said quickly.

'He's been far too busy amassing his fortune,' Alistair said. 'But he was also travelling a great deal and that doesn't leave much time for courting. Valbourg,' he said as the other man joined them. 'Glad you could make it.'

'Sorry I'm late,' the newcomer said. 'I'd forgotten how crowded London streets could be.'

'I doubt Lady Hincham noticed. Miss Bretton, Miss Winifred, allow me to make known to you my good friend, Lord Valbourg.'

Lord Valbourg was a handsome man, slightly heavier in build than Alistair, and perhaps an inch or two taller. He had dark-brown hair cut in a fashionable crop and a thoroughly warm and engaging smile. Victoria liked him at once. 'Good afternoon, Lord Valbourg.'

'Miss Bretton, Miss Winifred, pray forgive my intrusion into your conversation.'

'No apologies are necessary. Mr Devlin tells us the two of you are old friends.'

'Indeed, from our days together at Oxford.'

'And you are recently back from America,' Winifred said, green eyes sparkling. 'Are you planning to return there in the near future?'

'I am not. My time in the country served its purpose, but I am looking forward to settling down to the life of an English gentleman again.'

'And he's made a good start by taking a house in Berkeley Square,' Alistair informed them.

'Berkeley Square,' Victoria said with a glance at her sister. 'How nice.'

'Yes, though it is in desperate need of redecorating,' Lord Valbourg said. 'I was going to ask my sister for help, but with our mother being so ill, Mary's time is fully occupied looking after her.'

'Perhaps we could lend some assistance in that regard,' Victoria offered. 'Mama is likely to know where the best fabrics are to be found and Winifred has exceptional taste when it comes to colours and styles.'

Winifred blinked her surprise. 'I do?'

'Indeed. She helped Mama redecorate several rooms in our house in Kent last year,' Victoria informed the gentleman. 'She has a superb eye for that sort of thing.'

'Has she indeed?' Lord Valbourg turned an admiring gaze on a blushing Winifred. 'That would be delightful, of course, though I would hate to impose—'

'Oh, it would be no imposition,' Winifred assured him quickly. 'I would be happy to assist in whatever way I could.'

'Then I shall call upon you in the near future to make arrangements for a shopping expedition. Dev, will I see you at Jackson's tomorrow morning?'

'I'll be there.'

'Splendid. Then we can talk more about this project of yours and how I might be of assistance. Good afternoon Miss Bretton, Miss Wright, Miss Winifred.'

'Lord Valbourg,' Winifred said, a coquettish twinkle back in her eyes. When she turned to Victoria, her face was flushed and glowing. 'Well, perhaps I should go and see if Mama is in need of anything.'

Aware that the only reason Winifred was anxious to find their mother was to tell her about the handsome Lord Valbourg, Victoria made no demur. Given what an enviable match it could be for her sister, she really couldn't blame her.

'And we should probably go too, Cousin Alistair,' Miss Wright said, sounding less than enthused. 'Your sister has been glaring at us these past ten minutes.'

Victoria gazed across the garden to where the Archdeacon and his wife were seated under the shade of a large tree and saw that Mrs Baltham was indeed looking daggers in their direction. No doubt due, Victoria thought wryly, to the company her beloved brother was keeping. 'Then I shall bid you both a good afternoon.'

Alistair bowed. 'Miss Bretton. Thank you for your offer of assistance. I'm sure Lord Valbourg will be most grateful for the help.'

Their eyes met briefly, and though it did not last long, Victoria was startled by the intensity of his gaze. She couldn't tell if it was anger, or regret, or a combination of the two, but it left her wondering what thoughts really had been going through his mind.

The rest of the afternoon seemed strangely anticlimactic. Victoria wanted to put it down to a restlessness to get back to work, but she knew it had more to do with Alistair's leaving the gathering than it did with her own desire to be anywhere else. She wasn't sure when the nature of her feelings for him had begun to change, but she knew without question that they had and she was alarmed by the pace at which they were growing. Now the world seemed a far less interesting place when Alistair wasn't in it. And rather than avoid society events, Victoria found herself seeking them out, especially ones to which she thought he might be invited. She enjoyed being in his company. She liked listening to him talk and she loved watching his face when he expressed an opinion about something in which he was interested—like this unknown project Lord Valbourg had referred to.

Nothing more had been said about it, but Victoria had seen the glint in Alistair's eye when the topic was raised. She might have asked him about it had he not been forced to rejoin his sister and brother-in-law, and, given that she didn't see Lord Valbourg again, she was not provided an opportunity to ask that gentleman about it either. Nevertheless, Valbourg's name did come up frequently during dinner that evening, so much so that Victoria's father finally had to beg his wife and younger daughter to cease and desist.

'But this was a highly fortuitous meeting, Mr Bretton,' his wife said. 'Lord Valbourg is the Marquess of Alderbury's son. He would make a wonderful husband for Winifred, far better than Mr Fulton. Surely you realise that.'

'I do, and I have heard Lord Valbourg praised in more ways than any one gentleman has a right to be praised,' Mr Bretton said. 'But for pity's sake, can we speak of nothing else? He and Winifred are but once met and a long way from standing before the altar reciting their vows.'

So chastised, Mrs Bretton refrained from comment and the conversation moved on to other subjects. But a few minutes later, Victoria sincerely wished it had remained on Lord Valbourg.

'By the by, Lady Hincham told me this afternoon that Lady Kempton is hopeful of a match between her son and Lord Geldon's daughter,' Mrs Bretton said.

'Lady Sarah Millingham?' Laurence frowned. 'Isn't she a bit young for Devlin?'

'She is young, and flighty by all accounts, which is why Lord Geldon approached Lord Kempton about the match,' Mrs Bretton said. 'He feels Mr Devlin would be a steadying influence on his daughter, and apparently she is quite taken with him. It would be an excellent match for her.'

'But considerably less so for him,' Laurence observed. 'Devlin doesn't strike me as the sort of man who would be led willingly into his future, or who would enjoy the company of such a young girl.'

Victoria shared her brother's opinion. The

idea that Alistair might actually contemplate marriage to Lady Sarah Millingham caused her heart to wrench in the most painful manner. She might be guilty of discouraging him, but that was only because she knew there was no possibility of a relationship between them. Her uncle's startling revelations about Hugh Devlin had reinforced that. Nevertheless, if she had been of a mind to choose an aristocratic husband, Alistair would have been the only one she would have set her heart on and she would have done everything she could to attract him. If she felt that way about him, why would every other woman not feel the same?

'Well, all I know is that we must do everything we can to further this association between Winifred and Lord Valbourg,' Mrs Bretton said. 'And that means *you* must be more mindful than ever about what you say and where you are seen, Victoria. If things do not go well for Winifred with Mr Fulton, I don't want you jeopardising her chances with this other gentleman.'

'Rest assured I will not.' Victoria wearily got to her feet. 'Believe it or not, Mama, I am as anxious to see Winifred settled as you are. And I intend to do everything in my power to make sure nothing happens to put that at risk.'

Chapter Seven

As it turned out, Laurence was more than happy to escort Victoria to the seventh performance of her play. Having been informed of Miss Wright's belief that Valentine Lawe would be in the audience, he found it highly amusing that Victoria should be there to witness the excitement and he was quite prepared to go along for the ride. Naturally his accompaniment removed any possible hint of scandal being attached to Victoria's joining Alistair Devlin and his cousin in her uncle's box.

As well, in an attempt to keep up appearances, Victoria did not slip into the theatre through the stage door as she had in the past, but instead walked in through the front doors with everyone else. Several people nodded in her direction, but Victoria received no welcome as

enthusiastic as that of Miss Wright, when she arrived at the box to find her and Alistair already
seated within.

'Oh, I am so glad you came!' Miss Wright
said. 'I knew you would be as excited as I by
the prospect of finally seeing Valentine Lawe!'

'It was certainly a big part of my reason for
coming,' Victoria acknowledged, glad Laurence
wasn't around to hear the remark. 'Good evening, Mr Devlin.'

'Miss Bretton. Will your brother not be joining us?'

'He will, but he chanced to see one of his old
professors in the vestibule and stopped to have
a word.'

Settling into her seat, Victoria cast a surrep-
titious glance in Alistair's direction. He was
as handsome as ever in a black cutaway coat
over an exquisitely embroidered silver waistcoat. Black trousers made him look even taller
than he was and his cravat was tied elegantly,
but with a minimum of fuss. His hair looked to
have been freshly trimmed and his voice…oh,
yes, that was definitely a voice that could have
stirred the multitudes…

'—nice of you to offer us the use of your box,'
Miss Wright was saying. 'If I lived in London
I would always take a box for the Season. It's

such fun to watch everyone else. Oh, look, isn't that Lady Sarah?'

Victoria glanced across the theatre at the row of boxes below hers and saw the young lady in question gazing avidly back at them. Or, more to the point, at Alistair.

'I'll wager she's wondering who you're with, Cousin,' Miss Wright said with an impish grin. 'Are you acquainted with Lady Sarah, Miss Bretton?'

'I am not,' Victoria said, returning her attention to the stage where movements behind the curtain indicated that the last of the props were being set out. 'Except by name.'

'She's quite nice, though I can't imagine why anyone would think she would make a good wife for Cousin Alistair.'

'Isabelle, you speak of things you should not!' he said darkly.

'Do I?' His cousin blinked. 'I'm sorry. I thought it was common knowledge that your mother and father were hopeful of a marriage between the two of you.'

'Whether it is common knowledge or not, it is not the thing to speak of in situations like these.'

'Situations like what? We are here with Miss Bretton to watch a play. She must be aware of what people in society are saying about you. Everyone else is.'

'Evening, all,' Laurence said, stepping into the box.

'Laurence!' More grateful than she could say for her brother's arrival, Victoria grabbed his arm and drew him forwards. 'You remember Mr Devlin's cousin?'

'Of course. Good evening, Miss Wright.'

'Mr Bretton.' The girl's cheeks were two bright spots of colour. 'How nice to see you again.'

'And, of course, Mr Devlin.'

'Your servant, sir.' Laurence sat down in the chair next to his sister, the one on the other side already occupied by Devlin. 'My, my, another sold-out performance. This Valentine Lawe certainly knows how to pack them in.'

'Do you think he's here?' Miss Wright asked breathlessly.

'If he is, none of us will be any the wiser,' Alistair said. 'Unless he stands up and proclaims himself.'

'Which he is hardly likely to do,' Laurence said. 'Lawe has taken the art of concealment to a whole new level.'

'But what has he to conceal?' Miss Wright asked. 'Why would anyone so brilliant wish to hide his talent away? If I was that clever, I would stand up and invite the audience's applause.'

'Perhaps he is disfigured,' Alistair suggested. 'His face too ugly or scarred to be seen.'

'Or he could just be shy,' Miss Wright said. 'A man uncomfortable with all the accolades.' She turned her head to look at Laurence. 'What do you think, Mr Bretton?'

Laurence looked decidedly taken aback by the question. 'Me?'

'Well, surely you have an opinion as to why the man continues to shun society. Do you believe him ugly or disfigured as my cousin suggests, or do you think he is shy and has no wish for the company of others?'

'To be honest, I've never given it a moment's thought. I accept the man's brilliance, but as to his personal likes and dislikes, I have no opinion whatsoever.'

'And you, Miss Bretton?' Alistair said. 'You are keeping rather quiet on the subject.'

'Only because to speculate on Valentine Lawe's reasons for remaining anonymous would be a complete waste of time.' Victoria opened her fan and took care not to look at him. 'The man himself is the only one who can say why he does not seek recognition.'

'Oh, look, there is your uncle!' Miss Wright said, her gaze moving to the stage below. 'We are about to get underway.'

Fixing her attention on the stage, Victoria quietly exhaled a sigh of relief. She was beginning to hate all this talk about Valentine Lawe. She kept telling herself she had no reason to do so, that Alistair had no way of knowing who she was, and while she was sure his question had been motivated purely out of interest, she was growing more and more uncomfortable with the deception. If ever there was a time to reveal herself, it was now, yet fear of reprisal held her back. She would be risking a great deal more than her reputation if she was to offer up the truth now. There was Winifred's future to consider and her mother had made it very clear that no one was to do anything that might put that future at risk.

Confessing that she was Valentine Lawe would certainly do that.

More to the point, while it was highly unlikely that Victoria would ever see Alistair Devlin again once they returned to Kent, she would be forced to see her sister every day *and* to have to listen to her recriminations. She would be made to understand that if Winifred's marriage plans fell through, it would all be because of her. Somehow, keeping silent about the true identity of Valentine Lawe in the short term seemed a small price to pay for harmony in the years ahead.

* * *

That evening's production of *A Lady's Choice* was even more enjoyable than the one Victoria had watched on opening night. Signy's acting was inspired, her love for Elliot more convincing than in any of her showings thus far. And responding in kind, Victor gave one of the best performances of his life. The rest of the cast were equally impressive and, not surprisingly, the audience's approval rang long and loud at the end of the performance.

Victoria felt her heart thumping in her chest. To think that *her* words were having this kind of effect. That *her* characters and *her* story had brought the audience to its feet. It was a heady moment and if ever she needed proof that she was pursuing the right path, this must surely be it.

She shared a single glance with Laurie, but knew she dare not risk another. His pride was all too evident.

'Oh my, that was splendid,' Miss Wright said as they exited the box. 'Better even than the first time. Did you not think so, Cousin Alistair?'

'It was very impressive,' he agreed. 'Your uncle is to be commended, Miss Bretton. I thought Miss Chermonde's performance tonight outstanding.'

'I'm sure she would be delighted to hear you

say so,' Victoria said. Then, caught up in her enthusiasm and joy, said, 'Perhaps you and Miss Wright would like to meet her?'

No sooner were the words out of her mouth than Victoria realised she had made a dreadful mistake. She felt both Alistair's and Laurence's gazes on her and knew she should not have spoken, but the look of excitement on Miss Wright's face was not to be denied. 'You mean…we could actually go backstage and meet Miss Chermonde and Mr Trumphani?'

'That's what I was thinking, but it is up to Mr Devlin, of course,' Victoria said hesitantly.

He was watching her with narrowed eyes, his expression thoughtful. Victoria, who anticipated a quelling set down, was considerably relieved when all he said was, 'The offer is a generous one, Miss Bretton, but I do not think it would be a good idea. My sister and brother-in-law would not be pleased to hear that Isabelle was associating with…such people.'

Victoria felt the warmth start in her neck and travel upwards until her entire face was engulfed. Of course they wouldn't be pleased. In the afterglow of her success, she had lost sight of the fact that actors and actresses were not suitable company for people like Alistair Devlin and Isabelle Wright. To introduce Isabelle to Signy Chermonde would not have been to elevate Signy's standing. It would have been to lower Isabelle's. 'Yes, of course. Forgive me. I only thought—'

'No apologies are necessary,' Alistair said gently. 'I know your offer was well intentioned and I'm quite sure Isabelle would love to go backstage. However, there is a good possibility that someone would see her and that would not be good for her reputation. London may be a big city, but news like that makes the rounds very quickly.'

'Yes, of course,' Victoria said, biting her lip.

'We could, however, pay our respects to Uncle Theo,' Laurence suggested. 'Surely there could be no objection to Miss Wright meeting him in the privacy of the Green Room. He does, after all, move in very good society.'

Victoria looked up and saw Alistair watching her, the look in his eyes one she hadn't seen before. 'I don't think that would go amiss,' he agreed. 'Though it would be better if it were to take place in the vestibule rather than anywhere backstage.'

'Then I shall go and seek him out,' Laurence said. 'And ask him to meet us at the foot of the grand staircase.'

'Oh, yes, that would be lovely,' Miss Wright said, clapping her hands. 'Then he can confirm that I really did see Valentine Lawe in the theatre tonight.'

Victoria blanched. 'You *saw* him? Where?'

'In the first row of boxes. I noticed him when he came in. He walked in a very slow, dignified manner and he was dressed all in black and white.'

'As were most of the men in the theatre,' Alistair pointed out.

'Yes, but when he turned, I noticed that he was wearing a single red rose in his lapel! And I saw a number of the performers glance in his direction. It *must* have been Valentine Lawe!'

'Fine. While you speculate as to the likelihood of the playwright being in the audience, I shall go and speak to Lord Gavering,' Alistair said.

'And I shall search out Uncle Theo,' Laurence said with a pointed glance at Victoria. 'I think I know where he's likely to be.'

Left alone with Miss Wright, Victoria pointed to the red banquettes lining the wall. 'Shall we sit down while we wait for the gentlemen to return?'

'Yes, by all means.'

When they were comfortably seated, Victoria said with a smile, 'So, are you enjoying your stay in London, Miss Wright?'

'I am having the very *best* time, Miss Bretton.

Cousin Alistair has been so good to me. Taking me around, making sure I see all the sights and meet all the right people. It has been terribly busy, but very exciting. I shall be quite bereft when I return home. Of course, everyone is anxious that I meet a suitable gentleman and get married. I know that's why Mama agreed to let me come,' Isabelle said. 'But I'm quite happy to visit the shops and go to the theatre and experience all that London has to offer.'

'How do you like living with Lord and Lady Kempton?' Victoria asked in a casual voice.

'Oh. Well, they're very nice, of course,' Miss Wright said, blushing. 'And I know they mean well…'

'But?'

'But they are rather boring,' the girl admitted. 'It's not that they mean to be, and I suppose it is terribly ungrateful of me to say so, but it's just that…the way they carry on is so painfully…'

'Correct?' Victoria supplied helpfully.

'Exactly! Lord Kempton is very strict, and Cousin Julia and her husband even more so. But then I suppose an archdeacon and his wife must be more mindful of the proprieties than most.'

'Yes,' Victoria allowed grudgingly, 'which is why Mr Devlin has to be very careful about how you go on while you are here.'

'I suppose. Still, I should have loved to go

backstage and meet the cast of *A Lady's Choice*,'
Miss Wright confessed. 'If Cousin Alistair is allowed to involve himself with orphans, I don't
see why I can't—'

'*Orphans*?' Victoria interrupted.

'Oh dear, I don't think I was supposed to say
anything about that,' Miss Wright said. 'But I
suppose it's too late now. And I really don't see
why he doesn't want to tell anyone. It's not as
though he was doing anything wrong.'

'What exactly is he doing?' Victoria asked.

'Well, I don't know all the details, but I over-
heard him talking to Lord Valbourg the other
evening and I think he's bought a house with a
view to turning it into an orphanage. Apparently
he already has a place in town that he uses for
the purpose, but it's not big enough any more, so
he bought a larger house and plans to renovate
it. I think Lord Valbourg is going to help him.'

'I had no idea,' Victoria said, trying to imagine Alistair Devlin in such a benevolent role. Instead of squandering his wealth on prostitutes
and gambling, he was using it to help children
whose circumstances had forced them to find a
living on the streets. To think she had accused
him of being selfish. 'I wouldn't have thought
him the type to get involved in such a cause,'
she whispered.

'He doesn't talk about it much,' Miss Wright

admitted. 'I'm not even sure my aunt and uncle know, but I don't think they would be terribly pleased if they did.'

And then, Victoria had another disturbing thought. *Was that where he had been going the day he had come upon her at the Gryphon?* Was *that* the stop he had been intending to make? He'd made it sound as though he was on his way to visit a woman—and she had left him in no doubt as to how she felt about his doing so. But if he had been planning to visit an orphanage, why hadn't he told her? Why had he let her believe his destination was somewhere else, with an entirely different purpose in mind? Had he *wanted* her to think ill of him?

Regrettably, it was a question for which there was to be no answer. Laurence returned with their uncle and, at the same time, Alistair came back to join them.

'Well, well, Devlin, we meet again,' Uncle Theo said. 'I'm surprised to see you here a second time.'

'If someone had told me a few weeks ago that I would be heading to *any* theatre to see a repeat performance of a play, I would have told them they were mad,' Alistair said with a smile. 'But apart from my cousin insisting we come tonight, it was a pleasure to see the play again. The cast gave an even stronger performance than they did on opening night.'

'I am delighted to hear you say so,' Uncle Theo said. 'Did you enjoy the performance, Miss Wright?'

'Indeed, Mr Templeton! Especially once I realised that Valentine Lawe was actually *in* the theatre!'

Victoria knew her uncle to be a talented actor, but even she hadn't realised how talented until that moment. He looked at Miss Wright without blinking and said, 'And he did not come up and say hello? The bounder! Where did you see him?'

'In the first row of boxes, second from the left,' Miss Wright said. 'A very serious-looking man, with a red rose in his lapel.'

'A red rose.' Her uncle frowned, and then, started to laugh. 'My dear Miss Wright, I am sorry to disappoint you, but that was not Valentine Lawe.'

'It wasn't?''

'No. It was Sir Michael Loftus, the theatre critic.'

'It *was*?' It was Victoria's turn to be surprised. 'But…I thought he never attended plays more than once.'

'That was my understanding too, but I know

for a fact that he was here tonight and that he was sitting in that box.'

'Oh well, that *is* disappointing,' Miss Wright complained. 'I was *so* sure it was Valentine Lawe.'

'Never mind, cousin, at least you were able to see the play again,' Alistair said. 'I'm sure you will have a chance to meet the renowned playwright before you leave London.' He turned his head and looked straight at Victoria. 'If there is any possibility of that happening, I'm sure Miss Bretton will know how to bring it about.'

Victoria didn't hear what anyone said in response. How could she, given the staggering implication of what Alistair had just said? He believed his cousin would achieve the introduction she so desperately craved...and that Victoria would be the one to make it happen. There was only one possible conclusion she could draw from that.

Somehow or other, Alistair had figured out that she *was* Valentine Lawe!

Chapter Eight

Not surprisingly, Victoria passed a thoroughly wretched night. As the midnight hours stretched slowly into dawn, she stared up at her bedroom ceiling, wondering how Alistair could possibly have guessed her secret. Had she said something to give herself away? Indicated by some wayward glance that she was the elusive playwright?

She must have, for why else would he have made the comment?

And yet, as she thought back over every conversation the two of them had ever had, Victoria could pinpoint nothing that might have exposed her. She no longer started when Lawe's name was mentioned, nor did she blush when praise was heaped upon his work. She had learned to remain calm, as though the comments meant nothing to her. Even during her numerous conversations with Miss Wright, she was sure she had acted the part of uninterested bystander with a convincing lack of concern.

Still, she must have let *something* slip during their time together. Alistair's focused gaze and casually delivered remark were too pointed to ignore.

Needing to talk to someone who had been there during last night's conversation, Victoria waited for her brother to finish his breakfast before asking if he might like to join her for a walk. Thankfully, the morning had turned warm and, happy to get out of the house, Laurence agreed. Fifteen minutes later, they set off.

'So, what's really on your mind?' he asked after they had chatted about inconsequential matters for the first few minutes.

Victoria sighed. She might have known he would see right through her. 'I need to ask you a question. You were there last night, when Uncle Theo told Miss Wright it wasn't Valentine Lawe sitting in the fourth row, but Sir Michael Loftus.'

'Yes. So?'

'So, a few minutes later, Mr Devlin said something I haven't been able to forget.'

'That he was madly in love with you?'

Victoria coloured. 'Gudgeon! He would never say something like that to me.' And sadly, she knew all too well the reasons why. 'The point is, after Miss Wright said how disappointed she was that Valentine Lawe wasn't in the audience, Mr Devlin told her not to worry because he had every confidence she would meet the playwright before she left London. Then he looked right at me and said *I* would be the one to arrange it.'

Laurence gave her a blank stare. 'So?'

'So you don't think he was saying he knew *I* was Valentine Lawe?'

'No. He likely said that because he knows Theodore Templeton is your uncle and that if anyone was going to be able to effect an introduction to Valentine Lawe, it would be you by virtue of your relationship to him. Unless you've said something to make him think otherwise.'

'I haven't. I've gone over every word I've ever said and cannot think of one that might have given me away.'

'Then you have nothing to worry about.'

'Then why do I feel so guilty?' Victoria murmured.

'Because you don't like lying to the man. You feel guilty about having to deceive him and you're afraid he will think less of you if he finds out you haven't been telling him the truth. Of course, that only applies if you have feelings for him in return.'

'Don't be silly, Laurence, that has nothing to do with it.'

'Hasn't' it?' Laurence turned his attention to the road ahead. 'See that gentleman coming towards us?'

Victoria spotted the middle-aged man and nodded. 'Yes.'

'Do you care if he thinks your bonnet is hideous?'

Victoria frowned. 'Of course not.'

'Why not?'

'Because I don't know him.'

'And therefore care nothing for his opinion. However, if Alistair Devlin was approaching and I were to ask the same question, I doubt your answer would be the same.'

Victoria blushed. 'Of course it would be the same. I don't care what Mr Devlin thinks of my appearance.'

'Don't you?'

'No.' She turned to find Laurence's gently amused glance resting on her. 'Well, it's not as though I have any reason to care.'

'A woman doesn't need a reason to wish to look attractive for a man she likes, Tory,' Laurence said. 'And I think you do like him enough to care what he thinks. Unfortunately, right now I have to say your time would be better spent in trying to decide what to do about

Sir Michael's offer. You know exactly what *he* wants and you're going to have to give him an answer soon.'

Laurence was right. She did have to make up her mind quickly, both with regard to Sir Michael's offer and about going public with Valentine Lawe. She and Laurence had already agreed that the offer was an incredible validation of her talent, but that there were definite consequences to meeting with the man. Uncle Theo had blessedly bought her some time by saying she was abroad, but she couldn't stay in Europe for ever.

At some point, Sir Michael was going to want an answer, and she would have to have one ready. One she could live with…whatever the outcome.

The following day, Alistair left the estate agent's office well pleased with the morning's work. The papers were signed, the balance of the monies paid and the deed of ownership was finally in his hands.

He also had a new partner in his good friend, Lord Valbourg. Once he had described his plans for the old house, Valbourg had been only too happy to lend his assistance. Although money was not an issue for either of them, much of Alistair's was tied up in investments and would take time to release. Valbourg's was sitting idle, just waiting to be spent. When Alistair had shown him the list of projected expenses, Valbourg had been more than willing to make available whatever funds were necessary in order to get things going.

Yes, all in all it had been a very good morning, Alistair decided. The only hiccup had been his discussion over breakfast with his father concerning the subject of marriage to Lady Sarah Millingham. That was something Alistair had not been happy about and he had made it very clear to his father that such a marriage was *not* going to happen. For one thing, they had absolutely nothing in common. For another, she was too damn young. Alistair didn't want a schoolroom miss for a bride. He wanted a woman who knew her own mind; one who could match wits with him and meet him on his own terms.

Lady Sarah's mind was as vacuous as a butterfly's.

As to being a steadying influence in her life, Alistair couldn't imagine anything worse. The last thing he needed was a wife upon whom he constantly had to keep a watchful eye. One who was prone to doing silly, immature things. One who *giggled*.

That *would* drive him to distraction.

Besides, his feelings were already engaged.

No one knew that, of course, including the lady in whom they were invested. How could she know when the awareness of his feelings had come so recently to him? But because of what he felt for Victoria Bretton, Alistair could entertain no thoughts of any other woman in his life.

At first, it was just her loveliness that had appealed to him, though he had quickly discovered that there was far more to her than mere physical beauty. Victoria's ability to hold her head high and to ignore what people said about her was a quality he could admire, as was her desire to do what was right. She was funny, forthright, loving and honest.

Unfortunately, right from the start, she had been determined to keep him at arm's length. She believed they would not suit and that his position in society and her fondness for the theatre would always keep them apart. Added to that was her belief that he was a man who wasted his time in shallow pursuits and therefore not worthy of her time.

For that reason alone, he was determined to show her that there was more to him than she thought—and the best way of doing that was by introducing her to Mrs Hutchins and the children.

For reasons of confidentiality, Alistair had not discussed the details of his project with very many people. He'd had to tell his father about the house due to the financial ramifications, but he hadn't told him what it was for because he knew his father wouldn't have approved.

Pay others to do that, Lord Kempton would have said. *A gentleman does not dirty his hands with poverty.*

It was not an isolated opinion. Alistair knew that many affluent men had no wish to spend any part of their personal wealth on the welfare of the sick and the downtrodden, not even when those who suffered were children. But Alistair worked to a higher ideal. He had long been impressed by the example set by Thomas Coram, the gentleman who had founded a hospital for the care and education of young children cast aside by society, and he was convinced that the need for that type of housing was greater than ever. If those who had the wherewithal to help didn't make the attempt, countless innocents would die. He had the money and the time to invest in such a cause and he was happy to do it.

Besides, his reasons for establishing the orphanage went far deeper than any one knew. The day he had seen an eight-year-old girl purposely walk into the path of an oncoming carriage was the day his life had changed for ever.

There hadn't been time to react, either on his part or the coachman's. The carriage had thundered down on that poor child and she had been knocked aside by the lead horse, killing her on the spot. The carriage hadn't stopped. Alistair doubted the occupants were even aware of what happened. But he had made a vow, then and there, that whatever he could do to better the lives of children like that, would be done.

He wondered what Victoria Bretton would say about his inclinations. Would she look at him differently if she knew? Would she think better of him and perhaps be more willing to entertain his suit?

And then, as if conjured by thought alone, she appeared on the street ahead of him. She was strolling with her brother, the sound of her laughter drifting along the street towards him. She was dressed all in green and looked as beguiling as spring.

Alistair knew the moment she saw him. Her laughter stopped, but he saw the telltale rush of colour to her cheeks. And though that too receded, the fact it had been there at all gave him hope.

Unfortunately, there was still a feeling of unease between them as a result of the unfortunate conversation they'd had the day he had driven her home from the Gryphon Theatre. It had lessened slightly after their conversation at Lady Hincham's garden party, and he had hoped their evening together at the Gryphon would have resolved it entirely. It was the reason he had been so insistent that she join him and Isabelle for the seventh performance of Valentine Lawe's play.

But it had become clear to him right after the meeting with Victoria and her uncle at the foot of the grand staircase that she had still been very much on edge. She looked as though she had received news of a most disturbing nature, and it wasn't long after that she and her brother had left.

Alistair just wanted the distance between them to be at an end. He was desperate for a sign that she wasn't as unaware of him as he feared.

'Well, this is an unexpected pleasure,' he said, drawing his phaeton to a halt. 'Good morning to you both.'

'Good morning, Mr Devlin,' Laurence said. Victoria only smiled, but while her hand stayed in the crook of her brother's arm, Alistair noticed that her fingers tightened on his sleeve. 'You look very satisfied with yourself.'

'In fact, I have had a very productive morning and am on my way to share some good news with someone who will be very pleased to hear it.'

'May we enquire as to the nature of the business?' Victoria asked.

He looked down at her and knew the moment

was at hand. 'You may enquire, Miss Bretton, but rather than tell you, I wonder if you would allow me to show you what I am so pleased about.'

'I'm not sure how one shows another person good news, Mr Devlin.'

'That depends on the nature of the news. But if you would allow me, I think you will be pleasantly surprised.'

An expression of interest flashed across her face, as well as a flicker of curiosity—something Alistair knew very few women were capable of resisting. 'Very well, you have piqued my interest, sir.'

'Mr Bretton, you are most welcome to join us,' Alistair said, knowing it would be impossible not to extend the invitation to her brother as well.

Thankfully, Laurence declined. 'It is good of you to ask, but I have an appointment elsewhere. Victoria can tell me about it when she gets home. I trust you to take good care of her.'

Alistair smiled. 'I will do my best.'

Minutes later, he and Victoria were clipping along in the direction of the orphanage. Alistair knew it was too late to change his mind. They were set on a course and he was anxious to see what Victoria's response to his undertaking would be.

She was quiet as they drove through the narrowing streets. The house was located in an area north and east of the Gryphon Theatre, in a part of town Alistair doubted Victoria would be familiar with. There were no fine shops or attractions to which a young lady visiting London would have any reason to go, but it suited his purposes well enough. He had acquired the house some years ago as the result of a business transaction and, until a few months ago, it had been sufficient for his needs. But as the children kept coming, it had quickly grown too small, hence Alistair's decision to purchase a larger house.

He turned at last into the street and stopped the carriage in the usual place. Thomas appeared within moments, as if drawn by the sound of carriage wheels. After tossing the lad a coin, Alistair turned to help Victoria alight. 'Before we go in,' he said, 'I want you to know that if you feel uncomfortable at any time, or wish to depart, you have only to say so. But it was necessary that I come here today and I wanted to share this with you.'

'Why?'

A dozen answers sprang to mind. He gave her the most honest. 'Because your opinion matters to me.'

Intense astonishment touched her face, but

after a moment's consideration, she nodded. 'Then pray proceed, Mr Devlin. I am curious to see what this is all about.'

He unlocked the door and pushed it open.

Jenny was standing in the entrance hall. Blonde hair hung lank around her cheeks and, upon seeing Victoria, she gasped and ran back down the corridor, disappearing through a door at the end.

'Who was that?' Victoria asked.

'Jenny.' Alistair ushered her inside and rang a small silver bell on the table. 'She doesn't speak. At least, she hasn't since her arrival here.'

'Has she been injured?'

'Not physically. The doctor said her vocal cords are fine, but she witnessed—'

Alistair stopped, not sure how much of Jenny's sad story he should reveal. But while Victoria's face was pale, her voice was steady when she said, 'What did she witness?'

It was the calmness of her manner that decided him. 'A violent crime. She ended up here because it wasn't safe for her to remain where she was.'

Victoria kept her eyes on the door through which Jenny had just disappeared. 'Are there others here like her?'

'Yes. Their circumstances are all different, but their reasons for being here are the same,'

Alistair said, wondering where Mrs Hutchins was. 'They were all brought here to recover.'

Finally, Mrs Hutchins did appear, emerging from the same doorway through which Jenny had disappeared. 'Mr Devlin, I'm so sorry,' she said, wiping her hands on her apron. 'I heard the bell but I couldn't leave Molly. She's had a terrible bout of coughing. I've sent young Teddy for the doctor.'

Alistair felt despair well up in his soul. 'Take me to her.' He saw the housekeeper's gaze go briefly to Victoria and said, 'Miss Bretton, this is Mrs Hutchins. Mrs Hutchins looks after the children here.'

Victoria immediately put out her hand. 'I am very pleased to meet you, Mrs Hutchins. Please, take us to see Molly.'

The housekeeper nodded. 'I hope you don't mind the sight of blood, miss,' she said, turning to lead the way.

'I'm not squeamish. I was always the sister who fell out of the tree.'

The remark brought a faint smile to the older woman's face. 'You may find this is a little more unsettling. Mind your skirts there.'

Alistair tried to keep an eye on Victoria as they made their way down to the kitchen. He had complete faith in Mrs Hutchins's ability to look after the children, but if Molly was coughing up blood, it was just as well the doctor had been sent for. For all Victoria's claim that she had fallen out of trees, what she was about to see was something she likely didn't encounter in her everyday life.

Molly was lying on a narrow cot placed next to the fire. Her face was white and the front of her chemise was spattered with blood. A quick glance showed other towels spotted with blood, which Mrs Hutchins quickly gathered up. Molly's sister, Margaret, was standing a few feet away, her face stricken.

To Alistair's surprise, Victoria went straight to the child's cot. 'Oh, you poor little thing,' she murmured. She bent down, her skirts pooling like a field of green around her. 'Hello, Molly. My name is Victoria. Can you hear me?'

Molly's eyes were half-open and fixed on Victoria's face. When she nodded, Victoria looked up and smiled at the other child standing close by. 'Is this your sister?'

'That's Margaret, miss,' Mrs Hutchins whispered as she passed by.

'Hello, Margaret.'

The girl didn't answer, but Victoria didn't seem to expect her to. She returned her attention to Molly and gently brushed the hair back from her forehead. Then she took one of the girl's hands between her own and rubbed it gently.

'You've not been very well, have you, Molly? But the doctor is coming and he's going to take care of you.'

Molly nodded and her eyes drifted closed.

Alistair swallowed hard. He feared they were going to lose Molly—possibly her and Margaret both. The damage done by the mills was something even the finest doctors couldn't repair, and the knowledge that these little girls' early deaths could have been prevented made him angrier than he would have believed possible.

And then, four more children shuffled in, all huddled close together. He knew each of them by name because he had made it his business to, and they knew him. But they didn't know the lady crouching by Molly's cot.

'Will she be all right, then?' the tallest of them asked.

Alistair nodded. 'We've sent for the doctor, Thomas, and with luck, he'll be here very soon. Why don't you take Ruth and Alice upstairs and then gather the rest of the children together? There's something I want to tell you.'

'Aye, go along with you now, Thomas,' Mrs Hutchins said. 'Where's Robert?'

'Up in t' schoolroom,' Peter answered. 'With David and Beth.'

'All right. Go and find them and tell them Mr Devlin wants to talk to them.'

Alistair saw the look of fear on their faces and hastened to reassure them. 'Tell them I have good news. For all of you,' he said quickly.

That changed everything. The children disappeared, their footsteps clattering on the stairs in their haste to pass along his message. Alistair turned and saw Victoria watching him, the expression on her face one he had never seen before.

'Why don't the two of you go up as well?' Mrs Hutchins said quietly. 'I'll stay here with Molly until the doctor comes. I don't want to leave her alone.'

'Yes, all right. But I want you there to hear the good news as well, Mrs Hutchins,' Alistair said. 'This concerns all of us.'

Chapter Nine

All of us. He'd said it as though he was one of them, Victoria mused, yet he so obviously was not. These children were all orphans, or as near to it as mattered. They were here because their previous living conditions had become untenable. Clearly, Molly and her sister were ill, and while Victoria had no idea what the nature of their affliction was, she knew that for a child to be coughing up blood, the diagnosis could not be good.

Then there was Jenny, the silent one. She had witnessed something no child should ever have to and had been left emotionally scarred as a result. God only knew what had brought the other children to this haven, because that's what it was, Victoria acknowledged as she stretched out her hand to Margaret. A safe haven in the midst of a dangerous world.

Margaret glanced at her hand and then, slowly, put her own into it. She didn't say a word, but Victoria knew the girl trusted her to not do her any further harm. She looked at her sister as she passed the cot and briefly rested her free hand on Molly's cheek.

Molly's eyes opened and a tiny smile formed on her lips.

That smile broke Victoria's heart. Tears gathered in her eyes, and when she glanced up, she saw Alistair and Mrs Hutchins watching her. Her mother would have been horrified at the thought of her shedding tears for an orphan, but she would not cry in front of these children. They were the ones who should be crying. Not her. 'Come along then, Margaret. Let's go and join the others, shall we?' she said.

Obediently, Margaret nodded. Alistair had a brief word with Mrs Hutchins, then led the way up the steep and narrow stairs.

Victoria accommodated her step to Margaret's, slowing even more when she heard the sound of the child's laboured breathing. Clearly her lungs had also been damaged, but perhaps not to the same extent as her sister's. When they walked into the room where the other children were already gathered, it took everything Victoria had not to burst into tears.

There were seven of them, ranging in ages from four to about ten. All were thin, with gaunt faces and bones sticking out in places where bones were never meant to be seen. They all looked uncertain and a little afraid, but their clothes were mended and their faces clean.

Alistair Devlin seemed completely at home amongst them. One of the little girls, Alice, Victoria heard him call her, went to him, and the face she raised was brimming with trust. 'Have you brought us anything today, sir?'

'I've brought you good news,' Alistair said gently. 'But before I tell you what it is, I want you to say hello to Miss Bretton. She's come to visit you.'

The children looked at her with varying degrees of suspicion and fear, and Victoria couldn't help thinking how different they were from the healthy, well-dressed children she saw in the homes of the well-to-do. These little waifs had a reason to be suspicious of adults they didn't know, and all too sadly, to be fearful of the ones they did.

It was another half-hour before Mrs Hutchins finally joined them. She carried Molly in her arms and apologised for her delay, but as she explained to Alistair as she gently set the child on a cot, she wanted to be there while the doctor examined the little girl. Apparently he had given her something to ease her pain and Victoria saw Margaret's tension ease, her frown disappearing for the first time since she had arrived.

'Is she going to get better, then?' Margaret asked.

Victoria caught the look that passed between Alistair and Mrs Hutchins, and knew the answer wasn't good.

'We're doing all we can for her, Margaret,' Mrs Hutchins said. 'And you were very wise to let us know that she was having trouble breathing. We need you to keep doing that.'

The little girl nodded, looking years older than she should as she moved to stand at her sister's side. 'I will.'

'Good. And now,' Alistair said, 'I wanted you all here, because I have good news for you. You are going to be moving to a new home. A big house in the country, with lots of room inside and fields where you can play—'

'Are we all going?' one of the boys asked, a look of desperation on his face. 'You're not going to break us up, or send us away, like you did with the others?'

'No, I'm not going to do that, Peter.' For a moment, Alistair looked regretful. 'I had to send

the others away because there were too many of
you living here for Mrs Hutchins to look after.
But they have gone to a very good home where
they will be well taken care of, just as all of you
will be in this new place.'

'When will we be going?' Thomas asked.

'Hopefully in the not-too-distant future,'
Alistair said, obviously not wanting to put a definite time on it. 'Some renovations are required
and those are underway now.'

'We can 'elp,' David piped up.

Alistair smiled. 'Yes, you can. You and
Thomas and Peter will all have jobs to do.'

'Wot 'bout me?' the smallest boy said. 'I can
work, long as you don't send me up the chibney.'

'You won't ever be going up a chimney again,
my lad,' Mrs Hutchins said fiercely. 'I'm sure
Mr Devlin can find a job in the fresh air for you.'

'I most certainly can. We're going to need a
garden dug, Teddy, so I'm putting you in charge
of that. And the girls can sew curtains and help
in the kitchen,' Alistair went on. 'As well, you
will all continue with your lessons and eventually there will be other children joining you.
Not too many, because we don't want to end up
as crowded as we are here. But it's a big house
and it can hold others who need help, the way
all of you did when you came here.'

Victoria glanced at the children and saw a

wide range of expressions on their faces. Clearly, none of them was used to pampering of any kind and to learn that they were soon to have a new home where there would be fresh air for them to breathe and fields in which to play must have seemed like a miracle.

Moments later, when a hand gently touched her arm, Victoria looked around to see Margaret standing beside her. The child didn't smile, but in her eyes was a look of such profound trust that Victoria felt a lump rise in her throat. 'Yes, Margaret?'

'Molly wondered if you would read to her, miss.'

For some reason, Victoria looked to Alistair for his approval. She had no idea how much he wanted her to be involved with these children, but when she saw him smile and nod, she realised the tension between them was gone. A new bond had been established, one formed as a result of these children and of a mutual desire to help them. And it was strong, stronger than Victoria would have believed possible. 'Of course I will read to her. And to you, if you'd like.'

The girl's face lit up. 'Oh, yes, please, miss,' she whispered.

Somehow, a book magically appeared and, after the older boys went back downstairs,

Victoria sat down to read to Molly and Margaret Townsend, and to Ruth and Alice Harkness, and to Beth Lyton and Teddy Erskine. It was so easy being there with all of them gathered around her. Only Jenny Smith remained apart, the expression in her eyes enough to tear the heart from one's chest.

This must be how it felt to have children of one's own, Victoria realised. How strange given that she'd never really thought about being a mother before. The idea of having children naturally followed the necessity of finding a husband, but, given her reluctance to marry, the possibility of children had seemed remote. But now, as she ran her hand over Alice's silken hair and gazed down into her trusting eyes, Victoria realised she *wanted* a child of her own. One who would be loved and cherished and given all the things these children never had been.

How ironic that just a few short hours with Alistair's children had shown her what she was missing and made her long for something she'd never even known she wanted.

The visit had come all too soon to an end, but when Victoria had left, it had been with a promise to Margaret and Molly that she would come back and read to them again. It was only later, when she and Alistair sat in his high-perch phaeton driving back to Green Street, that she finally asked the question, 'What happened to Jenny? What did she see?'

Alistair was clearly reluctant to divulge the information. He kept his eyes on the road, but his sigh revealed much of what he was feeling. 'Jenny's father drinks. And when he drinks too much, he becomes violent. He beat Jenny's mother to death…and Jenny was in the room when it happened.'

'Oh, dear God!' Victoria closed her eyes, the image of what that poor child had witnessed too terrible to contemplate. 'No wonder she doesn't speak. I cannot imagine what that must have been like.'

'Who in our society can?' Alistair said softly. 'What these children have experienced is beyond the understanding of people like you and me. Our lives are pampered and indulged. We've never known what it is to be hungry or cold. We've never had to be afraid for our lives, or fear for the lives of those we care about.'

'How did all of these children end up in your care?'

'People know Mrs Hutchins round these parts. They know what she does and who she is associated with. And though we can't help them all, we do what we can.'

'And this house you've bought,' Victoria said

slowly. 'It is going to be a new home for these children, and perhaps more?'

'The house will easily accommodate twenty-five,' Alistair said. 'More than that and we'll begin to feel crowded again. Mrs Hutchins would take every child she could, but she knows what's involved and she has only so much energy. That's why I've already hired a cook and a gardener, as well as a tutor for the boys and a governess for the girls. Mrs Hutchins can engage more staff as she feels necessary. It won't be fancy,' he said, 'but it will provide them with a safe and, hopefully, a happy environment.'

Victoria stared at the houses around them and saw everything those children had never experienced: wealth, security and a life of plenty. 'You are doing a wonderful thing, Mr Devlin,' she said softly. 'You are giving those children a chance at a life they never would have had.'

'Some of them,' Alistair said. 'I doubt Molly or Margaret will live to see their twenties. The damage done to their lungs is irreversible. All I can give them is somewhere comfortable in which to live out their years. As for Jenny, her scars are emotional. She'll never forget what she saw, but hopefully the pain will ease over time and she will be able to lead a reasonably normal life again.'

'At least she won't die the same way her

mother did,' Victoria said. 'She might have, had she stayed with her father.'

They drove in silence for a while, each deep in their own thoughts. Finally, as he turned the carriage into Green Street, Alistair said, 'Thank you for coming with me today. I know it was difficult and I was very impressed by your composure. Your kindness was...a gift to those children. I watched Margaret's face as you read to her and her sister. She already adores you.'

For some reason, it suddenly grew hard for Victoria to breathe. 'She is easy to love. They all are. Even the boys, though they are trying so hard to be brave.'

Alistair smiled. 'Yes, and Mrs Hutchins loves every one of them unconditionally. I couldn't have found a better person to look after them. I don't know what I would do without her.'

Victoria managed a smile. Had Mrs Hutchins been twenty years younger, she might have been jealous of the warmth in Alistair's voice, but she knew it was just his appreciation for everything the woman had done. 'I don't think you will have to do without her. She is as deeply committed to those children as you are. Nothing short of death is going to separate her from them.'

Alistair drew the carriage to a halt. 'Perhaps, but everyone has the right to a life, Miss Bretton. Mrs Hutchins was married once and she may meet a man and wish to be married again. And then where will I be?'

'From what little I know of Mrs Hutchins, I suspect you'll find yourself with *two* people looking after the children,' Victoria said. 'I doubt she would marry anyone who wasn't willing to share what she does. She doesn't look on it as a job. To her it is a labour of love, and what better reason *could* there be for doing something so worthwhile?'

He turned to look at her. 'I can think of no better reason.' He watched her for a long time; his gaze filled with tenderness as it rested on her face. Then, slowly, he raised his hand and brushed his thumb lightly over one corner of her mouth. 'A crumb,' he explained huskily. 'From Mrs Hutchins's fruitcake.'

Victoria blushed, but didn't pull away. She wanted to close her eyes and lean into his touch to savour the intimacy of the gesture. When he smoothed his knuckles over her chin, she wanted to purr like a kitten. But to sit there in the street, exposed and open to view, was madness. They were in a public place...and Victoria knew she risked more than her heart by behaving in such a manner. 'I must go,' she said.

'I know.' But, like her, Alistair seemed reluctant to depart. They had shared so much today. It was as though a barrier had come down and, for the first time, she was able to see the man he truly was.

'I will not tell anyone where we were today,' he said. 'I doubt your parents would approve. But I am very glad you agreed to come.'

'As am I, Mr Devlin,' Victoria whispered. 'Very glad indeed.'

The visit to the orphanage marked a definite change in Victoria's feelings towards Alistair. She no longer saw him as a man concerned only with his own pleasures. He was as far from that as it was possible to imagine. If she lived to be a hundred, she would never forget the sight of him smiling down at little Molly Townsend. It suddenly made what she did for a living seem trite and unimportant. She wrote plays for the stage. Fictitious plays that mocked society and contributed nothing to its well-being.

It certainly did nothing for Alistair's children.

And yet, what boy or girl did not adore the theatre? As a child, Victoria had loved watching the puppet shows. She remembered laughing at the funny stories and knew without having to ask that none of the children in Mrs Hutchins's care had ever been inside a theatre. Their lives were rooted in a world where adults committed atrocities and life was harsh and unforgiving. Where a girl could be flogged for stealing a loaf of bread and a boy of eight could be forced up a chimney by setting fires beneath his feet. Their expectations were low, their hopes even lower.

'What's wrong, Tory?' Laurence said as he walked into the drawing room a few days later. 'You're looking very pensive.'

'Yes, I suppose I am.' Victoria pressed her hands together. 'I can't seem to forget what I saw at the orphanage.'

Her brother picked up a copy of the morning paper. 'I'm still surprised Devlin took you there. It isn't the sort of place a gentleman usually takes a lady.'

'No, but I'm very glad he did. The orphanage and those children mean the world to him. The fact he chose to share it with me says a lot about the man.'

'And about his feelings for you.'

She raised startled eyes to his. 'Why would you say that?'

'Because his wanting you to see what he is involved in tells me he cares about what you think. He wants to know that you approve of what he's doing.'

'But he would do it whether I approved or not.'

'Yes, but why bother to *tell* you about it if he

didn't feel it was going to have an impact on your relationship?'

Victoria didn't have an answer for that, but it did raise a very different question in her mind. 'What about what *I'm* doing, Laurie?' she murmured. 'If Mr Devlin cares enough to show me what he is doing, am I not obligated to tell him what I am?'

'Only if you have feelings for him. If you don't, there's really no point.' Laurence stopped, and turned to look at her. 'Do you care for him in that way, Tory?'

Victoria bit her lip. Yes, she did. She had tried to keep him at a distance because she truly believed nothing could ever come of it. Alistair's family was too well connected. They moved in the highest circles. Worst of all, his brother had eloped with an actress and died in disgrace as a result. His family would *not* be pleased to know that the infamous Valentine Lawe, a playwright known for poking fun at the aristocracy, was actually the woman their son wished to court.

But more to the point, how would Alistair feel when the truth about her was revealed? He was a man to whom honesty was of paramount importance. Victoria knew that his brief courtship with Lady Frances Shaftsbury had come to an end because he'd found out she was lying to him. Winifred had heard about it at a musicale.

And if Alistair truly had feelings for her, he would not be pleased at finding out that she had been deceiving him all along. He might not be able to accuse her of lying to him outright, but she was still guilty of a deceit. If that was going to make a difference in the way he looked at her, it was only fair that she tell him the truth now, before their affection for one another grew any deeper.

She would certainly have to tell him before she met with Sir Michael Loftus. Once that gentleman knew who she was, there would be no way of guaranteeing that he wouldn't make it public and she couldn't risk Alistair hearing it from someone at his club or fencing saloon. If nothing else, she was determined that there would be honesty between them. If he chose to stop seeing her as a result, at least she would be able to hold her head up and know she had done the right thing.

But when to do it? Tonight was Lord and Lady Drake's masquerade and, while she knew Alistair would be there, it was hardly the time for such a revelation. They needed time to talk with some degree of privacy. She wanted to be able to see his face when she told him she was Valentine Lawe. That was the only way she would be able to gauge what his feelings about it really were.

Tomorrow, then, Victoria decided. She would ask him to call upon her and she would tell him the truth. Then she would see first-hand just how much damage her lies had already done.

When hosting one of their elaborate masquerades, Lord and Lady Drake decorated the rooms in their palatial home to reflect the theme of the evening's entertainment. They insisted that everyone come in costume, and while they did not go so far as to specify any particular type of costume, Victoria knew they preferred costumes concealing enough so that it was difficult to tell who was beneath the mask.

For some, procuring a costume was a difficult process, but with an uncle who owned a theatre and an aunt who was adept at lengthening a hem or taking in the seam, finding something to wear was relatively simple. Victoria's costume for the masquerade was nothing short of spectacular. On one of her uncle's recent trips to Venice, he had been given access to a wondrous selection of gowns, many of them having been passed down from their original seventeenth-century owners. The materials were sumptuous, the designs spectacular, and the colours the rich, jewelled tones of sapphire, emerald, ruby and amethyst.

Victoria's gown was a glorious creation of gold antique moiré with an elaborate headdress and mask to match. Aunt Tandy had made the necessary alterations and Victoria had been delighted, if somewhat apprehensive, about the results. Used to wearing lightweight muslin dresses, the close-fitting gown took some getting used to. To accommodate the narrowness of the waist and the fullness of the skirt, the wearing of a corset was necessary, but that resulted in Victoria's breasts being pushed up so high, she actually blushed at the creamy expanse of skin visible above the gown's neckline.

She decided to keep her fan poised in front of her for as much of the evening as possible.

Winifred, on the other hand, surprised everyone by going as Diana, the huntress. She wore a gown cleverly converted into a one-shoulder affair that draped beautifully around her body, but that somehow managed to look not in the least bit scandalous. Her hair was coiled in ringlets around her head and she looked breathtakingly lovely. Victoria doubted that anyone looking at her, however, would have any trouble recognising who she was under the half-mask that covered her eyes and nose.

None of them was surprised that their parents had decided not to attend. Her mother did not approve of masquerades any more than she approved of the theatre. She grudgingly allowed her children to go because she knew it was another venue at which they might meet a prospective husband or wife, but she disliked the idea intensely—and Laurence's appearance, when he finally came downstairs, did nothing to improve it. He wore a long black coat, heavily embroidered with silver thread around the hem, over a white shirt with a froth of lace at the cuffs and throat. His legs were encased in tall black boots, a black mask covered his eyes and nose—and he wore a single red rose in his lapel.

Victoria stared at him in disbelief, then burst out laughing. 'I don't believe it,' she said, not sure whether to be shocked or delighted. 'You have taken Miss Wright's words to heart.'

His smile flashed. 'Indeed I have.'

'I don't understand,' Winifred said, looking at him. 'Who or what are you supposed to be?'

'Can you not guess?' her brother asked. 'I thought the rose would have given me away. It is his signature, after all.'

Winifred frowned. 'Whose signature?'

'Valentine Lawe's.'

'*Valentine Lawe*!' His mother's face went white. 'Laurence, are you mad? You cannot go out in public like that!'

'Why not? No one's ever seen Lawe so it's not as though I *don't* look like him.'

'But it is not a question of whether you look like him or not!' Mrs Bretton said. 'We don't want to publicise that he exists—because he does not!'

'Ah, but he does, Mama,' Laurence said. 'In the hearts of his most ardent fans, he is a legend. And his reluctance to be seen has created a great deal of interest about him. I simply thought to have a little fun with it.'

'But surely your attire is more last century than this one,' Winifred observed. 'Gentlemen haven't worn frock coats and lace in decades.'

'I know that, but given Valentine Lawe's propensity for privacy, I thought a little eccentricity was called for.'

'This is not at all like you, Laurence,' his mother said unhappily.

'No, it is not.' His smile was slow and puckishly charming. 'And I rather like the idea because of it.'

Victoria stared at her brother in amusement. There was no denying that the old-fashioned clothing suited him far more than the conservative clothes he wore every day. He had even left off his spectacles and styled his hair in a new and rather dashing way.

'Well, I think it's dangerous,' Winifred stated flatly. 'Fingers will be pointed at us.'

'Don't be silly,' Laurence said. 'I'm the one wearing the costume. Besides, people are supposed to dress up. Look at you pretending to be

a Roman goddess. Where did you get that bow,
by the way?'

'From Miss Jackson's brother. She asked him
if I could borrow it for the evening.'

'Very realistic. Just be careful you don't poke
anyone's eye out with it,' Laurence said, giving
her a wide berth. 'Thank God he didn't lend you
any arrows. By the by, Tory, you look glorious.
Is that one of the gowns Uncle Theo brought
back from Venice?'

'Yes. Isn't it magnificent?'

'It is stunning, as are you in it. And the mask
is very mysterious. I vow I wouldn't know it was
my own sister.'

'Good, because that is the idea,' Victoria
said, nevertheless setting the mask aside. She
would put it on just before they arrived at the
house. It did tend to get uncomfortably warm
very quickly.

'I am not happy about this,' Mrs Bretton said
as the three of them headed towards the door.
'You are inviting trouble, Laurence. Mark my
words!'

'Nonsense, Mama. It is a masquerade. What
could possibly go wrong?'

Chapter Ten

It was, Alistair decided, the *last* time he intended to give way to Isabelle's demands. He liked attending masquerades even less than he liked attending the theatre, but at least at the latter, *he* wasn't required to perform.

'I think you make a wonderful Prospero,' Isabelle assured him as the two mingled with a host of other masked guests. 'Very mystical, but very powerful. And it goes perfectly with my being Miranda.'

Alistair grunted. He had bluntly refused his sister's suggestion that he go as Mark Antony, but after hearing that Isabelle intended to go as the shipwrecked heroine from *The Tempest*, he'd decided that donning the robe-like costume of Prospero would not go amiss. If nothing else, appearing as Isabel's fictitious father would hopefully lay to rest any speculation that he was romantically interested in her—a ridiculous notion some miscreant in society had had the audacity to put about.

'I'm glad it meets with your approval,' Alistair said as a sword-wielding gladiator strode by. 'I would hate to disappoint on this, your very first masquerade.'

'It is exciting though, isn't it?' Isabelle said. 'All these beautiful costumes.'

Watching a rather tipsy Nero stumble past, Alistair was inclined to think otherwise, but given that enjoyment of the evening was not his main reason for coming, he kept the remark to himself. He was about to say something less controversial when Isabelle's hand suddenly gripped his arm. 'Oh, dear Lord, he's here!' she gasped.

Alistair turned in the direction Isabelle was staring. 'Who's here?'

'Valentine Lawe! Look there, standing next to the lady in that beautiful Venetian gown. It's him! It has to be!'

Alistair quickly picked out the couple in question, and though it was the gentleman who had caught Isabelle's eye, it was the lady upon whom Alistair fixed his gaze—because she was nothing short of magnificent. Her costume was exquisite: the rich golden gown liberally trimmed with lace, the bodice cut daringly low, the waist nipped in tight. Her hair was piled high and adorned with an elaborate headdress of feathers and jewels, and her face was hidden behind a white, three-quarters mask into which eye slits and small nose holes had been cut. She could have stepped out of a seventeenth-century gondola.

It wasn't until the couple started towards him, however, that Alistair began to smile. Only one woman of his acquaintance walked with that degree of confidence.

'I'm afraid you are destined for disappointment, cousin,' Alistair whispered in Isabelle's ear. 'The gentleman approaching is not Valentine Lawe.'

'He isn't?' Disappointment rang in the younger girl's voice. 'Then who is he?'

'I shall leave the determination to you, but I venture to say all will be revealed the moment he speaks.'

While his cousin waited breathlessly for the romantic playwright to approach, Alistair kept his eyes on Victoria. There could be no mistaking that measured gait. In the glorious Venetian gown, she could easily have taken her place on her uncle's stage. Her poise and confidence would have assured her of the audience's approval and her appearance would have inspired lust in the heart of every man present. Lord knew it did in his.

'Good evening,' he said as the pair drew close enough for conversation. 'Did you come by way of carriage or gondola, my lady?'

He saw her mouth lift in a smile, the patch placed next to the enchanting curve of her bottom lip encouraging the eye to linger. 'Alas, there are too few canals in England to allow the latter, good Prospero. But I see you have fled your enchanted isle to rejoin the ranks of us lesser mortals, along with your lovely daughter.'

Alistair bowed deeply. He should have known that Victoria would be familiar with the characters in one of Shakespeare's most popular plays. 'It would seem we are revealed, my dear,' Alistair said to his cousin. 'And though tonight Venice is missing one of its most radiant lights, we cannot be sure of the identity of her gallant escort. If I were to hazard a guess, I might think one of England's foremost playwrights had decided to honour us with his presence.'

The gentleman laughed, his blue eyes twinkling behind the mask. 'You would not be wrong, sir, for I am indeed the illustrious Valentine Lawe.'

'But in fact or only in fiction?' Isabelle enquired breathlessly. 'For truly you are everything I imagined him to be.'

'I cannot answer your question, dear Miranda. To do so would be to defeat the purpose of the evening,' Laurence said gallantly. 'Masquerade is, after all, about mystery and dark secrets.'

'And a certain degree of discomfort,' Victoria said, fanning herself. 'I cannot speak for the rest of you, but I am finding the wearing of a mask uncommonly warm.'

'Then, I wonder, dear lady, if I might suggest a stroll around the garden?' Alistair said. 'The evening air will serve as balm to your heated skin, and you need not fear any impropriety from a respectable father like myself. Besides, I suspect the garden is well inhabited by others seeking similar relief.'

'I should like that, good Prospero.'

Alistair smiled, then turned to address the playwright. 'Mr Lawe, I wonder if I might impose upon you to keep my fair Miranda company for a short time.'

'I should be delighted.'

'Excellent. I shall return your lovely partner in due course.'

As expected, the garden was crowded with masked harlequins and fine ladies laughing, flirting and generally enjoying the mood of the masquerade. Across the garden, Alistair was amused to see his good friend Valbourg in the guise of a pirate, enjoying a conversation with a young woman dressed as a shepherdess.

'The gentleman makes a very convincing pirate and the lady a most winsome shepherdess,' Victoria murmured at Alistair's side. 'Isn't it fascinating how clothes can change a person's appearance?' She turned her head to look up at him. 'Just as I look like a seventeenth-century Venetian, you appear every inch the powerful wizard you portray.'

'I am no wizard, beautiful lady,' Alistair said, looking around for a quiet spot where they might sit and talk. 'If I were, I would use my powers to make all these people disappear and leave you and I alone in this scented garden.'

'Ah, but that would not be proper.'

'What do I care for propriety when mystery is the order of the night? Masquerade is about being someone else, if only for a few hours. A man might come with his wife, but flirt with another's and no one would be any the wiser.'

'Except for the lady and the wife.' Slowly, Victoria began to smile. 'So we are indulging in make believe?'

'Until midnight, when we remove our masks and return to our everyday selves. Until then, let us enjoy these brief moments of supposed anonymity and speak of things we would not without the benefit of a mask.'

Victoria slowly raised her eyes to his. 'What would you say to me now that you could not say before?'

'Only that I am enchanted by you.' Alistair knew what he risked in saying the words, but whether it was the magic of the night or the playfulness of Victoria's mood, it was a risk he was willing to take. 'That I have been, ever since the first moment of having seen you.'

He watched her glance away, plying her fan even as her smile faded. 'You would do well to keep your flattery to yourself, good Prospero. I am no more suitable to you in that guise than I am in this one.'

'On the contrary, I may not know who you are tonight, but I know who you were yesterday and who you will be tomorrow.'

He saw dainty white teeth tug at her lower lip. 'I fear you do not. And while I have already decided that the omission will be set right, I think it only fair to tell you that…what you know of me now is not…all there is to know.'

'I don't understand—'

'And I would beg you not to ask. Not tonight. I do not wish to spoil the magic of the evening, for it *is* a night for secrets, as you say.'

'And for unspoken longings.' Alistair captured her hand and, raising it to his lips, breathed in the sweet scent of her skin. 'If I could, I would conjure a gondola to take us away into the night. I would quote poetry to amuse you and reach into the sky to make a necklace of stars to place around your throat.' He smiled and brushed his mouth against the softness of her fingers. 'I would tell you things I should not and hope you would answer in kind. And tomorrow, I would listen to what you wish to tell me, knowing it could not change my feelings for you.'

'You're wrong,' Victoria said sadly. 'A deception has been enacted and I fear that when you hear the truth, you will not look at me the way you do now.'

'I see no deception, beautiful lady. You have been truthful from the start. You told me there could be nothing between us. I was the one who took exception to the remark. But I will listen to what you have to say. And then I hope you will be willing to listen to what I have to say in return.'

'Mr Devlin—'

'Alistair,' he whispered.

'Mr Devlin,' Victoria repeated, closing her eyes, 'I beg you to listen to me—'

'I don't want to listen,' he said, drawing close. 'I want...this.'

And then...he kissed her.

Victoria had been kissed before: once by a fumbling youth in a childhood game and once by a friend in a Christmas theatrical. But she had never been kissed like this. Never been made to feel she as though was in danger of losing her mind. The searing heat of Alistair's mouth obliterated every rational thought and, for a moment, she didn't care that she must tell him a potentially damaging truth.

All she knew was that she was falling in love with Alistair Devlin. Whatever happened tomorrow would have no bearing on that.

Slowly, reluctantly, they drew apart, their eyes holding each other's in the dim evening light. Victoria hadn't known it was possible to feel like this, but she did know that things would never be the same between them again. Soon, she would have to tell him the truth. Soon, she would have to explain why this secret life had been imposed on her. But in the aftermath of his kiss, all she wanted to do was draw his head down to hers and kiss him again. She leaned in towards him, eyes slowly closing. 'Mr Devlin—'

'Alistair,' he whispered. 'Say it, my love. It's not difficult.'

My love. She wanted to laugh at the pleasure of the unexpected intimacy, to disappear into the darkness of the night with him and never return. 'Alistair…'

Smiling, he bent his head and kissed her again, deeper this time as he pulled her against him, the folds of his cloak enveloping them both. His mouth was soft, yet insistent, totally in control of the moment…and of her.

Strange. She had written about this desperate longing in her plays, framed scenes in which her characters had spoken of the depths of their feelings, but never had she imagined that it could feel like this. His fingers gently grasped her chin, angling her mouth, drawing her closer.

Victoria leaned into him, wanting this. Wanting him—

And then, a burst of feminine laughter…sensual and provocative…shattered the velvet darkness and broke the spell.

Muffling a gasp, Victoria drew back. Her heart was racing, her body heavy as a result of Alistair's caresses, but it was madness to carry on. They were no longer alone in an enchanted garden.

A couple had emerged from the ballroom to stand on the candlelit terrace. Believing themselves unobserved, they drew close in a lovers' embrace, the man's arms sliding around the woman's waist, the woman pressing her body wantonly against his. He wore the uniform of a naval officer; she was dressed in medieval garb, her long, titian hair streaming down her back. But while her face was hidden behind a full white mask, Victoria recognised the sound of her laughter and gasped in horror when she realised who the temptress was. 'Signy!'

'Signy?' Alistair stared at the other couple and slowly recognition—and anger—dawned. 'And that's Collins. What in God's name is he doing here?'

As they watched, the pair embraced, the passionate kiss they shared bringing the blood to Victoria's face.

'Fool!' Alistair ground out. 'He should have known better than to bring his mistress here.'

'I suspect he thought it would be safe,' Victoria said quietly. 'Everyone is in costume. I would not have recognized Signy but for the sound of her laughter. But I must speak to her. If Lady Drake were to find out—'

'No, it's Collins who must be taken to task,' Alistair said. 'With any luck, we can get them out of here before anyone is the wiser.' He strode across the grass and stopped at the base of the stairs. 'Collins, a word!'

The lovers guiltily sprang apart. Collins's expression reminded Victoria of a little boy caught doing something he knew was wrong. 'I say, Dev, is that you?'

'Fortunately for you, yes,' Alistair answered in a tight voice. 'What the hell do you think you're doing?'

'Enjoying the masquerade, same as everyone

else. But I say, what a splendid costume!' Collins said, swaying just a little. 'Don't know who you're supposed to be, but it looks damn fine.'

'Silly, it's Prospero, from *The Tempest*,' Signy said as she fell giggling against him. 'I should know, I played the part of Miranda last year. Mr Templeton said it was one of my finest performances.' She turned to stare quizzically at Victoria. 'But I don't know who you are.'

Victoria sighed. 'It's Miss Bretton, Signy. And you must leave at once. If Lady Drake finds out you're here, she will not be at all pleased.'

But Signy only laughed, too intoxicated to care. 'Why should I leave? I am a celebrated actress. Admired by my fellow actors and adored by my fans. Why should she not be pleased that I have come to grace her silly little gathering?'

'Because you are not a lady,' Alistair said quietly. 'And this is not a suitable place for the two of you to be seen together. Collins, take Miss Chermonde home.'

'Don't listen to him, Bertie!' Signy said. 'I don't want to leave.'

But Collins was already wavering. 'Perhaps this wasn't such a good idea—'

'But nobody knows who I am!' the actress cried. 'And no one *need* know if we don't say anything. We can leave just before midnight. Right before everyone takes off their masks.'

'I think it best you go now, Signy,' Victoria said. 'Before someone recognises you and tells Lady Blake you're here.'

The change in the woman was alarming. In a matter of seconds, her pretty smile vanished and her eyes turned hard. 'I don't answer to you, Miss Bretton. Your uncle is the only one who has the right to tell me what to do.'

'That may be true, but I think we both know that if he were here, this discussion would not be taking place,' Victoria said, purposely keeping her voice calm. 'I would rather not have to tell him I saw you, but I will if I think it in everyone's best interests. You know how he feels about members of his cast stirring up gossip.'

The actress hissed like an angry cat. 'I don't like being threatened.'

'And I'm not threatening you. I am simply stating facts. The choice is yours.'

A tense silence followed as Victoria waited for Signy to make up her mind. The actress was clearly debating whether to stand her ground or to do as she had been told and make a hasty exit. Her focused stare was clearly an attempt to intimidate Victoria and to make her change her mind. But Victoria was prepared to make good on her threat. She would not risk her uncle's reputation by allowing a scandal to take place that centred on a member of his troupe, no matter how valuable that actress believed herself to be.

Thankfully, it didn't come to that. Signy drew herself up, as though stepping into a role, and, tossing back her glorious hair, said, 'Very well, I'll go. I have no desire to repay Mr Templeton's kindness by embroiling him in a scandal. But I owe *you* no such loyalty, Miss Bretton, and you have overstepped yourself tonight. You would do well to remember that I'm not the only one who plays a part, but at least I don't try to disguise who or what I am.'

She made as though to return to the ballroom, but Alistair gently but firmly took hold of her arm. 'Not that way. Collins, take Miss Chermonde out through the garden and on to the road. It would be better if neither of you ventured into the house again.'

Victoria remained silent as the drunken pair stumbled past, too stricken by the venom in Signy's parting remark to offer any kind of retort. What had Signy meant when she'd said she wasn't the only one playing a part? Did she know Victoria was Valentine Lawe? And if so, did she intend to expose her?

Signy knew she was the company's most valuable actress. She was used to being admired for her beauty and fêted for her talent. The fact she had been told she wasn't a lady and advised to go home would not sit well with her. She had an ego the size of London and Victoria knew she would take this as a personal slight. Her parting threat had been unmistakable...which made the necessity of telling Alistair the truth more important than ever.

'Is everything all right, Victoria?' he asked, sensing the change in her mood.

'Yes, of course.' Victoria tried for a smile, but failed. 'But I think we should go back inside. It is nearly time to unmask. Besides, Laurence and Miss Wright will be wondering where we are.'

She turned to go, but was stayed by the touch of his hand. 'They can wait a little longer. What's wrong, Victoria? Are you sorry I kissed you?'

The sweetness of the memory engulfed her and, aware that nothing could have been further from the truth, Victoria said, 'I would be lying if I said I was. But it was foolish to behave that way in a public place.' She cast an uncertain glance towards the departing pair. 'Our embrace may have been witnessed.'

'By those two?' Alistair shook his head. 'They were too caught up in each other to notice anything going on around them. But there's something you're not telling me. Something that's still troubling you.'

Victoria shook her head. This wasn't the time to alarm him over her fears about Signy. Not when she still had to tell him the truth about Valentine Lawe. 'It's nothing. Other than my concern over Miss Chermonde's reaction. She did not take kindly to my asking her to leave.'

'She is used to being the one other people bow to. But tonight she crossed a line and she had to be told. Collins, too.'

'Will he be angry that you asked him to leave?'

'I really don't care,' Alistair said. 'He should have known better than to bring his mistress here, given Lady Drake's feelings about such things, but it was clear they had both been drinking. I'm sure by the morning this will all have been forgotten.'

Victoria wasn't so sure. While she *hoped* Signy would forget everything the moment she fell into Lord Collins's arms, it was hard to forget the look of resentment in her eyes. Signy had wanted to come to the masquerade. She had enjoyed playing the part of the fine lady and had likely played it very well. Victoria doubted anyone who had seen the beautiful woman on Lord Collins's arm suspected her of being an actress and his newest mistress. Why would they? Bringing a woman like that one to one of Lady Drake's gatherings simply wasn't done.

But tonight it had been done and they had been caught in the act. Alistair might have been the one to tell Signy she wasn't a lady, but it was

Victoria's asking her to leave that the actress had taken exception to. And as they headed back into the ballroom, Victoria couldn't help but feel that this wasn't the last she had heard of it.

The news broke four days later.

Victoria was in her bedroom when it did, recovering from a wretched cold that had come upon her the morning after the masquerade. It had kept her to her bed and so prevented her from speaking to Alistair as she had planned. Even now, on her first day out of bed, she still found herself drifting in and out of sleep. The maid had to knock twice before Victoria heard it and when she finally opened the door, it was to learn that her father wished to see her at once.

Upon descending to the drawing room, she found both her uncle and her father waiting for her. The fact her mother and Aunt Tandy were not present said a great deal, but it was only when Victoria looked at her father's face that she began to fear the worst. 'What's wrong?'

The brothers shared a glance, but it was her father who spoke. 'I'm afraid there's no easy way to say this, my dear, so I'll just come right out and say it. I have been informed that there are rumours circulating about you.'

Victoria swallowed hard. 'What kind of rumours?'

'Rumours that you are…Valentine Lawe.'

Victoria abruptly sat down. 'Who started them?'

'We don't know—'

'Tell the girl the truth, John,' Theo interrupted impatiently. 'She deserves to know what she's up against.'

There was a brief moment of silence before her father sighed and said, 'Yes, I suppose she does. But I hate having to be the bearer of bad news.'

'It's all right, Papa, you're not,' Victoria said slowly. 'This doesn't come as a complete surprise.' She turned to look at her uncle. 'Signy Chermonde told Lord Collins I was Valentine Lawe, didn't she? And his lordship did the rest.'

Her uncle's eyes caught and held hers. 'How do you know that?'

'Because I happened to encounter Signy at Lady Drake's masquerade.'

'Lady *Drake's* musicale? What in blazes was Signy doing there?' Theo demanded. 'The countess isn't the type to invite actresses to her gatherings.'

'Signy wasn't invited,' Victoria said unhappily. 'She was there…with Lord Collins.'

'Collins?' Her uncle's shock yielded quickly to anger. 'He took his mistress to such a gathering? That little fool! He should have known better!'

'Yes, but he did not, and Signy took exception to my asking her to leave,' Victoria said. 'She accused me of...playing a part I wasn't brave enough to own up to. I suspect she informed Lord Collins of her suspicions that night. It was too much to hope that he would keep silent about it.'

'For your sake, he should have!' her father snapped, his usual complacency gone. 'If he believed there was any truth to the story, he must have realised there was a good reason why you weren't publishing the plays under your own name.'

'I know, Papa, but it doesn't matter any more. If Lord Collins hadn't been the one to expose me, someone else would. Signy wanted to humiliate me. She resented my interfering in her evening and this is how she is repaying me.' Victoria got up and walked slowly across the room. Her head was pounding and her nose was so stuffed she could hardly breathe, but she had to stay and hear it all. 'How widespread are the rumours?'

'I don't know,' her father said honestly. 'Theo heard it at his club. Said someone asked him outright if it was true.'

Victoria glanced at her uncle. 'What did you say?'

'That it was a lie, of course, and that he should have known better than to listen to such gossip.'

'But it *isn't* gossip,' Victoria said. 'It's the *truth*.'

'That doesn't mean we have to acknowledge it as such. We can fight this, Victoria,' her uncle said. 'No one outside the family knows you're Valentine Lawe, so no one outside the family is in a position to confirm or deny the rumour.'

'Some of the servants here know,' Victoria reminded him.

'True, but those who do have been sworn to secrecy and I pay them well enough to guarantee their loyalty. And when it becomes known that an actress started this rumour, I guarantee it will lose *all* credibility.'

'Unfortunately, a rumour doesn't have to be true to do damage,' her father pointed out. 'It is enough that it exists. By the time anyone bothers to find out how and where it started, the harm to Victoria's reputation will have been done.'

'Perhaps, but if we stand firm in our denials, it may die a faster death,' Theo said. 'I'm quite prepared to call Signy a liar. She doesn't know for certain that Victoria is Valentine Lawe, and unless someone in this family let it slip, there's no way anyone outside this house can confirm it.' He turned to Victoria. 'This may seem like an insensitive question, my dear, but is there *any* chance Winifred might have said something?'

'Absolutely not. She and Mama live in fear

of this very thing happening,' Victoria said. 'She would never expose me for fear of what it would do to *her* reputation. And I know Laurence wouldn't say anything.'

'So this is purely speculation and mischief-making on Signy's part.' Theo sighed. 'Pity. I shall have to dismiss her. I will not tolerate this kind of conduct in my troupe.'

'But you can't let her go!' Victoria cried. 'She is your finest actress. You need her.'

'I won't disagree that she is talented, but I've no time for petty jealousies and I will *not* have someone I cannot trust in my company.'

'But she hasn't violated your trust. I *am* Valentine Lawe,' Victoria said unhappily. 'What she told Lord Collins was the truth.'

'If only Collins had had the decency to keep it to himself,' her father muttered.

'Yes, well, as it turns out he did not, and I still say we have no choice but to present a united front,' Theo said. 'Deny it at every turn. Make it sound as laughable as it is unbelievable. Unless you've had a change of heart, Victoria, and don't care that people know you're Valentine Lawe.'

Victoria's first thoughts were for her mother and sister, who would never forgive her for exposing them in such a way. Her next were for Alistair and for entirely different reasons. She had to talk to him as soon as possible. If he hadn't already heard the rumours, he *must* hear about it from her. 'No. For the sake of the family, I think we must continue to deny it,' Victoria said with a heavy heart. 'I never wanted this to happen. I never *thought* it would happen. But now that it has, I have to deal with the consequences. Mama and Winifred will be furious, of course, but I think for now, we must do as Uncle Theo suggests.'

'*Can* you do that, Victoria?' Theo walked up to her and put his hands on her shoulders. 'Can you convince the world that you don't care what they're saying about you and that it is all a lie?'

'I have to try,' Victoria said. 'For the sake of everyone involved, I really have no choice.'

Chapter Eleven

Unfortunately for Victoria, Alistair did hear about the rumour and in the worst possible manner. He was standing with Lord Mortimer and Sir Nigel Gunstock, two of society's most malicious gossips, along with the rest of his family at the Bentley-Hydes' ball, when Lady Sarah Millingham came running up to them, positively bursting with the news. 'Have you heard the rumour about Miss Victoria Bretton?'

Alistair stiffened, but Isabelle was already asking the question. 'What rumour?'

'Shame on you, Isabelle,' Lady Kempton said. 'A lady does not encourage gossip.'

'But you will hear it spoken of before the night is over,' Lady Sarah said. 'There are those who are saying Miss Victoria Bretton is actually

Valentine Lawe! I heard it this afternoon at the milliner's and it was causing ever such a stir.'

Alistair was so astonished that for a moment he could think of nothing to say. Victoria Bretton the celebrated playwright? Impossible! She would never pretend to be someone she was not. And she would never wilfully mislead him. 'I'm afraid someone's been having sport with you, Lady Sarah,' he said. 'Miss Bretton is not the type to masquerade as someone else, and certainly not as a playwright.'

The young lady quailed slightly under his gaze. 'I cannot swear it is the truth, Mr Devlin, but the source was said to be very reliable.'

'And who is the source?' Lord Kempton demanded.

'Lord Collins.'

Alistair hissed, 'Bertie?'

'Really,' the Archdeacon said, raising an eyebrow. 'I wonder where he came upon the knowledge.'

'I understand he has been spending a lot of time at the Gryphon of late,' Lord Mortimer commented with a smirk. 'Perhaps he heard it from someone there.'

Sir Nigel chuckled, but Alistair did not find it in the least humorous. 'That doesn't explain why Miss Bretton would pretend to be someone she was not. Or why she would write plays under an assumed name.'

'I can think of several reasons why she would do that,' Sir Nigel said. 'Her mother is dead set against the theatre and everything to do with it. Apparently, her father was one of those fire-and-brimstone ministers who lived by the word of God and refused to allow any member of his family to indulge in such wickedness. No doubt Mrs Bretton raised her children in the same way and it galls her to no end that her brother-in-law owns a theatre and that both he and his wife were once actors. So if her daughter wished to write plays, it would have to be under an assumed name.'

'Not only that, Lawe has a particularly cutting wit and has made fun of society in more than one of his plays,' Lord Mortimer observed. 'Do you really think a young lady of good birth would wish people to know she was making fun of them? It certainly wouldn't help her marital aspirations.'

'If she has any,' Sir Nigel said. 'For all her beauty, Miss Bretton doesn't seem all that inclined towards marriage.'

'Still, it is not the thing for a young woman of good birth to be so closely associated with the theatre,' the Archdeacon said. 'I remember the first time I met her. She took leave to tell me what she thought of the calibre of the performers. I was astonished by her temerity.'

'There is nothing wrong with a woman being knowledgeable about the performing arts,' Alistair said as patiently as he could. 'Miss Bretton is exceptionally well read and her appreciation for the theatre would naturally be strengthened by her relationship with her uncle.'

'And I like her very much!' Isabelle said fiercely. 'She is admirable in every way, and while I am disappointed that Valentine Lawe is not the dashing playwright I imagined him to be, it doesn't bother me in the least to know that Miss Bretton is the brilliant author behind his works. I only wish I were so talented!'

'Hold your tongue, Isabelle!' Lord Kempton admonished. 'I will not hear you say such things in my presence. It does not please me to hear you defend a woman who has obviously been lying to all who know her. It speaks very poorly of her character, and of her family's.'

'Indeed, they must have known what she was about,' the Archdeacon said, 'so they are all party to the deception.'

'In which case,' Lord Mortimer said, laughing openly, 'who knows what other manner of skeletons are likely to fall out of the closet. Best not open that door at all.'

Alistair didn't stay to hear any more. It was

more than he could bear to hear Victoria made a laughing-stock in society. He refused to believe that she had lied to him. What he knew of her character would allow for no error in that direction. It was impossible to think that the woman he'd held in his arms and kissed with such passion would ever deceive him.

No, far more likely Collins had made a mistake. Or that Signy Chermonde, incensed by Victoria's taking her to task, had decided to exact her own kind of revenge. Either way, he would resolve the matter before the night was out. No matter where he had to go or who he had to track down, he would find out what he needed to know. And he intended to make damn sure the guilty party was at Victoria's house tomorrow morning, offering her the apology he knew without question she was due.

The search for Lord Collins took Alistair to Bertie's favourite hell, a club on Bennett Street that while not as disreputable as some, still had a reputation for high-stakes gambling and the fleecing of young aristocrats too naïve to know any better.

Collins was in one of the upstairs rooms, watching a game of faro. It was evident from his heightened colour that he had been drinking. Upon seeing his good friend standing in the doorway, he got up and staggered across the room. 'Dev, old man!' He threw an arm about Alistair's shoulders, his lopsided grin showing no signs of remorse. 'To what do I owe the pleasure?'

'I doubt you'll find it a pleasure when I tell you why I'm here,' Alistair muttered, shrugging off the man's arm. 'I need to speak to you in private.'

'Ah. Well, you won't find much of that in here,' Collins said, glancing at the crowded tables close by.

'Fine. Then we'll step out into the corridor.'

Alistair led the way, making sure to close the door behind them. He could still hear the sound of laughter from within and so proceeded down the hall until he could not. Finally, he turned to face Collins, whose expression was still blissfully ignorant of any wrongdoing. 'What's the matter, Dev? You seem a little upset.'

'I'm a damn sight more than a little upset,' Alistair snapped. 'Is it true you started this ridiculous rumour about Victoria Bretton being Valentine Lawe?'

'Of course not!' Collins blustered, though his face went as red as a beetroot. 'Whoever said that was lying.'

'Why would they lie?'

'I don't know. Why would you accuse me of

making up a rumour about Miss Bretton being Valentine Lawe?'

'Because your mistress is Signy Chermonde,' Alistair said in a silken voice. 'And we both know she resented Miss Bretton's telling her to leave the masquerade the other evening. Now she is seeking revenge by making up this ridiculous story and she told *you* because she knew you would put it about in society.'

The remark had the effect of banishing the grin from Collins's face, leaving him looking somewhat confused. 'Ah. Well, now that you mention it, Signy did make reference to something of that nature the other night. And in fact, I may have let something slip at Jackson's the other morning,' he admitted sheepishly. 'But I swore them all to secrecy and they assured me they wouldn't breathe a word of it to anyone.'

'Then I suggest you find more trustworthy friends,' Alistair ground out. 'Why did you say anything, Bertie? You must have known it was all a hoax.'

'Signy doesn't seem to think so. In fact, she's convinced Victoria Bretton *is* Valentine Lawe.'

'That's ridiculous!'

'Is it? The facts would indicate otherwise.'

'What facts?'

'Apparently, Miss Bretton is often to be found at the theatre during rehearsals, but only when

one of Valentine Lawe's plays is being staged.
And Signy says she's heard Templeton talking
to Miss Bretton about Lawe's plays on a number
of occasions,' Collins said. 'Consulting with her
as to how a character should be portrayed or a
particular line spoken.'

'So, the lady has an eye for that sort of thing,'
Alistair said, unwillingly recalled to Victoria's
emerging from the theatre at half past ten in
the morning. 'That doesn't mean she's Valentine
Lawe.'

'But it doesn't mean she isn't, either,' Collins
pointed out. 'Besides, when you think about it,
why couldn't she be Lawe? No one's ever seen
the fellow. Keeps himself hidden away like a
bloody monk, and to what purpose? His plays
draw sold-out crowds. The critics love his work,
so why go to all the trouble of keeping his identity secret?'

'I would have thought that was his business,'
Alistair said drily. 'If I choose to become a re-
cluse, it's no one's business but my own.'

'But think, Dev. No one's *ever* seen Lawe.
And he's been writing for…how many years?
Don't you think it's a little strange that no one
has *any* information about where he lives, where
he dines, who his servants are, or what he does
when he's not writing?'

Alistair hadn't thought it strange because

until that moment, he hadn't given it a passing thought. But faced with the question now, he had to admit that Collins had a point. Not one of his acquaintances had ever claimed to have seen the famous playwright, and there wasn't so much as a whisper of substantiated gossip about the man, even from servants. It was almost as though he didn't exist.

Was he wrong to believe so completely in Victoria's innocence?

Alistair had trusted women before, only to find out they had deceived him. Lady Frances Shaftsbury. Celeste Fontaine. Both had led him to believe something that wasn't true...which likely explained why he'd wanted so desperately to believe that Victoria was telling him the truth. After all, *she* was the one who'd run from him; the one who'd said right from the beginning that they would not suit. Had she said that because she'd known there was something she couldn't tell him and didn't want to risk being found out?

The very idea left a bad taste in his mouth.

'Nevertheless, it doesn't give you the right to spread a rumour about Miss Bretton when you have no way of knowing whether it's true or not,' Alistair said, not about to express doubts within Collins's hearing. 'She is a lady in every sense of the word. This could do irreparable harm to her reputation.'

'I venture to say her reputation was already tarnished when you met her, my friend,' Collins said. 'I told you as much that first night. Take my advice, marry the Millingham chit. She's a pretty little filly and once she bears you an heir, you can look for compatibility elsewhere. It's what gentlemen like us do.'

Alistair took his leave shortly thereafter. Having heard all he needed to from Bertie—and not liking any of it—he headed for the Gryphon, determined to uncover the truth. It was not yet midnight. With luck, Signy would still be there and he would deal with her personally. If not, he would speak to Templeton and find out what that gentleman knew.

He was in luck. Templeton was just walking down the front steps as Alistair drew his carriage to a halt. 'Templeton, a word, if you don't mind.'

'Mr Devlin,' Templeton said. 'I'm surprised to see you at this hour.'

'I have business with Miss Chermonde. Is she still here?'

'Good God, no, she left over two hours ago.'

'Fine. Then I'll deal with you. I was made aware of a very disturbing rumour earlier this evening and I was informed that one of your cast members started it.'

Templeton frowned. 'I don't like the sound of that. You'd best tell me what this is all about.'

'Are you saying you haven't heard the rumour that your niece, Victoria Bretton, is Valentine Lawe?'

'The playwright?' Templeton started to laugh. 'Good Lord, how intriguing.'

'Forgive me if I don't share your amusement. I find it anything but.'

'Yes, of course, but surely you don't believe the rumour?'

'No, but I have it on good authority that a member of your cast started it in the hopes of embarrassing, and perhaps even of disgracing, Miss Bretton. That person is Signy Chermonde.'

'Signy?' Templeton's look of amusement abruptly vanished. 'Why would she do such a thing?'

'Because Miss Bretton and I came upon her and Lord Collins at Lady Drake's masquerade, and though we both told them to leave, I believe Miss Chermonde took exception to Miss Bretton's telling her to do so and this is her way of seeking revenge.'

'You make a serious accusation, Devlin,' Templeton said, all traces of good humour vanishing.

'And I do not make it lightly. But I will not

see Miss Bretton's reputation tarnished by the irresponsible behaviour of a spiteful actress.'

'If that is true, I can assure you that Miss Chermonde will be reprimanded,' Templeton said. 'It does no one any good to have these scurrilous rumours spread around. Imagine anyone thinking that Victoria could be Valentine Lawe.'

'My thoughts exactly,' Alistair said, starting to feel a measure of relief that Templeton, who was perhaps the *only* person who knew Valentine Lawe and was willing to state that he was *not* Victoria Bretton. 'Unfortunately, given that no one but you has ever seen Lawe, there are many who are willing to believe it. Sometimes I wonder if he truly does exist.'

'Oh, he exists. Someone had to write those plays,' Templeton said. 'I certainly didn't.'

'Then set the record straight and *tell* people who Valentine Lawe is! For your niece's sake, if not for yours or mine.'

'I'm afraid I can't do that, Mr Devlin,' Templeton said regretfully. 'I gave my word I would never reveal his identity and I must hold true to that promise. But it is a travesty that Victoria should be made to suffer in order to appease Signy's petty need for revenge. I will speak to her first thing in the morning.'

Alistair was happy to settle for that, his concerns about Victoria having been laid to rest.

He should have known better than to doubt her. She was a lady and had been raised with a lady's sensibilities. She knew the difference between right and wrong, and Alistair would *not* allow a pretty actress to blacken her name, no matter what his father, his brother-in-law or society thought. He would show them all what he thought of their ridiculous charge.

He loved Victoria and he believed in her. And he would prove it by doing the one thing that would leave no room for doubt in anyone's mind.

Despite the family's concerted efforts, the rumour about Victoria being Valentine Lawe did not go away. It went without saying that her mother and sister were furious. It seemed Mr Fulton had suddenly directed his interest elsewhere, and that even Lord Valbourg was nowhere to be found.

'This is all your fault, Victoria!' Winifred cried waspishly at breakfast the next morning. 'Had you not engaged in such scandalous behaviour, I might even now be engaged to Mr Fulton! But he has heard the rumours and is paying court to Miss Daversham. How could you do this to me? How *could* you!'

'I didn't do anything to you, Winifred,' Victoria said wearily. 'It was never my intention that you or any other member of this family should suffer.'

'But we *are* suffering and if you cared for us, you would stop it at once and try to make everything right,' Winifred said.

Quince entered the room with a letter and handed it to her father. Her father, upon seeing that it was addressed to Victoria, duly passed it down the table.

'Victoria is receiving mail?' Winifred said between mouthfuls of toast. 'From whom?'

'I'm sure if your sister wishes you to know, she will tell you,' her father said, returning his attention to the newspaper.

'Well, who sent it?' Winifred demanded as soon as it was in her sister's hands.

Victoria broke the seal and blanched when she saw the signature. 'It is from…Mr Devlin.'

'Devlin?' Her father put down his paper. 'I wasn't aware you knew the gentleman well enough to be receiving letters from him, Victoria.'

'What does he want?' Laurence asked, looking up from his book.

Victoria scanned the contents of the letter. They were brief and to the point. 'He wishes to call upon me at two o'clock this afternoon,' she said. 'On a matter of…considerable importance.'

'Considerable importance?' Her mother

gasped. 'Oh, dear Lord! He is coming to *propose*!'

'He is not coming to do anything of the sort!' Victoria said, quickly refolding the letter. 'I suspect he is coming to talk to me about the rumour. What shall I tell him…if he asks?'

'You must tell him what you think best,' her father said.

'Except the truth!' Laurence added. 'Remember what Uncle Theo said. We must continue to deny the rumour whenever we hear it. Present a united front. I, in fact, was questioned about it just yesterday and denied it most vehemently.'

'But how can I lie to *him*, of all people?' Victoria asked. 'When he has been nothing but honest with me?'

'How would Mr Devlin react if you were to tell him the truth and ask him not to say anything?' Winifred enquired.

'I can't do that! It is bad enough I have to lie to him. I could never ask him to keep silent about it as well.'

Victoria glanced at the clock. Alistair was coming at two o'clock—and it was half past ten now. She had three and a half hours in which to make up her mind. Three and a half hours to decide whether to be honest with the man she loved and risk losing his good opinion—or to perpetuate the myth and lose hers.

Chapter Twelve

As always, when anticipating the arrival of an unsettling event, the hours flew all too quickly by. Before she knew it, Victoria heard the sound of the clock on the mantel chime the quarter hour. Fifteen minutes to go.

Thankfully, her mother and sister were not at home. Contrary to Winifred's fears, Lord Valbourg had not taken her in disgust over the rumours about Victoria being Valentine Lawe. He had simply been preoccupied with his mother's illness and had had no time to spare on the redecoration of his new house. Once Lady Alderbury turned the corner, however, he had written to ask if they might arrange the shopping expedition, and today he had collected them to do just that. They expected to be gone for a few hours.

That, at least, gave Victoria some breathing room. The thought of her mother being present as she tried to explain herself to Alistair was decidedly offputting. However, given that someone had to be in the room when he came to call, Victoria decided it should be Laurence. The presence of her father might definitely indicate hopes of a proposal.

For that reason, at ten minutes to two, brother and sister walked into the drawing room and took up their respective positions. Victoria sat down on the loveseat to the left of the fireplace and Laurence set up an easel in one corner of the room. He thought it would be easier for all of them if he was actively engaged in doing something, and so positioned the easel in such a way that the focus was away from the seating area. So it was that when Alistair was shown into the room at precisely two o'clock, he found Laurence at his painting and Victoria with her head bent over her stitching. He acknowledged Laurence's presence with a brief nod, then turned to bestow a warm smile on Victoria. 'Miss Bretton, thank you for agreeing to see me.'

'Not at all, Mr Devlin. Won't you sit down?'

He chose the high-back chair across from her, effectively putting his back to Laurence. 'I think you must know why I've come,' he said after a moment.

Victoria bit her lip, her gaze falling before his. 'Yes, I rather think I do.'

'Good. Given what passed between us at the masquerade, I hoped you would be anticipating my visit.'

Victoria's eyes shot up. 'What happened…at the masquerade?'

'Yes.' Alistair leaned forwards and lowered his voice. 'Surely you haven't forgotten?'

A rush of warmth suffused Victoria's face as memories of that intimate and most pleasurable encounter returned. Of course she hadn't forgotten. If she lived to be a hundred she would never forget. But not for a moment had she thought it might be the reason he had come today. 'I haven't forgotten, but I thought we were…indulging in an impossible fantasy.'

'I didn't think of it as impossible,' he said. 'I was entirely serious.'

'But how can you wish to pursue this in light of some of the…other things you must have heard about me?'

'You mean the ridiculous rumour that you are Valentine Lawe?'

A crash from the corner—the sound of breaking glass—was followed by a muffled oath and a hasty apology. 'Sorry! Terribly clumsy of me,' Laurence said. 'Knocked the water jar clean off the ledge.'

'That's…all right,' Victoria said, forcing a smile. 'These things happen.' But when she saw her brother heading towards the door, she added quickly, 'Where are you going?'

'To fetch a rag. I doubt Mama would appreciate me using the edge of her tablecloth to wipe up the mess. I'll be back in a moment.'

Victoria chewed on her bottom lip, but Alistair only smiled as the door closed. 'Convenient, your brother knocking the jar over just then. I think he must have guessed at my reason for coming.'

Then he was the only one, Victoria thought anxiously. The way Alistair was looking at her… the gravity of his expression…surely he wasn't about to—

'Victoria, I know you're not expecting this,' Alistair said quietly. 'But over the past few weeks, I've come to feel something for you that I've never felt for anyone else in my life. I can't stop thinking about you and I want you to know what is in my heart.'

No, this couldn't be happening, Victoria thought, alternating between delight and despair. It was clear now that he hadn't come to discuss the rumour that she was Valentine Lawe. He had come to propose! And with Laurence's timely exit, that's exactly what he was about to do.

But he mustn't! Not when he wasn't acquainted

with all of the facts. If he knew what she was up to, he would not be coming to her with his heart in his hands. He would be coming to her with words of condemnation and blame. For his sake as well as her own, she had to stop him before the words were uttered. 'Mr Devlin—'

'Alistair.'

'No, there can be no intimacy between us. Not without you knowing the truth.'

'The truth?'

'Yes. About me. About…the rumours that I am Valentine Lawe.'

'Dearest girl, I already know they aren't true. I am aware of how honest and straightforward you are. You warned me right from the start that you and I would not suit,' Alistair said. 'You told me you were outspoken and opinionated and that I would damage my reputation by being seen with you. But I have since come to know you so much better than that. Nothing in your behaviour has led me to believe you would be anything but honest in your dealings with me and with others.'

'But…what Signy said about me—'

'Stemmed from petty jealousy and resentment,' Alistair said flatly. 'She didn't like you telling her to leave the masquerade and thought to settle the score by starting this ridiculous rumour. But I refused to believe it. I told Collins as much when he tried to convince me it was true.'

Victoria gasped. 'You've spoken to Lord Collins about this?'

'Of course. The moment I heard he was the one responsible for spreading the rumour. I tracked him down and told him exactly what I thought of him.'

'Oh, please say you did not!'

'I did, and in no uncertain terms. I said that no gentleman, and certainly no friend of mine, would ever allow a lady to be so insulted. As far as I'm concerned the same goes for Miss Chermonde. She should be dismissed for spreading such lies and I told your uncle as much.'

'You spoke to my uncle as well?' Victoria blanched. 'What did he say?'

'That he was very disappointed and that he would take care of it at the first opportunity.'

Victoria began to feel physically ill. It was even worse than she had feared. Not only had Alistair defended her to his best friend and called an honest woman a liar, he had asked her uncle to act accordingly. Truly, she had to bring this to an end. 'Mr Devlin, I beg you will listen to what I am about to say and try to understand.' Needing to distance herself from those hypnotic eyes, she abruptly got to her feet. 'It was never my intention to deceive anyone—'

'No one has been deceived.'

'Yes, Mr Devlin, I fear they have,' Victoria said quickly. 'Particularly you. Because as much as I hate to tell you this, the truth is, I *am*… Valentine Lawe.'

There was a short, tense, silence. '*You* are… Valentine Lawe.'

'Yes.'

'Impossible.' He stared at her, unsmiling. 'You never said a word to me—'

'Because I *could* not say anything to you. I *promised* Mama I would not,' Victoria said unhappily. 'It was bad enough when she found out I had written a play. She was horrified when she found out my uncle was going to put it on the stage. She was so upset she became ill. So, I made her a promise. I told her I would never tell anyone what I do and that I would write under a pseudonym so no one would know it was me.'

There was another silence, longer and more ominous than the first. 'So you lied to me,' Alistair said in a cold, flat voice.

'No! I never said I was *not* Valentine Lawe—'

'But you never said you *were* either and I seem to recall any number of occasions where you might have done so,' Alistair said. 'The night we first met, when I told you how much I enjoyed the play. That evening at the Holcombes, when we talked about your love of the theatre. Even that morning in the park, when Isabelle told you how desperate she was to meet Valentine Lawe. You never let on. Never so much as a whisper that *you* were the person she was describing and admired so much. How could you do that to her? How could you tell such barefaced lies?'

'It wasn't like that,' Victoria said desperately. 'I *couldn't* say anything, don't you understand? I had given a promise to my family. To my mother. But I didn't lie.'

'Unfortunately, I've never been overly fond of truth by omission,' he said distantly. 'I stood up for you, Miss Bretton. I called a good friend's integrity into question and defended you to my family. But it seems they all knew better than I who you really were.'

His words of brittle condemnation broke her heart. 'I'm sorry,' Victoria whispered. 'At one point, I thought you knew. That night…when you told your cousin she would meet Valentine Lawe before she left London, you looked at me—and I thought you had guessed—'

'I guessed nothing. I was simply sharing my amusement with you over Isabelle's silly infatuation with an unknown playwright. I said what I said in the hopes of making her feel better. Had I known the famous playwright was standing right in front of me, I wouldn't have made such a damn fool of myself.'

'But you did not—!'

'Yes, Miss Bretton, I did. And I compounded my foolishness by telling your uncle to dismiss Signy Chermonde for what I believed to be a conscienceless act of malice. How he must have laughed at my gullibility—'

'He would never have done that!' Victoria cried. 'We weren't trying to deceive anyone!'

'Not deceive anyone? You deceived half of London!' Alistair snapped. 'Everyone who went to your plays. Everyone who ever talked to you about Valentine Lawe. You deceived them all! And you did a damn fine job of deceiving me.'

'Alistair, please—'

'No! I trusted you, Miss Bretton. I admired you because I thought you were different from all the others. I respected you for having the courage to say what you thought. Believe it or not, I could have accepted the fact that you wrote plays, but I cannot come to terms with the extent of your dishonesty. To lie so convincingly to my face—how can I ever be sure you would not lie to me again?'

'I'm sorry,' Victoria said, feeling her heart shrivel up and die like an old woman's hopes. 'I never meant to hurt you—'

'Pray, do not trouble yourself, my sensibilities are not so easily wounded,' Alistair said in a voice that was chillingly cool and aloof. 'Perhaps it is just as well I found out when I did. I suspect it has saved us both a great deal of heartache in the long run.'

He turned and started for the door, hesitating only long enough to say, 'You need not fear that I will be the one to expose you. For the sake of…what I once felt for you, I will keep silent. But I have already given more to you than any other woman. Do not ask me for anything more.'

Victoria kept to her room for the rest of the week. She did not entertain visitors and she refused to pay calls. Nor did she write a word. She kept remembering the look of disgust on Alistair's face, the surprise that had turned so quickly to revulsion. She kept hearing the cold ring of finality in his voice and it tore her apart. She couldn't eat, couldn't sleep, couldn't think.

From her brother she learned that talk about her being Valentine Lawe had finally started to abate. Likely because the men in her family continued to deny the rumour whenever and wherever they heard it, and her mother so chilled anyone who brought it up that people stopped mentioning it in her presence. And, as her father predicted, it was soon displaced by a new rumour about a certain titled lady whose staggering losses at cards had all but bankrupted her new husband.

But because Alistair knew the truth and wanted to have nothing more to do with her, Victoria felt no relief at hearing the news. In point of fact, she could not have been more despondent. Because in the days following their final interview, she came to realise how deeply and irrevocably in love she was with Alistair Devlin. And how, as a result of her own stupidity, she had lost him.

The pain was debilitating; the razor-sharp edge of grief made her long for the darkness of night when she could lose her sadness in sleep. But upon waking, the agonising bleakness returned, and with it, the tears. Her brother knew how she had suffered. A week after her meeting with Alistair, he took her to Astley's Amphitheatre so that they might enjoy the delights of the equestrienne ballet. But though he was a delightful companion and the performance highly entertaining, the memory of Alistair's bitterness refused to be shaken.

'You must try to get over this, Tory,' Laurence said as they left the theatre at the end of the show. 'It is not healthy for you to take on so. You will go into a decline.'

'I can't help it, Laurie. I miss him so much,' Victoria said. 'I never thought I would feel this way about any man, let alone him.'

'Dashed uncomfortable thing, love,' her brother

acknowledged softly. 'Especially when it's with the wrong person.'

Something in his voice prompted her to glance at him. 'You're not still harbouring a tendre for Signy, are you?'

'No.' He laughed, managing to look a little sheepish. 'I realise now it was just a silly infatuation. I always knew there was no future in it. But that doesn't mean we can't indulge ourselves in dreams.'

'There is someone out there for you, dearest,' Victoria said, slipping her arm through his. 'You are going to make some girl very happy one day…if you pull your head out of your books long enough to notice one.'

He grimaced. 'I don't spend all of my time with books. I went to a rather disreputable club for cards the other evening and, though you mustn't tell Mama, I visited a peep-show in Coventry.'

'Laurie, you didn't!'

'Indeed I did. Saw the wonders of the Orient, the splendours of the Taj Mahal, and a very pretty young lady bathing on a Caribbean island.'

'I hope she was decently clothed.'

'Scantily, but decent,' Laurence admitted. 'I was far more interested in the palm trees and the remarkably blue water than I was in admiring her rather obvious charms.'

'Wretch!' Victoria said, squeezing his arm. 'You would send Mama to bed for a week if she knew.'

'Which is precisely why I have no intention of telling her. She is in enough of a tizzy over—' He broke off, blushing. 'That is—'

'It's all right, I know what you were going to say and you're right,' Victoria said, her momentary smile fading. 'The entire family is in a twitter for one reason or another. Winifred barely speaks to me, Mama is chilly at best, and even Papa seems unusually distracted. I wouldn't have thought it possible that one person's actions could disrupt a family so completely, but it is clear that mine have. That's why I have decided...' she stopped and swallowed hard '...that I am not going to write any more plays.'

'*What?*' Laurence stopped dead in his tracks. 'You can't stop writing plays!'

'Yes, I can. I've given this a great deal of thought, and it really is the only solution. When *A Lady's Choice* finishes its run, there won't be any more Valentine Lawe plays. I have already brought too much public attention and disgrace to the family and made everyone miserable as a result. You know that was never my intention.'

'Of course it wasn't, but you can't stop writing, Tory. People would kill for a talent like yours. You can't just…throw it all away or pretend it doesn't exist!'

'Actually, I can,' Victoria said, refusing to let herself dwell on it. She had thought long and hard about this over the last few days and, while knowing she would not write another play only added to her feelings of despondency, she also knew it was the only logical answer. 'I can bear the humiliation for myself, but not for Mama and Winifred. Every time I see their long faces, I am reminded of what I've done and hate that everyone has to lie for me. That truly is the worst,' she said, remembering the look on Alistair's face when he had thrown the accusation at her. 'So, in future, there will be no more need for lies because there won't be any more plays. Eventually, everyone will forget about Valentine Lawe and life will return to normal. Winifred will marry someone suitable, as will you—'

'And what about you, Victoria?' Laurence said. 'What are you going to do, if not write?'

'I don't know. Travel, perhaps. I've always wanted to visit Florence and Rome.' Victoria stared at the bustling street, seeing it all through a grey mist of tears. 'Who knows? Maybe I'll even go to Venice and ride in a gondola.'

'Oh, yes, that will make Mama happy,' Laurence

muttered. 'Her eldest daughter following in the footsteps of Lady Tavistocke. A blow from which she might *never* recover!'

Her brother's quip brought a faint smile to Victoria's lips, but it was not enough to keep the sadness at bay. She feared nothing had the power to do that any more.

Not surprisingly, the days following his interview with Victoria were not ones of joy or satisfaction for Alistair. Contrary to the belief that he would feel nothing but relief at being free of her, he was in fact ill tempered, impatient and a bear to be around. He found fault with everything and everyone and was quick to criticise and even quicker to dismiss…because the simple truth was, he missed her. He missed her beautiful smile and her wonderful disregard for the things that seemed to matter so deeply to everyone else.

He heard her spoken about, of course. Frequently, a salacious mention of Valentine Lawe would work its way into a conversation and he would be forced to listen to remarks that ranged from the mildly censorious to the openly condemning. It seemed that while no one could deny that Miss Bretton had a formidable talent, the majority agreed that it was not the thing for a lady to deceive people by writing plays under an assumed name, especially when those plays often hit so close to home.

Of course, there were those who refused to believe that Victoria *was* the famous playwright. Men, for the most part, who believed that *no* woman was possessed of that degree of talent. But in literary circles, she was highly praised, and while no confirmation was ever given by a member of her family or by the lady herself, bluestockings and those of an intellectual bent continued to support the claim that Victoria was the author and they celebrated her achievements accordingly.

Sadly, none of that took away from the fact that Victoria had lied to him. Or that she had done so in such a way that made it impossible for Alistair to go back and apologise to Lord Collins, or to his family or friends. He had given Victoria his word that he would not expose her and he intended to stand by that promise. But in losing her, he had also lost any and all interest in marriage. He informed his parents of his decision and while his father had been furious and his mother dreadfully put out, he had stood fast, saying he would not marry for their pleasure or convenience. Because in the midst of all the confusion, there was one thing about which Alistair was very sure.

He had to get over Victoria Bretton before he stood any chance of falling in love with anyone else.

Chapter Thirteen

Victoria knew it wasn't a good idea to go to the orphanage. For one thing, the area was hardly the sort of place a lady visited, even in a closed carriage with a maid as a companion, and for another, there was the distinct possibility of running into Alistair.

That alone was enough to make her think twice about her decision.

But, for days now, she had found herself wondering about the children and how they went on. Ever since Alistair had taken her there, Victoria had felt a connection to those poor little waifs. To Molly and her sister, and to poor little Teddy, whose treatment at the hands of a cruel master could have scarred him for life. And of course, to Jenny, who had been exposed to the type of violence no child should ever have to witness.

Had she spoken yet? Victoria wondered about that as the carriage drew to a halt in front of the grey stone building. Perhaps Mrs Hutchins had succeeded in breaking through the wall of silence and fear the child had built around herself. She would find out in the next few minutes.

'Je ne pense pas que c'est une bonne idée,' Angelique whispered, glancing through the window at the unprepossessing house.

'I'm not sure it is a good idea either,' Victoria agreed. 'But we are here now and I am not going to leave without seeing them. I could not go on with my life without making some small effort on their behalf.'

The decision to make a donation to the orphanage had come to Victoria late last night as she lay awake in bed thinking about her future. It was one of several decisions she had made over the past week, and it was by far the easiest. By contrast, her decision to tell Alistair the truth about Valentine Lawe, followed by her decision to give up writing, had been the hardest. The others—to go away for a while and to set herself up in her own establishment upon returning home—had fallen somewhere in between, but the more she thought about them, the more sense they made.

It was unlikely she would ever marry. The possibility of having someone in her life other than Alistair was too unpleasant to consider. She would rather spend her life as a spinster than constantly be comparing her husband to another man and find him lacking.

No, it was better that she dedicate herself to other causes. She would go abroad and spend a few months travelling around the continent with Angelique or a companion—an older woman, perhaps, who was well read and shared her interests. Then, when she returned to London, she would take a house on some quiet London street and go on with her life.

She certainly had the wherewithal to do it. The plays had afforded her the income to live independently and, contrary to what she had told Laurie, she did intend to continue with her writing, but in the form of novels rather than plays, and more directed towards children than adults. She could publish them under her own name and become one of those women society didn't know how to deal with: a strong woman of independent means and esoteric tastes. No doubt she would become part of a literary circle and hold intellectual gatherings at her home.

All in an attempt to forget the man she had fallen in love with and the life she would never have.

It was as she was approaching the front door that Victoria caught a movement out of the corner of her eye. She smiled when she realised the boy was trying to watch her without being seen. 'Teddy, is that you?'

Identified by name, the little tyke stiffened. 'Might be. Don't know you, though.'

Victoria wasn't disappointed by the boy's lack of recognition. She would have been more surprised had he remembered her. 'I'm Miss Bretton. I came a while back with Mr Devlin.'

He stuck out his lower lip. 'You're the one wot read to Molly.'

'That's right. I've come to see how she is.'

The little boy shrugged. 'She's aw'right. Doc's not been round this week. Mrs 'utchins said there weren't no need.'

'I'm very glad to hear it,' Victoria said, hoping the housekeeper's reasons for not summoning the doctor had more to do with an improvement in Molly's health than the alternative.

'Wot's in there, then?' he asked, glancing at the hamper Angelique was carrying.

'A few little treats,' Victoria said. 'I thought they might be nice to have with your tea.'

Teddy briefly considered this, then, to her surprise, walked up to the front door of the house and pounded his fist against it. 'You've got to bang 'ard sometimes,' he said. 'They don't alus 'ear a light knock.'

'Thank you, Teddy. I am most grateful for your help,' Victoria said as the door swung open.

'Why, Miss Bretton!' Mrs Hutchins looked far more surprised to see Victoria than Teddy had been. 'Whatever are you doing here?'

'I've come to see the children, if that's all right. And to bring them a few things.'

'Is Mr Devlin not with you?'

'No. He doesn't know I'm here and I would rather he not learn of it,' Victoria said.

'Well, you'd best come in then. Don't worry about the carriage; Thomas will keep an eye on it. Won't you, Thomas?'

Victoria looked around and saw the lanky young man who had been there the first time she'd visited, leaning against the wall. He didn't smile, but he did nod in a very serious fashion. Victoria made a note to herself to leave something for him when she left.

'You'll have to excuse the mess,' Mrs Hutchins said as she led the way upstairs. 'I've already started to pack. Mr Devlin says we're going to be moving the end of next month as the work he's doing on the house is coming along better than he thought. And look, here's Margaret come to say hello. You remember Miss Bretton, Margaret?'

The little girl with the spectacles glanced up

at Victoria. She didn't smile, but she did nod. 'Hello, Miss Bretton.'

'Hello, Margaret. How are you?'

'I'm fine. Molly's all right, too. She hasn't been coughing as much.'

'I'm very glad to hear it.' Victoria glanced at the housekeeper. 'Do you think we could go up and see her?'

'I don't see any problem with that,' Mrs Hutchins said. 'Margaret, take Miss Bretton and her maid up while I put the kettle on for tea.'

'Actually, I was thinking Angelique could stay here with you,' Victoria said. 'She could help you put away the things in the hamper. I won't be long.'

Angelique seemed happy enough to stay downstairs, no doubt hopeful of a gossip, and with Margaret once again taking her hand, Victoria made her way upstairs. She arrived to find most of the younger children there. They were all a bit shy at first, but Victoria soon set them at ease. Some of them remembered her, likely because seeing a lady of quality wasn't something that happened often.

At least, Victoria hoped it wasn't a common occurrence. She couldn't bear to think that Alistair had already brought another lady here, someone with whom he hoped to share his life and his interests. But, then, what did it matter what he did with his life now? He had made it perfectly clear that she had no place in it.

Molly was no longer in bed. She was sitting at a small table, drawing on a piece of paper. Victoria didn't have to feign pleasure when she looked at it. 'How very pretty, Molly.'

'It's a princess,' the child said.

'Yes, I can see that,' Victoria said. 'She's wearing a crown and has a lovely dress—'

'It's blue,' a soft voice said behind her.

Victoria turned and caught her breath. Jenny was standing by her shoulder. She was looking down at the drawing and her attention was focused on the picture, as though it was the most important thing in the world. 'You can't see that it's blue,' she went on, 'but it is. As blue as the sky. And her crown is gold and has all sparkly bits in it.'

'Of course it does,' Molly said, seeming not in the least surprised by Jenny's comment. 'Mrs Hutchins showed me a book with pretty ladies in it. But they didn't have crowns.'

'I know, but they did look very nice.'

Refusing to act as though Jenny's conversation was in any way out of the ordinary, Victoria said, 'I've brought some books with me today that have pictures of pretty ladies in them. And some of them do have crowns.' They were actually fashion magazines Victoria had picked up for her sister, but she decided the needs of these little girls far outweighed Winifred's. 'I'll leave them with Mrs Hutchins, shall I?'

Molly was intent on her drawing, but her nod was indication that she had heard.

Jenny sat down at the table. Victoria watched her for a while and was relieved to see definite signs of improvement in her appearance. Her hair had been trimmed and no longer hung down into her eyes and her complexion was brighter too. She also looked to have put on some weight, no doubt a result of Mrs Hutchins's excellent cooking. Any loud noise from the outside still caused her to her flinch, but overall she seemed far more settled in her surroundings. As she flipped through the pages of a book, she looked like a child again rather than the frightened girl/woman she had been when Victoria had first seen her.

She spent almost an hour with the children. She would have stayed longer, but was all too conscious of the passage of time. The longer she stayed, the greater the risk of running into Alistair. Besides, she still had business to transact with the housekeeper.

'I have to go and speak to Mrs Hutchins now,' she told Margaret.

The girl nodded. 'Will you come and see us again?'

'I'd like to.'

'You can come and see us in our new 'ouse,' Teddy said. 'The guv'nor says we're going there soon. I'm going to dig a garden.'

Victoria smiled, hard pressed to think of Alistair as 'the guv'nor'. 'Then I shall certainly try to get out and see you.' She wouldn't, of course, but the children didn't need to know that. They had more important matters to concern themselves with. Such as living.

She bid a reluctant goodbye to the girls, gave hugs to those who would allow it and shook hands with those who would not, and then, strangely teary, made her way back downstairs to Mrs Hutchins's room.

'Ah, there you are, Miss Bretton,' the house-keeper said. 'We've been having a nice chat, Angelique and me.'

'I 'ave been asking Mrs 'utchins about Monsieur Devlin,' Angelique said, handing Victoria a cup of tea. ''E sounds like a very good man.'

'One of the best as far as I'm concerned,' Mrs Hutchins asserted. 'He's made a world of difference in these children's lives.'

'I think you've done a great deal yourself, Mrs Hutchins,' Victoria said. 'You're the one who has the responsibility of looking after them day after day.'

'Aye, but without his generosity, none of this

would have been possible. These children would have suffered the same fate as so many others if he hadn't stepped in. Me, I'd help them all if I could, but there's only so much one person can do. But Mr Devlin is doing all that and more.'

'That's another reason for my visit today, Mrs Hutchins.' Victoria reached into the hamper Angelique had set on the floor and took out an envelope. 'I'll likely be going abroad for a few months, but I wanted to give you this before I left. It's a donation. For the children. Use it however you think best.'

Mrs Hutchins took the envelope and when she glanced inside, her eyes grew wide. ''Pon my word, miss, this is very generous.'

'I wanted to help. But I'd prefer you not tell Mr Devlin where the money came from.'

'Not tell him? Why ever not?'

'I have my reasons. Just say, if he asks, that the money came from an anonymous source.'

Mrs Hutchins glanced at the contents of the envelope again and then at Victoria. 'I don't understand why you wouldn't want him knowing, miss, but I'm not one to pry and all I can say is thank you very much.'

'You're welcome. And now, we won't keep you any longer.' Victoria finished her tea and stood up. 'Come along, Angelique, it's time we went home.'

The ladies said their goodbyes at the door, but it wasn't until Victoria climbed into the carriage and saw the magazines lying on the seat that she remembered her promise to the girls. 'Angelique, I have to run back inside. Would you mind giving these to the boys?' she said, digging in her reticule for some coins. 'One to Thomas and the other to Teddy.'

The maid took the coins and smiled. 'I never knew you 'ad such a soft spot for children, *mademoiselle*. Zey will remember you.'

Victoria sighed as she slipped back into the building. She liked to think the children would remember her, but not because she had given them gifts. It was far more pleasant to think they would remember her for the time she had spent with them.

That was certainly what she would take away from all this. If and when she published her first children's book, it would be dedicated to them, to Alistair's orphans, who by their very existence had inspired her to do something different with her life.

Thankfully, the front door was still open, but when Victoria called Mrs Hutchins's name, there was no answer. No doubt the woman was busy in the kitchen. Victoria decided she might as well take the magazines up herself.

She was halfway up the stairs when the front

door opened again. Thinking it was one of the children, she cast a glance over her shoulder—and her heart plummeted. *Alistair!* The last person she wanted to see.

Unfortunately, judging from the look on his face, she was the last person he had been expecting to. 'Miss Bretton? What are you doing here?'

There was no warmth in his eyes, no welcome in his voice, and, recalled to a time when there had been both, Victoria felt unutterably sad. 'I wanted to see how the children were getting on. They've been on my mind ever since I was here last.'

'You could have asked me about their welfare,' he said. 'Sent me a note.'

'I wasn't sure you would answer. I thought that…by coming here, I would be able to see for myself.'

He nodded and, for a moment, smiled. 'I might have known you would take matters into your own hands. Even to venturing alone into a part of town no well-bred lady would ever consider visiting.'

'You know me well, Mr Devlin,' Victoria said, striving to keep her voice light. 'But I am not alone. My maid is waiting for me in the carriage.'

His glance fell to the books in her arms. 'And those?'

'Magazines, for the girls,' Victoria said, 'They like pictures of pretty ladies.'

When he turned to shut the door, Victoria briefly closed her eyes. She hadn't thought it would be this difficult, carrying on a normal conversation with him, but she had underestimated the power of her love. She wanted nothing more than to fling herself into his arms and to forget everything that had happened. To cast aside propriety and tell him how much she loved him.

But she would not. He would not welcome such an admission. Not from her. Not now.

His head came up again and Victoria held her breath. She wasn't sure whether to carry on up the stairs or just hand him the magazines and leave. But all he said was, 'By all means, go up and give them what you promised. I would not wish them to be disappointed.'

Victoria swallowed hard and continued up the narrow staircase, painfully aware of Alistair following a few steps behind.

The children were much as she left them. Margaret and Molly were both sitting at the table, though Jenny was standing by the window looking out. She turned upon hearing the visitors and her eyes went immediately to the magazines. 'You remembered!'

'Of course I remembered,' Victoria said. 'I told you I would bring them back.'

'But you were gone so long. We thought you'd forgotten.'

A wave of guilt washed over Victoria. She hadn't stopped to consider that to these children, five minutes would seem like an hour. 'I had a cup of tea with Mrs Hutchins and the time slipped away on me,' she said. 'But I wouldn't have left without bringing the books. Here,' she said, holding the top one out to Jenny, 'this one has some very pretty ladies in it.'

'Are there any princesses?' Molly asked.

'I don't think so, but there are a few ladies wearing crowns.'

The little girl thought about that for a moment, then nodded, as though satisfied with the answer.

Victoria was very aware of Alistair standing behind her as she placed the magazines on the table. The girls, accepting her now as someone they could trust, gathered around and pushed close in an effort to see the pictures. Victoria felt the softness of Jenny's breath on her hand and had the strongest urge to draw the girl close and smooth her hand over the softness of her hair. To let her know that someone cared…

'Go ahead,' Alistair said softly. 'I don't think she'll pull away.'

Victoria turned, and as their eyes met over the girls' heads she felt her heart shatter like glass. She loved him so much—and he would never be hers. She would never know what it was to feel the gentle caress of his hands in the dark, or the softness of his kisses against her neck. She would never hear those sweet, sweet whispers in the night, or turn to him for warmth and comfort.

She glanced at the little girl standing so close to her and realised she might never have a daughter of her own. She would certainly never have a child of his…and the realisation made her want to weep.

She turned her head away and squeezed her eyes shut, praying the tears wouldn't slip through. For everyone's sake, she had to be strong. She had to get through the next few minutes and then leave, knowing she would never see Alistair or the children again. Just a few more minutes and it would all be over—

'Why did you really come back?' he whispered close to her ear. 'I thought I'd never see you again.'

The words shattered her resolve, the softness of his voice almost her undoing. But she couldn't tell him the truth. She couldn't admit that the reason she had come back was to be close, one last time, to something that was so very important to him. How foolish that would sound to a man like Alistair Devlin.

Instead, she drew a deep breath, mustered a smile and said, 'I told you, I wanted to know that the children were all right, and to see with my own eyes that they were happy.' She bent down to pick up a magazine that had fallen to the floor, using the opportunity to dash tears from her eyes. 'I hear they will be going to their new home next month.'

'Did they tell you that?'

'No, Mrs Hutchins. We had a very pleasant chat.'

'No doubt she was surprised to see you.'

'I believe she was.' Victoria straightened. 'Well, I think it's time I was on my way.'

'I'll walk you to your carriage.'

'There is no need—'

'I said, I'll walk you to your carriage.'

Their eyes met again, and this time Victoria didn't look away. She wanted to remember his expression and to lock it away in her heart. No face would ever be as dear, no man ever so deeply loved.

Victoria didn't see Mrs Hutchins again. She walked down the stairs and stood back to let Alistair open the front door for her. When they were both outside and he closed the door again, she put a hand on his arm, knowing it would be the last chance she had to ask. 'Why are you so committed to these children, Mr Devlin?' she whispered. 'Why would a man who has everything bother with children who have nothing?'

He was silent for a long time. Numerous people walked by the house, some casting curious glances at the fine lady and gentleman standing by the door, but it was clear that Alistair would not be rushed. The furrow in his brow told Victoria he was thinking very carefully about whether or not to answer her question, and his reluctance to do so only added to her curiosity, convincing her there was something very personal at the heart of all this.

'Are you familiar with the story about…my older brother?' Alistair asked in such a quiet voice that Victoria had to lean in close to hear it. 'The one who fell in love with an actress.'

She nodded. 'Yes, my uncle told me about it.'

'Of course. Everyone in the theatre knew about Hugh and Sally. Knew how they fell in love and eloped after my father wouldn't allow them to marry. Most people even knew they eventually had a daughter, Helena, and that after my brother died, my father refused to see her. For most people, that's where the story ends,' Alistair said quietly. 'But for me, it's where it really begins. Because I found Hugh's daughter— and, sadly, I was the last person to see her alive.'

'She *died*?' Victoria whispered. 'How? When?'

'It's a long story—'

'I'm not going anywhere.'

He glanced away, the muscles in his jaw working. 'After my father turned Sally away, she went back to the theatre where she had been performing when my brother met her. I suppose she thought to pick up where she left off,' Alistair said. 'But she couldn't remember her lines any more and an actress who can't memorise lines is of no use to anyone. So, she tried turning her hand to something else. She rented a small room over a milliner's shop and took in sewing, hoping to earn enough money to take care of her and Helena. Sadly, there wasn't enough money, and when Helena got sick, Sally turned to…other ways of making money. But it was a desperately hard life, and eventually, she fell ill. So much so, that Helena often ended up having to look after her.'

Victoria could scarcely breathe. She wanted to stop him, knowing how painful it must be to talk about it again, but she had to know how it ended.

'Sally died not long after that,' Alistair continued in a low voice. 'A few of her friends from the theatre took up a collection and got enough to give her a decent burial, but there wasn't enough left over to look after Helena and no one was willing to take her. So, she ended up on the streets, as so many children do. She drifted from place to place, stealing food, picking pockets, learning the trade so she could keep clothes on her back and food in her stomach. But it was no life for a child and after she was caught and beaten for stealing a loaf of bread, she never really recovered.'

'How do you know all this?' Victoria whispered.

'I made it my business to. I never forgot the day Sally and her daughter came to see my father,' Alistair said quietly. 'I was present for that interview because my father thought it would be a good lesson for me to learn. He called me into the room and I remember looking at that lovely young woman, because Sally *was* still beautiful then, and feeling totally removed from her and her daughter. As though they had nothing to do with me. Because I honestly believed they *had* nothing to do with me.'

'Then you agreed with your father?' Victoria said.

'At that time, yes. I thought he'd done the right thing in turning Sally away. I couldn't imagine my brother throwing away everything he'd been born to for the love of a woman who was clearly so far beneath him. I couldn't understand because I'd never been in love. And then, ironically, I did meet someone,' Alistair said. 'She was a few years older than me and was unhappily married. It had been an arranged marriage and, though both parties benefited financially, there was never any love between them. It wasn't long before we became lovers,' he said, his voice softening. 'Her husband found out, but he didn't try to stop us. He didn't care. He travelled a lot and, as long as we were discreet, he was willing to turn a blind eye. But I came to love her desperately. I would have done anything for her. Anything to be with her.'

Alistair paused, and after a moment carried on. 'Eventually, her husband came back and decided it was time for our affair to end. Someone told him they had seen us together and he didn't like that, so he arranged to take her away. He owned some property in Scotland and decided it would be best if she stayed there. He, of course, continued to live in London and to travel throughout Europe, but I never saw her again.'

'Did you write to her?' Victoria asked, trying to imagine how hard it must have been.

'In the beginning. But after a while her letters stopped coming. I suppose she realised how hopeless it was. But I came to understand how love changes a person. For the first time in my life, I understood what my brother had gone through and what he'd felt for Sally. And

I realised how important it would have been to Hugh to know that his wife and daughter were taken care of. It broke my heart when I realised how badly we had failed him.'

Victoria blinked hard, feeling tears trembling on her lashes. 'What did you do?'

'I started to look for them,' Alistair said. 'I wrote endless letters, asked endless questions. I went to the theatre where Sally had worked, hoping to find some answers. It was from some-one there I found out that she had died, but it took another six months before I found Helena. I had only seen her the one time, but I remem-bered her. She was a beautiful little girl, with the brightest red hair I'd ever seen. And she had... my brother's eyes,' Alistair said, lost in memo-ries of the past. 'I knew she was his the moment she walked through the door.'

'Your father must have seen that.'

'He didn't want to see it. He called Sally a whore and turned her away, saying she was less than nothing to him, even though she gave him the letter Hugh had written—'

When he broke off, Victoria put her hand on his arm. 'You don't have to go on. I can see how painful this is for you—'

'Nowhere near as painful as it was for them,' Alistair ground out. 'As I said, I eventually found Helena. She had been living in a brothel.

The worst kind of place. I wasn't surprised she ran away before I got there. It took me another two months to find her again, but I did, entirely by chance in a part of town I'd never gone to before. I knew her at once. She was standing at the other side of the road and, though she was thin and dressed in old clothes, she still had the brightest red hair I'd ever seen.'

'She must have been so happy to see you.'

Alistair shook his head. 'She didn't know who I was. To her I was just another man. Another customer, for all she knew. I called her by name and she looked up, but she made no move to come closer. But our eyes met across the street, and when I saw that she was crying I knew I had to do something.'

Victoria didn't want to hear any more. She knew the story didn't have a happy ending. Alistair's next words confirmed it. 'At that moment, a carriage turned on to the street,' he said woodenly. 'A large carriage, drawn by four young horses. It was travelling too fast, the driver having lost control of the team during the turn. Everyone got out of the way and everything should have been fine. But Helena looked at that carriage, looked back at me and then, calmly and purposefully, walked out into the street.'

'Dear God!'

'There was nothing I could do,' Alistair said softly. 'She was in the street before I even realised she was moving. The carriage didn't stop. The people inside never knew what happened. But I knew. She was my brother's only child,' Alistair said, drawing a long, painful breath. 'And I watched her die in front of my eyes. I've never forgiven myself for that.'

'But it wasn't your fault!' Victoria said desperately. 'You said it yourself, you didn't have time to do anything. Everything happened so fast.'

'I know, and I don't blame myself for what happened that day,' Alistair said. 'I blame myself for not having done anything in the years that led up to it. For not reaching out to her and Sally sooner, when I could have made a difference in their lives—' Alistair broke off, ran his hand through his hair. His eyes were bleak and filled with sadness. 'After Helena's death, I made enquiries into her life. I couldn't imagine what would have driven an eight-year-old child to throw herself under the wheels of a carriage, but sadly, I found out. When I learned what her life had been, I came to understand the sense of desperation she must have felt. The feeling of utter abandonment. And the day I watched her die was the day my life changed,' Alistair said. 'The very next week I hired Mrs Hutchins, installed her in this house and set about the business of collecting children. I didn't want to see what happened to Helena happen to someone else. I might not have been able to save her, but I was damned if I was going to sit by and let it happen to children like Jenny and Alice.'

It was a heartwrenching story, one of the most tragic Victoria had ever heard. But it explained why Alistair had been so determined to set up the orphanage. It also brought home to her just how noble was the man she had fallen in love with. 'I am...so very sorry,' she said, knowing how totally inadequate the words were. 'I can't imagine how terrible it must have been for you.'

'Helena's death is something I live with every day,' Alistair said quietly. 'And every day it inspires me to do more. I suppose if there's anything good to have come out of all this, that would be it.' He looked up, blinking hard. 'But now, I've kept you talking long enough. Come.'

Together they walked towards the carriage. Alistair opened the door and helped Victoria to get in. After he closed the door behind her, she watched him take a step back, then saw him signal the coachman to drive on.

As the carriage moved off, she had to fight the urge to turn around and look back.

Angelique showed no such restraint. '*Merde*, 'e is so good looking!'

'Turn around, Angelique.' Victoria's voice was stiff. 'It is not polite to stare.'

'Pah, you English. You do not know when it is good to look and when it is not.'

'I am perfectly aware of when it is appropriate to look,' Victoria said. 'This is *not* one of those times.'

'But 'e likes you! Did you not see ze look on 'is face? 'E is in love wiz you!'

Victoria squeezed her eyes shut. 'Don't be ridiculous. Mr Devlin is *not* in love with me!'

'But—'

'And we will not talk about this any more.'

'But 'e is ze one you 'ave been crying over… and now I see it is for no good reason—'

'Enough!' Victoria said firmly. 'This conversation is at an end!'

Angelique grudgingly subsided as Victoria opened her eyes and stared blindly through the window. Her composure was badly shaken and her confidence even more so.

She hadn't expected to run into Alistair today. Nor had she been prepared for the heartwrenching story he had just told her. She hoped more than ever that Mrs Hutchins would honour her request and keep silent about the money. The last thing she needed was to have Alistair seek her out to express his thanks.

She wasn't strong enough to see him again.

Besides, she *hadn't* made the gesture to be recognised by him. She had done it for the children, just as he had. Everything he'd done, he had done in memory of Helena—a child who should never have died and whose tragic life story Alistair had just shared with her.

The less she saw of him now, the better off they would both be.

Alistair watched the carriage until it turned the corner and drove out of sight. Only then did he turn around and start for the front door.

The encounter had shaken him. He'd tried telling himself that he wasn't in love with Victoria Bretton. He had almost convinced himself that his feelings were under control and that when he saw her again, he wouldn't feel this burning desire to pull her into his arms and kiss her senseless. But he was wrong. The sight of her a few minutes ago, of those beautiful blue eyes and that tempting mouth, had shattered his illusions and brought home to him all that he had lost… and everything he had been trying to forget.

Victoria Bretton would *not* be shaken. For all her duplicity, she still remained uppermost in his heart.

He went inside, not in the best of humours, and found his housekeeper clearing up the remnants of her visit.

'Such a delightful lady,' Mrs Hutchins said. 'Imagine a fine lady like her coming all the way down here just to see the children. I never heard the like.'

'Did you know she was coming?' Alistair asked quietly.

'Hadn't a clue. I was that shocked when I opened the door and saw her standing there. But she's got a good heart, has Miss Bretton,' Mrs Hutchins said. 'Not like those society ladies who think about nothing but their own pleasures. Very generous, she is.'

'Generous?' Alistair said. 'Did she bring something for the children?'

The housekeeper flushed. 'Indeed, a lovely big hamper of food and sweets, as well as magazines for the girls and books for the boys. They'll think it's Christmas when I take it all up to them.'

'Hmm.' Then he saw the envelope lying on the table. 'What's that?'

Mrs Hutchins followed his gaze—and blanched. 'Nothing. Just some letters I was going through.'

'You were looking at letters while Miss Bretton was here?'

'No. I was looking at them…before she arrived.'

But Alistair's instincts were raised. 'Mrs Hutchins, what is in that envelope?'

'I told you, sir. Letters, that's all.'

'Only letters.' Alistair put his hands behind his back. 'Show one to me.'

The housekeeper's cheeks burned. 'Sir!'

'I don't want to read it. Just to see it.'

'I'd really rather not.'

'Very well. Then simply hold open the envelope and let me look inside.'

This request had the effect of flustering the housekeeper even more, but as if realising she wasn't going to win, she sighed, and handed him the envelope.

Alistair took it and glanced at the contents. He didn't say a word. After a few minutes, he handed it back. 'Thank you.'

'You might as well keep it, sir,' she said. 'It's for the children and I don't like having that much money around the place.'

He nodded and slipped it into his pocket. 'Thank you, Mrs Hutchins.'

It was clear the housekeeper didn't know what to say, so, being an intelligent woman, she said nothing.

Alistair went upstairs to check on the children. He spent forty-five minutes with them, talking of everyday things, checking on the state of their health as he read to them and making sure everything was as it should be. He was uncommonly pleased at how well Jenny was progressing, convinced for the first time that she would recover from her ordeal. Even Molly and Margaret looked better and Teddy was definitely on the mend. They would all benefit from their move to the country where the fresh country air would do wonders for their spirits.

With that thought in mind, Alistair bid good afternoon to Mrs Hutchins and returned to his carriage where, climbing up into the seat, he sat thinking for a few minutes. Then, reaching a decision, he flicked the reins and set off, his destination not Berkeley Square, but Green Street.

Victoria did not immediately return home after her visit to the orphanage. Having no desire to face her mother or father in the aftermath of everything Alistair had told her, she directed James to take her to Hatchard's where, surrounded by books and papers, she took time to think about everything that had happened, about her relationship with Alistair and what her prospects for the future were.

Now more than ever she had to get away. To put distance between herself and the man she loved. To give herself room to breathe and hopefully to forget about her impossible dreams.

Her parents wouldn't be pleased at her plans to go abroad, of course. To her mother, the idea of a woman travelling alone would be incomprehensible. There were dangers untold for young ladies who undertook such voyages and the sooner such outlandish ideas were laid to rest, the better.

No, her mother would definitely not be pleased.

Her father, on the other hand, would hopefully be more open-minded. He knew his elder daughter had a good head on her shoulders and that she was unlikely to do anything foolish. He would simply miss her and wish her to stay home for that reason.

As to setting up her own establishment, Victoria suspected neither of them would be happy about that. But, she had made up her mind and she intended to see it through. It was the best for all concerned. The time she planned to spend abroad would give her the breathing space she needed to settle matters in her own mind without reminders of home or Alistair Devlin serving as distractions, and having a place of her own when she returned would give her the freedom to live her life independently of anyone else.

It was the right thing to do. Not in the eyes of her family or society, but in her own. At the moment, that was all that mattered.

There was a line of carriages in the road when Victoria finally arrived in Green Street, but, preoccupied with her thoughts, she didn't trouble herself to look at them. All she wanted was the peace and quiet of her own room where she could start making lists of what needed to be done.

Unfortunately, when Quince greeted her at the front door, it was with the message that her father wanted to see her in the drawing room as soon as she returned.

Wondering what could have prompted the request, Victoria took a moment to check her appearance in the hall mirror. She was uncommonly pale and pinched both cheeks several times to bring out some colour. Then she smoothed her hands over her skirt, adjusted her shawl and opened the door.

Her father was not the only person in the room. Laurence was leaning against the credenza with his arms crossed over his chest and another gentleman was standing with his back to her.

He turned around—and Victoria blanched. 'Mr Devlin!'

She was so shocked to see him she didn't notice the other gentleman standing by the window. A man who suddenly stepped forwards and said, 'Have I the pleasure of addressing Miss Victoria Bretton?'

Confused and off stride, Victoria inclined her

head. 'You have, sir, though I confess you have the advantage of me.'

The unknown gentleman was well dressed, his jacket a masterpiece of tailoring, his boots polished to a brilliant sheen. He wore no jewellery other than a gold signet ring on his right hand and, while he was not handsome, he exuded an air of authority that must have been apparent to everyone in the room. 'I hope you will forgive my calling upon you at home, Miss Bretton, but when I heard the news, I was determined to seek you out, since your uncle was not good enough to give me your direction.'

'My uncle?' Victoria glanced in bewilderment at her father. 'Papa?'

'Victoria, allow me to introduce Sir Michael Loftus,' her father said, with an uncertain glance in Alistair's direction. 'He has come in the hopes of speaking to you. Or rather…to Valentine Lawe.'

Victoria had heard that one's legs could give way during times of stress, but until this moment had never experienced how singularly unpleasant a sensation it could be. She reached for the back of a nearby chair, her fingers digging into the soft upholstery. 'Sir Michael,' she whispered. 'How…do you do?'

'Very well, given what I hope to hear in the next few minutes.'

Alistair, who had been directing curious glances between her and Sir Michael, said, 'Would someone be good enough to tell me what is going on?'

'Mr Devlin, forgive me,' her father said quickly. 'This is Sir Michael Loftus. Theatre critic for the *Morning Chronicle*.'

'Devlin,' Sir Michael said with a slight bow.

'Sir Michael. I've read a few of your critiques,' Alistair said. 'You speak your mind.'

'I see no point in doing otherwise,' the gentleman said with an arrogant twist to his lips. 'I have a responsibility to the theatre-going public. If a performance is brilliant, I am happy to say so. If it is flawed, I am equally quick to make my opinion known, though in as constructive a manner as possible.'

'I'm not sure constructive would be the word I'd use,' Alistair observed drily. 'In some cases, your reviews have been harsh to the point of condemnation.'

The other man shrugged. 'I am not to blame if the material is substandard. I only offer my professional opinion based on what I see. However, as to my reason for being here, I heard a very interesting rumour and decided it was worthy of following up.'

'Indeed?' Mr Bretton said. 'What rumour might that be?'

The critic stared at him for a moment, then smiled. 'Come now, Mr Bretton, you must have heard that your daughter is reputed to be the famous playwright Valentine Lawe?'

'Oh, that rumour. Yes, we've heard it, but we paid it no mind.'

'Why not?'

'Because it isn't true.'

Victoria saw Alistair's head whip round, but Sir Michael was already speaking. 'Really? Then I wonder if you would be good enough to tell me how it came to be? I'm not sure if you are aware,' that gentleman said, 'but I have been trying to arrange a meeting between Lawe and myself for quite some time now, but Templeton has been singularly effective at putting me off. Most recently, he informed me that Lawe was travelling on the Continent. It would seem…' he said, turning to stare at Victoria, 'that he was not being entirely truthful in that regard.'

Victoria's mind was spinning. A quick glance in Alistair's direction gave her no indication as to what he might be thinking. His features could have been cast in stone for all the emotion she saw on his face.

By contrast, her brother seemed almost at ease as he walked towards the fireplace, his hands clasped loosely behind his back. 'Why did you wish to meet Mr Lawe in person, Sir Michael?'

'Because I would very much like to talk to him about his next play. I have had discussions with Mr Elliston at Drury Lane, and he is interested in seeing Lawe's work performed there. The Gryphon is all very well, but everyone knows it hasn't the reputation of Drury Lane or Covent Garden,' Sir Michael said in a condescending tone. 'When I advised Templeton of this, I was told I would have to wait because Lawe was out of the country. Not once did he mention that the fellow was actually a relative, or that he was in fact living right here on Green Street.' There was a brief silence as Sir Michael glanced around the room. 'Well? Is no one going to tell me what I want to hear? You're all looking at me as though I were mad.'

'No, not mad, Sir Michael,' her father said with a regretful smile, 'just misinformed. The rumour is not true. My daughter is not Valentine Lawe.'

Victoria stopped breathing. She was aware of Alistair's head again turning in her direction, but she couldn't meet his gaze. Not after her father had just contradicted everything she'd told him.

'What about the rumour that Miss Signy

Chermonde started the story?' Sir Michael continued. 'Do you also deny that?'

'No, because I am not in a position to deny or confirm it,' Mr Bretton said. 'I'm not even aware if my daughter is acquainted with the actress.'

'But if she were, why would Miss Chermonde tell such an outlandish story? What has she to gain? Surely only a personal grievance would prompt her to lash out in such a way?'

By now, Victoria's heart was beating so hard she was finding it difficult to breathe. She had to say something—but what? What could she possibly say that wouldn't make matters worse?

'Sir Michael,' she began slowly, 'I…regret that Miss Chermonde felt the need to talk about me in such a way. I am aware that she is…one of the actresses in my uncle's troupe and that she is an extremely talented young woman. I think I can safely say we have always enjoyed an amicable association—'

'Until a few weeks ago,' Alistair spoke up unexpectedly, 'when Miss Bretton and I chanced to meet Miss Chermonde at a society gathering. I believe that particular incident prompted Miss Chermonde to make this claim.'

'Why?' Sir Michael frowned. 'What precisely was the nature of the incident?'

'Suffice it to say that Miss Chermonde was discovered at an event to which she had not been invited,' Alistair said. 'Fearing for the reaction of the hostess, Miss Bretton and I advised her to leave. Unfortunately, Miss Chermonde took exception to Miss Bretton's asking her to do so and I believe she started this rumour in the hopes of humiliating her. A rumour which, as you've just heard, has absolutely no basis in fact.'

Victoria froze. Alistair was *lying* for her? Why on earth would he do such a thing? He *knew* the truth about her. Why would he compromise himself by saying something he knew to be utterly false?

'Well, I must admit this is all very disappointing,' Sir Michael said, considerably put out. 'Here I thought I had discovered the identity of Valentine Lawe, only to find out now that it has all been a hoax.' He levelled a blistering gaze at Victoria. 'Are you telling me, Miss Bretton, that there is absolutely no truth to the rumour that you are Valentine Lawe?'

The room went so silent that Victoria could hear people talking outside on the street—and wished with all her heart that she might be one of them. Anything, rather than be here in this room facing Sir Michael's interrogation. If she lied, the whole affair would continue to spin out of control until they were all so deeply mired in the deceit they wouldn't have a hope of emerging unscathed. But if she told the truth, their reputations would be destroyed—every last one of them.

Her father had just told an out-and-out lie. Her brother had pleaded ignorance of events he knew to be true. Even Alistair had perjured himself by ignoring her guilt even as he condemned Signy for hers. How would it look if she suddenly admitted to Sir Michael that Signy was the one telling the truth and everyone else the lies?

On the other hand, how could she maintain a shred of self-respect if she did not speak up now and clear the air once and for all?

Every person in the room was waiting for her to answer. Her father was watching her with an expression of loving concern, Sir Michael with one of avid curiosity. Her brother's face was harder to read and she could make nothing of Alistair's at all, but she could certainly guess at the direction of his thoughts. He must detest her for having put him in this distasteful position. How would *she* feel, if she ever found herself forced into such a situation?

'Sir Michael,' she began slowly, 'I'm sorry you had to go through all this. It was never my intention that anyone should be deceived, and had I not believed that my reasons for doing what I did were entirely justified, I would never have done it. But at the time, I truly believed I had no choice.'

'Miss Bretton, I don't have all day,' Sir Michael said irritably. 'What exactly are you trying to say?'

'Well, it's just that—'

'What my poor sister is trying to say,' Laurence cut in unexpectedly, 'is that she cannot tell you she's Valentine Lawe because that would indeed be telling a lie.'

'It would?'

'Yes.' Laurence moved away from the fireplace and went to stand directly in front of Sir Michael. 'My sister did not write *Penelope's Swain*, *Genevieve*, *A Winter's Escapade*, or *A Lady's Choice*.'

'Fine,' Sir Michael snapped. 'Then who did?'

'I did,' Laurence said without hesitation. 'I wrote those four plays and gave them to my uncle to produce. Because the truth is, *I* am Valentine Lawe.'

Chapter Fourteen

His words fell into a stunned silence broken only by the measured ticking of the mantel clock—and by the sound of blood rushing through Victoria's ears.

Her brother was claiming to be Valentine Lawe? Had he lost his mind?

'*You're* Valentine Lawe?' Sir Michael said, sounding equally sceptical.

'That's right.'

'But I thought your sister was the one who wrote the plays.'

'That is what the rumours would have you believe,' Laurence said. 'But they are not true. I *am* Valentine Lawe. Would you like me to recite a selection from one of my plays? I can do so without difficulty.'

'That won't be necessary, anyone can memorise lines,' Alistair said, his voice like granite. 'The question is *why* did you wait until now to make this claim?'

'The reasons are many and varied. Mainly, I suppose, to protect my privacy,' Laurence said. 'I've never sought the spotlight, nor do I crave the adulation of an audience.'

'Then why do you write?' Sir Michael asked.

'Because I must. The ideas flow like water from a well and cannot be stopped by wish or inclination.' Laurence smiled, a rather fatalistic smile to Victoria's way of thinking. 'It is difficult for anyone not of a creative nature to understand, but that is the way it is.'

'And your reason for employing a pseudonym?' Alistair drawled.

Victoria couldn't look at him. She heard the derision in his voice and knew he didn't believe Laurence's claim. Why would he when she had done everything she could to convince him that *she* was Valentine Lawe?

'I took the name to protect my family,' Laurence said. 'My plays are, by nature, controversial, and I had no wish to see anyone in my family suffer for the association. People tend to think that opinions expressed by one member of a family are shared by everyone else, but that simply isn't true. It would have been unfair to expose my mother and younger sister, who though aware of my passion, have never been fully supportive of it, to that type of censure. It is the reason I have kept my identity secret even from them.'

'Are you telling me your own *family* don't know you're Valentine Lawe?' Sir Michael asked incredulously.

'Some of them do. Victoria and my father knew of my hopes in that direction, as did my uncle, who kindly undertook to produce the plays at his own expense.'

Sir Michael gave a snort. 'And why would he not? Templeton's no fool. He knows good material when he sees it. He knew those plays would make him—and you—a lot of money.'

'Not at the outset,' Laurence said. 'I was an untried commodity. Just another aspiring playwright trying to sell his work. My uncle only read my play because I was his nephew. And though he liked the material, he couldn't guarantee that an audience would, too. He simply took a chance and it paid off.'

'An understatement if ever I heard one,' Sir Michael muttered.

'A theatre doesn't run itself, Sir Michael,' Laurence said quietly. 'Salaries have to be paid. Maintenance and repairs carried out. It behoves a theatre owner to seek out the best material he can in order to achieve the highest return. If my plays are able to do that for him, so much the better.' For the first time, Laurence glanced at his father, and this time, his smile was almost apologetic. 'Forgive me, Father. We knew we couldn't keep this a secret for ever. You were right to believe that as the popularity of my plays increased, so would the risk of exposure. But I think we've had a good run, don't you?'

Mr Bretton looked shaken, as it was expected he must by his son's unanticipated disclosure. 'Yes, I suppose we have.'

'Laurence, why are you doing this?' Victoria whispered finally. 'There is no need—'

'Yes, dearest, there is. You have been my most valiant supporter and you have done everything you could to ensure my anonymity. Even to compromising your own reputation. But I was wrong to let it carry on as long as I did and I apologise for having done so,' Laurence said, giving as fine a performance as Victoria had ever seen. 'I should have said something as soon as the rumours began, but even then I was reluctant to expose my identity. I regret that deeply. When I think of all you've had to endure, of the abominable way you have been treated, I am ashamed of myself. However, that is all at an end now. The truth is out in the open and I for one am glad of it.'

'Then you do not mind if I make this information public,' Sir Michael said.

'Not at all. The sooner, the better as far as I'm concerned,' Laurence said. 'I am tired of hearing my family whispered about in society. I want my sister's reputation restored. I want her to be able to lead a normal life again.'

Victoria sank weakly into the chair. It was too late. There was nothing she could do. Nothing, short of calling her brother a liar, would change the situation. Sir Michael *believed* Laurence was Valentine Lawe—and he intended to make sure everyone in London knew it.

'Well, I must say this has been a most enlightening interview,' the gentleman said, looking considerably happier than he had a few minutes earlier. 'While I don't understand your reluctance to admit to your talent, I respect your reasons for having done so and I commend you for your honesty in having finally lifted the burden of responsibility from your sister's shoulders. I hope, Miss Bretton,' Sir Michael said, turning to offer Victoria an apologetic smile, 'that you can find it in your heart to forgive me. And to appreciate how such a misunderstanding came to pass. Now that the truth has been made clear, I see how foolish I was to have believed the rumours. A lady of your genteel manners would never think to enact such a hoax, except, as your brother said, in your valiant defence of him. You are to be applauded for your unselfish support. I'm sure you are equally relieved to have everything out in the open.'

'Truly, I am…without words,' Victoria said weakly.

'As we all are. Your brother is a gifted writer and the public is anxious for more of his plays. I dare say his life is going to be very different from now on. Travelling on the Continent, indeed!' Sir Michael said, starting for the door. 'I shall have words with your uncle when I get back!'

'You're going away?' Laurence asked quickly.

'For a few weeks. I'll contact you as soon as I return. We have a lot to talk about, young man, and I am anxious to get started. Well, good afternoon, Miss Bretton. Gentlemen.'

In the moments that followed, no one said a word. It was almost as though no one knew what to say. They could all have been actors in one of Victoria's plays, each waiting for the other to recite his or her lines, without having any idea what those lines were or whose turn it was to speak. Victoria certainly didn't. Never in her wildest dreams had she imagined that her quiet, unassuming brother would stand up in public and claim to be Valentine Lawe. Why would he? There had never been any need.

'Well, that was… enlightening,' her father said, a deep line furrowing his brow.

'Enlightening, but not entirely unexpected,' Laurence said. 'We knew it was only a matter of time before the truth came out. Perhaps you should send Uncle Templeton a note, Father, warning him of Sir Michael's intention to call. I don't think the gentleman was very pleased at the manner in which Uncle Theo put him off.'

A glance passed between the two men and Victoria knew exactly what they were thinking. It wasn't a warning letter her father intended to send Uncle Theo; it was a call to arms.

'Yes, I think you're right, I shall do that at once,' he said. 'Mr Devlin, pray excuse my having to leave you. I hope you will stay and take some refreshments.'

'That won't be necessary.' Alistair's tone was brusque. 'I must be on my way as well.'

'In that case…' Mr Bretton turned to regard his son '…perhaps you would care to join me in the study, Laurence? There are one or two things we need to discuss before your mother and sister get home.'

His words held a wealth of meaning and Victoria knew the upcoming meeting would not be easy. Nevertheless, Laurence's smile remained cheerfully optimistic. 'Of course. I shall return directly, Victoria. Good afternoon, Mr Devlin.'

Alistair did not look up as he pulled on his gloves. 'Bretton.'

And then he and Victoria were alone, the few feet between them feeling like miles.

'Alistair, I am so sorry,' Victoria said, glad to have a few minutes of privacy. 'I had no idea my brother was going to say what he did, but I think I can explain—'

'I'm sure you can, but there really is no need,' Alistair interrupted curtly. 'I have seen and heard all I need to and I must say it was a superb performance.'

Victoria faltered. 'Performance?'

'Indeed. What I just witnessed could have graced the stage at Drury Lane. I tip my hat to you, Miss Bretton. I had no idea you came from such a theatrical family, or that you yourself were such a talented actress.'

'Actress?' Shocked, Victoria took a step backwards. 'I don't understand—'

'I think you do. That day, in the drawing room when you told me you were Valentine Lawe, I must say you were convincing. You had me believing every word.'

'Because I was telling you the truth! I *am* Valentine Lawe!'

'Really? Then how do you explain your brother

having just made *exactly* the same claim in front of a man who could ruin your family if he ever found out he had been lied to and made a fool of?'

'I can't explain it,' Victoria said. 'That's why I wanted to talk to you. I had no idea Laurence was going to say what he did, and I don't know why he— Alistair, wait! Where are you going?'

'It is not appropriate that we be alone here to-gether,' he said, making for the door. 'I suppose I shouldn't be surprised, coming from the type of family you do, but—'

'The *type* of family I come from?' Victoria stopped dead. 'What exactly do you mean by that?'

'A family of actors and storytellers who have no qualms about making up roles to suit them-selves,' he threw back at her. 'In your case, a fictitious playwright by the name of Valentine Lawe. But it really wasn't necessary, you know. If you'd wanted to discourage me, you could simply have told me the truth.'

'Discourage you?' Victoria's eyes opened wide. 'Is that why you think I told you I was Valentine Lawe? To *discourage* you?'

'Well, what else am I to think? You said from the beginning that we should not suit,' Alistair said. 'I don't go to the theatre. I don't care for masquerades, and I don't have to work because of the circumstances of my birth. You made it quite clear you thought me no different than men like Lord Collins or Mr Bentley-Hyde, but fool that I was, I was determined to change your mind. So I took you to the orphanage so that you could see we *did* have something in common. A mutual concern for those less fortunate than ourselves and a genuine wish to make life better for the people we care about. But more than that, I wanted to be honest with you. I wanted to share a part of my life with you I've felt compelled to keep from others, only to find out now that you haven't been honest with me at all!'

Victoria recoiled. 'How can you say that! I told you the truth—'

'*Your* truth, Miss Bretton. Not your father's or your uncle's, or even your brother's. *They* all defended you in public. *They* all stated that you were *not* Valentine Lawe. Even today, when your brother stepped forwards to make his claim, your father made no move to contradict it. When the question was put to him, he stated very clearly that you were *not* Valentine Lawe. So what, I asked myself, am I to make of that? That your father is not an honourable man?'

'Of course he is honourable—'

'Then why would he lie? Why would your brother and your uncle lie? And how, in light of everything I've heard, am I to believe that the only one *not* telling a lie…is you!'

Victoria closed her eyes, her stomach knotting against a black wall of despair. She didn't say a word as Alistair walked out of the house. She was fighting not to break down, desperate to hang on to the last vestiges of self-control. She was bleeding; every bitter word he'd flung at her had torn a gaping hole in her heart.

He couldn't have hurt her more had he picked up a knife and stabbed her with it.

'Was he very angry?'

Victoria turned to see her brother standing at the bottom of the stairs, and suddenly, she was livid. 'How *could* you, Laurence! Have you *any* idea what you've just done?'

'Yes.' His voice, unlike hers, was dispassionate. 'I have saved your reputation.'

'*Saved* it? Thanks to you, Mr Devlin now thinks I lied to him and wishes to have nothing more to do with me!'

'I am sorry to hear that, but there is more at stake than just your relationship with Mr Devlin,' Laurence said quietly. 'Had I let you stand there and proclaim yourself to be Valentine Lawe only moments after Father had said exactly the opposite, our family would have been ruined. We would have lost all credibility in the eyes of society and Loftus would have had a field day with it. He doesn't like Uncle Theo to begin with. Can you imagine what he would have done had he been handed the ammunition to humiliate our uncle in public?'

'You don't know that he would have done that,' Victoria muttered.

'Yes, I do. What little I know of Loftus doesn't induce me to think he would take kindly to being made a fool of. I did what I had to do, Victoria, and I had no time to think about it beforehand.' Laurence glanced at the front door. 'What did Mr Devlin say?'

'He accused me of…twisting the truth to suit my own purposes.' Victoria's chin came up even as tears scalded her eyes. 'He called us a family of actors and storytellers, then accused me of lying to him when I told him I was Valentine Lawe.' She shook her head and the tears spilled over. 'I always knew there was very little chance of my having any kind of future with Alistair, but I *never* wanted it to end like this.'

'I'm sorry,' Laurence said. 'Truly I am. If there had been any other way, I would have taken it, but this was the *only* way out of a bad situation.'

'No, it wasn't,' Victoria flung at him. 'You could have told me what you were planning to do. Given us time to talk about it.'

'There wasn't time. I didn't even *know* what

I was going to do until Sir Michael asked you the question. And even if there had been time, I'm not sure I would have told you.' He stepped towards her and took her hands in his. 'I knew you wouldn't have gone along with it.'

'Of course I wouldn't!' Victoria jerked her hands free. 'Not only is Mr Devlin thoroughly disgusted with me, but now *you* have become an integral part of the deceit. You have thrown yourself into the fire, Laurence, without sparing a thought for what it will do to your future!'

'Yes, well, let's not worry about that right now,' Laurence murmured. 'There are more important considerations, like the fact that by this time tomorrow, most of London will have heard that I *am* Valentine Lawe.'

She wanted to stay angry with him and to lash out at him for everything he'd done, but when she stopped to consider the bigger picture, Victoria realised that hers was not the only life that had changed this afternoon. Her brother's confession might have taken her out of the public eye—but it had dropped him squarely into the middle of it. 'Do you really think Sir Michael will put it about so quickly?' she asked.

'I do. It will puff up his consequence to be known as the man who revealed the identity of Valentine Lawe…which means *we* have no choice but to prepare ourselves for what lies ahead. Father is writing a note to Uncle Theo as we speak and we must tell Mama and Winifred as soon as they return.'

'They are not going to be happy about this,' Victoria said grimly.

'Trust me; they're going to be a damned sight happier than if we had to tell them it was *you* who had confessed rather than me!'

The truth of Laurence's words was borne out in a very short time. Within half an hour, Theo and Tandy arrived at Green Street and, not long after, Mrs Bretton and Winifred returned from their shopping expedition. They all gathered in the drawing room and were told the startling news.

'Gracious, Laurence, whatever prompted you to make such a claim?' Aunt Tandy asked in wide-eyed astonishment. '*You*? Of all people… a famous playwright?'

'I had no choice,' Laurence said. 'Had I remained silent and allowed Victoria to admit to her part in the subterfuge, we would all have been cast in a terrible light.'

'We still are,' Victoria muttered. 'All we've done is cover a lie *with* a lie.'

'Be that as it may, I think it exceedingly decent of Laurence to step into the role,' Uncle

Theo said proudly. 'I see where he felt it was the right thing to do.'

'Oh, yes, you would, wouldn't you!' Mrs Bretton snapped. 'In fact, you're very happy that it is now Laurence who has taken ownership of this wretched lie, rather than Victoria.'

'I don't see it as being the problem you make it out to be, sister-in-law.'

'Really? Has it not occurred to any of you that Laurence has never so much as *written* a word?' Mrs Bretton said. 'And now he is going to parade around London as a famous playwright? How long is *that* deception going to hold up, do you think?'

The same thought had occurred to Victoria, though she hadn't had the heart to say anything. She was the only one who knew that a few years earlier Laurence had written a novel that had been turned down by several London publishers. It had been a difficult pill for him to swallow, especially given that her second play had just opened to such rave reviews.

Laurence, however, having committed himself to the part, was clearly intent on carrying it through. 'It's really not so bad when you think about it. After all, I have only to play the public face of Valentine Lawe. Victoria can still write the plays and Uncle Theo can continue to produce them. In some ways, it really is an ideal solution to the problem.'

'You'll forgive me if I do not share your optimism,' his mother said tightly.

'Nor do I,' Winifred spoke up. 'Since when did telling lies become an ideal solution to anything?'

'Generally, I would agree that it is not,' Uncle Theo said in an effort to be conciliatory. 'But in this instance, I think Laurence is right. When telling a small untruth protects the names and reputations of so many without doing any real harm, surely the ends justify the means.'

'A *small* untruth?' Mrs Bretton repeated aghast. 'Do you really expect me to think of this as a small untruth?'

'You *must* think of it that way, Mama,' Laurence said quietly. 'It's not as though I've hurt anyone. There is no stigma attached to a gentleman being a playwright, and now that I have proclaimed myself to be Valentine Lawe it frees all of us from the taint of scandal. Victoria and Winifred need have no fear about moving in society again and they will be free to receive the attentions of whichever gentleman cares to offer them. I dare say even Mr Fulton will show an interest in you again now, Winnie, though I'm not sure I would be as welcoming towards him if this is all it takes to turn him up sweet.'

'You have no idea how Mr Fulton is going

to react,' Winifred said stiffly. 'And I think it grossly unfair of you to accuse him of being fickle. We don't know the rumours about Victoria are what drove him away.'

'You seemed fairly settled on that score a few days ago,' Victoria pointed out.

'Let us not stray from the matter at hand,' her father said. 'The fact is, the news about Laurence's being Valentine Lawe is going to make the rounds very quickly and, while I agree it is not the course of action any of us would have chosen, I think it behoves us all to go along with it.'

'Mr Bretton, surely not!'

'Well, what would you have us do, my dear?' he asked his wife in frustration. 'You've told me more than once that our daughters' chances of making good marriages have suffered for Victoria's occupation and now you have been offered relief in the form of Laurence taking up the role. I'm not saying I *like* the deceit any better than you, but under the circumstances it does seem to be the answer to several of our most pressing problems. It is Laurence who must bear the burden of what is to come. I just hope, for his sake, he is ready for it.'

Her father's words turned out to be strangely prophetic. Within days, word of Laurence's transition from quiet scholar to celebrated playwright swept through the drawing rooms of society and the reaction to the news was both unexpected and gratifying.

The most immediate benefit was that invitations began arriving again, both from people with whom the family had socialised in the past, and from those with whom they had not. Hostesses who had been censorious of Victoria suddenly became welcoming again and all were anxious to hear more about the dashing brother who had been revealed as the romantic playwright.

Laurence himself began receiving invitations to literary gatherings and readings, and while in the beginning Victoria went with him with a view to lending assistance, it soon became evident that no such help was required. While he was not at home in the public eye, his knowledge of Shakespearean literature was actually superior to hers and his familiarity with a wide range of other topics carried him easily through evenings with learned gentlemen who believed themselves superior in intellect to a mere playwright.

But it was his reluctance to talk about his literary accomplishments that made Laurence the darling of society. He was reserved when people showered praise upon him, and even those who criticised his work were forced to acknowledge a grudging admiration for his unassuming nature. About any future works, he was noticeably reticent, acknowledging only that while there were many ideas swirling around in his head, he had yet to put anything down on paper.

Watching him, Victoria could only marvel that her bookish and thoroughly unpretentious brother had stepped so successfully into the role of celebrated playwright. Fame, contrary to being anathema to him, was a mantle he wore with grace and humility. And while they all knew that an inadvertent slip could expose them, nothing like that came to pass and eventually, Victoria was able to breathe a sigh of relief that the eye of society had finally turned away from her.

Sadly, it did nothing to heal the rift between Alistair and herself. The memory of his anger stayed with her through the days and weeks that followed, and his bitter disappointment pierced her soul. She wrote to him twice, but both letters were returned unopened. It seemed he really did intend to have nothing more to do with her.

Strangely enough, however, as the weeks passed, his continued avoidance of her began to have its own unexpected results.

Victoria got angry. Angry that he wouldn't listen to what she had to say and that he didn't believe her when she'd tried to tell him the truth. *She* hadn't tried to cover a lie with a lie. She had confessed to being Valentine Lawe that day in the drawing room because she had wanted there to be honesty between them. Even though she had known what the confession would do, how it might affect his opinion of her, she had still done it—and he had thrown it back in her face! He had accused her of lying and had sided with her brother when Laurence had made his outrageous claim.

What did that say about his feelings for *her*? How could *any* man who professed to love her believe what someone else said when it was so radically different from what she did?

She thought they had established a rapport. That day at the orphanage, when they had stood together over poor little Molly, each had shown the other a side of themselves they had never revealed before—a side that was honest and caring and so very worthy of love. When Alistair had gone on to tell her about Helena, a tragic story no one else knew, Victoria felt sure he had been opening up to her in a manner that signified a deeper level of trust and affection than he had ever shown her before.

And yet, what he had said to her in the drawing room after Laurence's confession had totally contradicted that. It had destroyed the fragile trust building between them and had put paid to everything they'd said to one another. And as the days went on, Victoria realised she wasn't willing to forgive him for it.

As a result, *she* began to avoid him. She did not seek him out at events to which they were both invited and she no longer went for early morning rides in the park. When she did go abroad, it was either with her maid or Winifred, who suddenly, like her brother, had become the toast of the town.

'Isn't it strange,' Winifred said to Victoria at the coming-out ball for Lord and Lady Brookston's daughter. 'Instead of being shunned by society as we feared your being exposed as Valentine Lawe would do, we are now embraced by it. We receive more invitations than ever and I am constantly approached by silly young girls asking for an introduction to our brother. Even when I am in conversation with a gentleman, questions about Laurence inevitably arise. Frankly, I fail to comprehend what all the fuss is about. You would think he had been elevated to the peerage, for goodness' sake!'

That was Victoria's other big concern—that her shy, retiring brother, having been literally thrust on to centre stage, would not be able to deal with the pressure that would inevitably come his way. He said he did not mind and repeated that he had no intention of going back on his word, but Victoria knew he didn't really enjoy it.

When Laurence started losing weight and began spending a lot more hours shut up in his room, her concern blossomed into genuine worry and she sought her uncle out to talk about it.

'It's just that Laurence has never looked for this kind of notoriety in his life,' Victoria said as they strolled along Oxford Street together. 'He has always been the quiet one. Happiest when his head is in a book.'

'Yes, and been viewed as a boring intellectual because of it,' Uncle Theo said in a wry tone. 'Personally, I don't think it's a bad thing. The boy already seems to have acquired a dash more confidence.'

'Only when he steps out in public,' Victoria said ruefully. 'It's as though he puts on a mask the moment he becomes Valentine Lawe.'

Her uncle shrugged. 'If wearing a mask allows him to be convincing in the part, I'm all for it. It really is no different than one of my actors stepping into a role.'

'But this is not the stage, Uncle Theo. This is real life. And in real life, bad things happen to good people.' Victoria bit her lip. 'Speaking of such things, how do matters stand between you and Signy? I have to admit, I'm relieved you didn't dismiss her.'

'It would have been folly to do so,' her uncle agreed. 'Knowing she was the source of the rumour, but not of the lie, I would have been hard pressed to be convincing in my criticism of her conduct. But I did reprimand her for speaking out against her betters and for attending Lady Drake's masquerade. I told her it was a foolish thing to do and she accepted the chastisement meekly enough. She even said she would apologise to you, though I wouldn't hold out any hopes of it being sincere.'

Victoria wrinkled her nose. 'I cannot like this, Uncle. Signy has no need to apologise as both you and I know.'

'Yes, but we are well and truly launched on the path now and there is no turning back. Otherwise, we shall all be made to look like a hopelessly ramshackle lot. For my own part, I would hate to give Loftus a reason to verbally assassinate me. Which, I can assure you, he would.'

Recalled to the comment Laurence had made, Victoria said, 'Is there really so much animosity between the two of you?'

'I'm afraid there is. Oh, we hide it well enough,' Uncle Theo said. 'Professional courtesy and all that. But as a critic I've always thought him unnecessarily harsh. I know of actresses who've never set foot on the stage again after reading one of his reviews and there have been any number of occasions where he and I have differed on the quality of an actor's performance.'

Victoria smiled. 'Including some of your own?'

'I admit he had the temerity to say that my Hamlet fell far short of expectation,' Uncle Theo said grudgingly. 'And that the first play I ever produced suffered for my participation in it. But we're both older and wiser now and we agree to disagree with civility. But how do *you* feel about all this, Victoria? It is still your work, after all, but now it has become the source of Laurence's fame.'

'I have mixed emotions,' Victoria said, gazing at the road ahead. 'On the one hand, I am relieved to be able to write my plays and know they will be thought the product of my brother, but on the other, it seems even more dishonest than it did when I was publishing them anonymously. I have involved another person in my deceit, and while I love Laurence with all my heart, I'm afraid he will be caught out and be made to suffer for his participation.'

Uncle Theo stopped and turned to put his hands on Victoria's shoulders. 'My darling girl, I trust you know I would not say this if I didn't believe it, but I honestly feel that what

Laurence did *was* for the best. He removed any possible stigma that might have attached itself to your name and, in doing so, cleared the way for you and Winifred to make good marriages. Your mother need no longer fear that her family will be ignored by society, and while she will never be happy that one of her children is doing something so closely associated with the stage, at least the idea of her son doing it is more palatable to her than one of her daughters. All things considered, I think we got off lightly. What would have happened, for example, if Mr Devlin had learned the truth about Valentine Lawe— ?'

'He did learn of it, Uncle,' Victoria said softly. 'I *told* him the truth before Laurence made his announcement.'

'Good God, why would you do that?'

'Because I couldn't live with the fact that I was lying to him,' she said. 'He is such an honest man, and I knew he had…that is, that he held me in…some regard.'

Her uncle regarded her in all seriousness. 'Did he make you an offer?'

'No, but I think he was about to…and I could not permit it. Not when he believed me to be something I was not. Now there is no question of the disgust in which he holds me.'

'Did he say that?'

'There was no need,' Victoria said. 'I heard it in his voice.'

'But you told him the truth because you felt honesty was the best policy.'

'Of course.'

'Did it ever occur to you that loyalty is also a quality much to be admired?'

Victoria sighed. 'I see no evidence of loyalty in all this.'

'Do you not? I see loyalty to your mother, to whom you gave a promise of silence, and to your sister, about whose future you were so concerned,' her uncle said. 'I see it in your conduct towards your father and myself, who have always been so supportive of your talent, and to Laurence, whom you did not wish to embarrass. Honesty is a valuable commodity, Victoria, but so is loyalty. And sometimes, in being loyal to those we love, we must do things that are not entirely honest. Be truthful with me. How much happiness do you think you would have brought the family had you been honest with Sir Michael that day?'

'Not very much,' Victoria said truthfully.

'Absolutely none,' her uncle said. 'Society has embraced Laurence in this new role because it is acceptable to them, but you would not have been such an easy fit, and your mother would have been very unhappy at seeing you ostracised by those whom she believed mattered. And we both know she would have blamed you had Winifred been unable to make a good marriage.'

'It almost came to pass. Mr Fulton did briefly turn to someone else.'

'Of course, because he is young and foolish and more concerned with appearance than with substance. Frankly, Winifred is better off without him, but she won't thank me for saying it and your mother won't be brought around to that way of thinking. She would have continued to resent you, me, and anyone else who had a hand in it. So, all things considered, you chose the right path,' Uncle Theo said. 'You told Devlin the truth. Your conscience need not be anything but clear.'

'But I did not refute it when Laurence told Sir Michael that *he* was Valentine Lawe. And now he hates me because of it.'

'From what your father tells me, you had precious little opportunity to do so. Laurence cut you off at every turn.'

'Nevertheless, I should have found a way,' Victoria muttered.

'If you had, it would only have ended up damaging your reputation and destroying Valentine Lawe into the bargain. You've read Loftus's reviews. You know how cutting the man can be. If he took it into his head to question what he had seen at your house, he could have done far more damage than good. As I said, I've known Loftus a long time and while he can be very helpful to those he likes, trust me when I say that he is entirely capable of destroying those he does not. Far better it end like this. The sooner you are able to come to terms with that, the better.'

Chapter Fifteen

Alistair gave much thought to his feelings for Victoria over the next few weeks—something that in and of itself surprised him. He usually dismissed people who lied to him without a second thought, unwilling to invest any more time or effort into something that was so obviously destined to fail. But he wasn't able to dismiss her that easily and he wasn't sure why.

The day he had gone to her home with a view to speaking to her about his hopes for the future was the day she had revealed that about herself which he, in his wildest dreams, had never imagined. That *she* was the renowned playwright, Valentine Lawe. Then when he had gone a second time to see her and had encountered Sir Michael Loftus in her drawing room, he had been forced to bear witness to that astonishing scene in which her brother had boldly proclaimed the playwright's identity as his own—and Victoria had not refuted it.

Was it any wonder he had reacted the way he had? It was only in deference to her that he had not said anything at the time. Because when, after listening to her brother's explanation of the claim, including his reasons as to why he chose to keep his identity hidden, Alistair had had no choice but to face facts.

Victoria had lied to him. Again. In a moment of clarity, he had seen her 'confession' for what it really was: a well-enacted attempt to discourage his attentions by establishing herself as a playwright and, therefore, someone who would be unacceptable to him and to his family. Clearly, any woman who would go to such lengths to put him off could have no genuine feelings for him.

It had all been an act—and because he loved her, he'd believed every word.

'I like what you've done in here,' Valbourg said as he gazed around the room that would one day be a classroom. 'Knocking down the wall and opening this up allows in a lot more light.'

'I didn't want them studying in a dark, windowless space,' Alistair said without enthusiasm. 'A child needs to be able to look out a window and dream.'

His friend glanced at him in surprise. 'Hardly

the type of comment I'd expect from you. I always thought you were more grounded in reality.'

'If I'm going to give these children a better environment than the one from which they came, such things must be considered.'

'Then you might like to think about knocking out the end wall in the dining room and putting in a conservatory,' Valbourg suggested. 'It faces south, so as well as being an additional source of sunlight, it could be used as a greenhouse for herbs and vegetables.'

'Capital idea. I'll have the architect rework the drawings,' Alistair said. 'But it will raise the costs.'

'Not a concern. I'll make available the necessary funds. Just let me know what you need.'

The two men strolled for a time in silence, examining what progress had been made. Alistair was pleased at how well the renovations were coming along. With luck, he would be able to move the children in before the end of the next month, giving them time to enjoy the warm summer sunshine before the cool winds of autumn blew in. It should have made him happy, yet as he and Valbourg made their way back downstairs and out into the garden, all he could think about was Victoria.

Why was it that everything to do with that damned woman was so wretchedly convoluted?

'What's on your mind, Dev?' Valbourg asked, his eyes on the distant hills.

Surprised, Alistair looked around. 'Nothing. Why?'

'You've been preoccupied these last few weeks.'

'Have I?'

'You know damn well you have.' Valbourg turned his head to meet his gaze. 'And that's not like you.'

Alistair's jaw clenched. He'd forgotten how insightful his friend could be. 'I've simply had a lot on my mind. Setting all of this up, finalising the plans for the renovations, engaging tradesmen. Not to mention arranging for furnishings and bringing in additional staff. It all takes time and thought.'

'True, but the Alistair Devlin I remember thrived on that kind of pace,' Valbourg commented. 'You made the rest of us look like hopeless laggards at school.'

'That's because most of you were hopeless laggards,' Alistair said drily. 'But you know me. I'm happiest when I have a lot to occupy my mind.'

'Then why do I get the feeling there's still something you're *not* all that happy about?'

Alistair smiled, but left the question unanswered. 'I'm thinking of buying some boats. Thought the older boys might enjoy rowing across the pond.'

'It would be good exercise for them. I could look into it, if you like.'

Alistair nodded. 'Thank you, I would.'

They walked on a bit further before Valbourg said casually, 'I had an interesting conversation with Miss Winifred Bretton the other day.'

'Did you?' Alistair let his gaze roam over the still waters of the pond. 'I wasn't aware you were seeing her.'

'I'm not. I went with her and her mother to look at fabrics for the dining room. But I gathered from her conversation that she thinks you're quite taken with Victoria.'

'Then she is mistaken,' Alistair said distantly. 'I have no feelings for the lady one way or the other.'

'Yet I understand you've spent a good deal of time in her company.'

'We've encountered one another at society events.'

'And been seen with her in her box at the theatre.'

'That was for Isabelle's benefit.'

'And you took her to visit Mrs Hutchins and the children?'

That was one harder to explain. 'I offered to drive the lady home, but had to pass by the orphanage on the way.'

'Dev, I may have been living in America for the past six years, but I haven't forgotten where things are in London. Green Street is nowhere near the orphanage, so what's really going on between the two of you?' Valbourg turned a keen eye on his friend. 'Did you offer for Miss Bretton and get turned down?'

'Certainly not.'

'But you do have feelings for her?'

Alistair wanted to refute it. The words of denial sprang hot and ready to his lips, but he couldn't utter them because he knew damn well that anger or regret couldn't live in a vacuum. They could only exist where there had once been strong feelings of love and affection. 'I *had* feelings for her,' he said tersely. 'But after being made aware of certain truths, my opinion of her changed.'

'Certain…truths,' Valbourg echoed. 'Strange. In the short time I've known Miss Bretton, she has always struck me as being a most admirable young woman. Intelligent. Well spoken. Thoughtful.'

'If you like her so much, why don't *you* propose to her?' Alistair bit off.

'Because my affections are engaged elsewhere.'

'With Winifred?' Alistair asked in surprise.

'No. You are not acquainted with the lady, and do not ask me to give you her name because I have no intention of doing so,' Valbourg said, though the smile that accompanied his words removed any possibility of Alistair taking offence. 'But with regard to the state of affairs between you and Miss Bretton, I hope you will at least make an effort to clarify the situation.'

'I see nothing that needs clarifying,' Alistair said, more with bravado than belief.

Clearly, Valbourg knew it too. 'I disagree. Depending upon from whom you heard these *truths*, you may wish to ask the lady herself if they are correct.'

'And if I were to say there was no point?'

Valbourg shrugged. 'That would depend on how much stock you're willing to put in the source. If you believe it credible, fine. If you do not…'

'The source is such that it would be difficult to ignore what was said,' Alistair replied. Because the source was Laurence Bretton, a man for whom Victoria felt the deepest respect and admiration. Emotions she was never likely to feel for him.

Still, Valbourg was right. He needed to speak

to her again. His emotions at the time had been raw. He hadn't been thinking straight and his reaction had been one of anger and disappointment. Of confusion. But now, having had a few weeks to reflect on the situation and the events of that day, Alistair knew the time was right to broach the subject again and to listen to what Victoria had to say. If she had any feelings left for him at all, surely they would be able to eke out some kind of common ground?

Lord knew he loved her enough to try.

At Lady Morgan's soirée that evening, Victoria moved perfunctorily through the steps of a country dance. Her partner, Mr Tifford, was an adequate dancer and a pleasant enough man, but she was not in a mood to appreciate either. She was deeply unsettled and had been ever since Alistair's abrupt departure from Green Street. Even her conversation with her uncle had done little to mitigate her concerns.

Perhaps she *should* have felt better, as her uncle tried to make her see, for certainly there were more benefits to the lie than disadvantages. Now Alistair would see that it had never been her intention to mock him or Miss Wright by denying any knowledge of Lawe because she'd had a very good reason for doing so. Perhaps, as Laurence had suggested, Alistair would be able to find it in his heart to forgive her for trying to protect her brother from the prying eyes of society.

But if that was the case, why hadn't he sought her out?

The dance ended and Victoria was returned by her partner to the chairs lining the wall. She watched her sister being escorted from the floor by Mr Fulton, and saw Sir Anthony Deverill waiting for the next dance. Gone were the worry lines from Winifred's pretty brow. She was happy and gay, content in the knowledge that she was no longer an outcast and that her situation had, in fact, been improved by her brother's elevation to the literary world. Would that Victoria could say the same for hers—

'Miss Bretton, are you engaged for the next dance?'

Victoria's head snapped round. She had no need to check her card. She knew she was not engaged for the waltz. She simply hadn't expected Alistair Devlin to ask for it. 'I am not, Mr Devlin, though I am surprised you would wish to dance with someone you believe to be an actress and a liar.'

She was gratified to see a flush darken his cheeks. 'My cousin is convinced that you and I have taken each other in dislike. I do not wish her to think that is the case.'

'Why not? It is the truth.'

'From your perspective, perhaps.'

'From *both* our perspectives. I was left in no doubt as to how you felt about me the last time we parted.'

'Can you blame me?'

'Not entirely,' Victoria said, prepared to be fair. 'But I resented your unwillingness to give me a chance to explain.'

'How was I to know that what you told me would be the truth?' Alistair countered. 'I believed you when you said you were Valentine Lawe the first time. You did not deny it when your brother made the same claim.'

'Because I *could* not deny it!' Victoria said in frustration. 'Laurence cut me off every time I attempted to interrupt. Besides, how could I make him look like a fool in front of a man like Sir Michael Loftus? No matter what I said, it would all have come out sounding dreadful.'

'All right.' Alistair held out his hand. 'Then explain it to me now.'

Her eyes widened. 'What, here?'

'Why not? The waltz allows us to dance close enough for conversation and the music will cover our words.'

'I'm not sure I *wish* to talk about it,' she said contrarily.

'Fine.' His hand stayed where it was. 'Then

dance with me regardless and I shall have no choice but to believe you lied to me for the reasons I put forward at the time.'

'I did no such thing!' Victoria said hotly.

When he raised his brows, Victoria realised that her voice had risen and that eyes were turning in their direction. Reluctantly, she put her hand into his. Neither of them could afford to give the gossips anything to talk about. Now that Alistair's decision not to marry Lady Sarah Millingham had been made public, speculation was rife as to whom he *did* intend to propose to, and any woman with whom he spent time was viewed as a possible candidate.

Her mother made no secret of the fact that she hoped it might be her elder daughter, but Victoria knew better. Whatever respect Alistair might have felt for her at the beginning of their association was now gone.

She had disappointed him twice. She would not be allowed to do so a third time.

'You have a noticeable frown between your brows, Miss Bretton,' Alistair said as he drew her into his arms. 'Either my company is distasteful or you are deep in thought.'

'If your company was distasteful, I would not have stood up with you,' Victoria said, hoping he wouldn't see how furiously her heart was beating. 'And I can assure you, my mind is not engaged to any purpose other than the enjoyment of the dance.'

'I'm glad to hear it. I would not like to think you were dancing with me out of a sense of obligation.'

Victoria averted her gaze. 'You should know by now that I don't do anything I have no wish to.'

'I wonder. Your brother said you claimed the role of Valentine Lawe in order to protect *his* anonymity, but you must have known what it would do to your reputation if the truth ever came out,' Alistair said. 'I cannot believe that was something you anticipated with joy.'

'You don't know me well enough to comment.'

'I thought I did…once.'

Embarrassed, Victoria stopped dead. She tried to back away, but he only tightened his grip. 'We are being watched and unless you wish to give society something to talk about, I suggest you remain calm in manner and appearance.'

'I would very much like to do that, Mr Devlin,' Victoria muttered through clenched teeth, 'but you do provoke me.'

'I know.' Then, unexpectedly, he smiled. 'Has anyone ever told you how lovely you are when you are provoked?'

He swept her into a turn and in doing so,

curved his hand around the small of her waist, drawing her close against his body. Victoria felt the warmth of his breath on her temple, the hardness of his chest against hers, and though the contact was brief, it sent pleasurable shivers through her body. It was the first time they had been in such close proximity since her brother's revelation and it brought home to Victoria just how much she missed him. No man had ever had this kind of effect on her before and she doubted one ever would again.

'By the way, I meant to thank you for your most generous gift,' Alistair said.

Her eyes rose to his. 'Gift?'

'The envelope you left with Mrs Hutchins. I doubt she expected me to arrive so closely upon your heels. The envelope was still lying on the table.'

Victoria felt guilty warmth steal into her cheeks. The urge to deny was strong, but she had made up her mind that there would be no more lies between them. 'It was not my wish that you should find out the money came from me. I wanted to do something for the children.'

'Why would you feel the need? I am more than capable of providing all they require.'

'I know, but having spent time with them, I wanted to do something special myself,' she said. 'To feel I had contributed in some way to their betterment, whether it was ribbons for the girls or new shoes for the boys. Or, perhaps, just sweets for their tea.'

His brows rose in amusement. 'What you left will keep them in sweets well into their dotage.'

The remark surprised a laugh from her. 'Yes, I suppose it could. But they have so little.'

'As I said, it is my mission to make sure they have everything they need. But your gift was most thoughtful and I thank you for it.'

Victoria nodded, unable to meet his eyes. Oh, why was this so hard? She had told herself over and over again that it was futile to harbour any hopes of recapturing this man's good opinion. That she could never live with a man who thought so poorly of her. Why couldn't she bring herself to believe it?

'By the by, I recently heard another rumour making its way around town,' he said. 'About a certain young lady planning to go abroad.'

Victoria's lips compressed. There was no need to wonder at the source of *that* rumour. 'I'm sorry to hear it has become public knowledge. I did ask Winifred not to say anything.'

'How do you know it was your sister?'

'Because I can trust Laurence to keep my secrets.'

'Can you?'

For a moment, their eyes met and Victoria felt

her cheeks burn. Not surprisingly, she was the first to look away.

'So I take it the rumour is true?' he said.

'It is.'

'Why?'

'Because I wish to travel.'

'Not to stay in London and find a husband? Your mother cannot be pleased.'

'She is not, but the decision was mine to make.'

'And will they pay for a trip they do not wish you to make?'

'No. I shall,' Victoria said with an edge of defiance in her tone. 'The money I earned from my plays will cover any costs I incur.'

'*Your* plays,' Alistair said quietly. 'How curious, when you consider how firmly ensconced your brother now is in the role of Valentine Lawe. I hear he has been called upon to speak at literary gatherings. Some even say he boasts about his newfound fame.'

'Then they have not spoken to him,' Victoria said quietly. 'My brother does not boast. It is not in his nature.'

Alistair met her gaze, held it through a turn, then said, 'Will you be travelling alone?'

'No. I intend to set off with my maid, but Laurence has expressed an interest in joining me when he can.'

'Really?' His gaze sharpened. 'And will he write his next play while the two of you are away?'

Victoria missed a step. He didn't believe her. He still thought Laurence was Valentine Lawe. 'I have no idea what he intends to do,' she said stiffly. 'If he wishes to write, I shall not stop him.'

'And what will you do while your brother pens his next great opus? You once told me that writing was *your* passion. Will you take pen to paper and begin a turbulent love story about a young couple who fall in love against the backdrop of ancient Rome?' he murmured. 'A passionate recounting of love won and lost? Or will you be content to while away the hours drinking sweet wine in Florence and painting pictures of sunsets over the rolling Tuscan hills?'

Victoria briefly closed her eyes. Oh, but he was cruel! To ask such questions in a room full of people where the slightest blush, the merest gasp, would give her away. Truly, he cared nothing for her feelings if he could slight her in such a way. 'I may do all of those things or none of them,' she said quietly. 'But I shall enjoy the freedom of being my own person, of that you can be sure.'

'And will you think of anyone while you are gone?' he asked.

The dance came to an end…and Victoria stepped out of his arms. For all her inclination to tell him the truth, there was no way on earth she was going to be honest with him about that. 'One must have a reason for missing someone, Mr Devlin. I have not been given that reason. In fact, I have been given a great many more reasons for *not* missing anyone. Good evening.'

She did not wait for his response. What was the point? Nothing he said now was going to make any difference. He had not apologised to her for his conduct, or made any attempt to smooth over the unresolved issues that lay between them. He had simply asked her a few questions, offered her a meaningless compliment, and then changed the subject. They were no closer to a resolution at the end of the dance than they had been at the beginning.

And when she saw him later that evening, smiling into the face of a pretty young lady with whom she was not acquainted, Victoria knew Alistair had no intention of settling matters between them. The proof was staring her in the face. Was it any wonder that the future suddenly seemed bleaker, and stretched out longer, than it ever had before?

That night had been by far the worst as far as sleep went. Nightmarish images of Sir Michael

Loftus being stabbed by a grinning Prospero while she, not Miranda, wept false tears to the sound of Laurence's laughter and the audience's applause, had played havoc with Victoria's sleep. With such dreams to disturb her slumber, was it any wonder she felt nothing but relief when Angelique arrived to shake her awake in the morning?

Nor did the rest of the day improve. Victoria went through the motions of paying calls with her sister, but no matter how she strove to occupy her time the reality of her situation did not change. There was no future for her with Alistair Devlin. And it was that realisation in the end that prompted her to make her decision.

She would leave England now, before her spirits plummeted any further. She would head to the sunny climes of Italy and spend languorous days enjoying the warm Tuscan sun. After all, what reason was there for her to stay in London any longer? Her sister was being courted by any number of eligible gentlemen, Laurence was launched on his new literary career, and her father was once again happily immersed in his books. Even her mother seemed to have accepted the status quo and had taken up her busy social life again. Victoria was the only despondent one now, so why should she not make plans to leave a city that held nothing but unpleasant memories?

'But how can you go without telling him the truth?' Laurence argued with her over breakfast the next morning.

'Because there is nothing to be gained by it.' Victoria put down her knife and fork and pushed the plate away. 'I did everything I could to convince him of the truth, but he doesn't want to believe I'm Valentine Lawe. Why would he when society has embraced you so whole-heartedly in the role? And with Mr Fulton so close to proposing to Winifred, why would I do something that would only put all of that at risk again?'

'Because your conscience demands that you do!' Laurence replied. 'You just said you cannot sleep for the nightmares that fill your head and that your stomach is queasy much of the time. Those feelings won't go away unless you settle matters between you.'

'There is nothing to settle. If Mr Devlin was open to changing his mind, he would have done so by now. But he has not and I will not go grovelling to him,' Victoria said. 'The first lie was mine, but the second was not and he must be the one to apologise now. And he has made it quite clear that he has no intention of doing so!'

'Then I've ruined everything, haven't I?' Laurence said quietly. 'Here I thought I was doing the right thing by claiming to be Valentine Lawe, when all I've done is cost you the man

you love. I'm truly sorry, Victoria. I never meant
to hurt you.'

'Oh, Laurence, I know that,' she said, reaching for his hand. 'You were only trying to protect
me. How can I blame you for putting everyone's
needs ahead of your own? It was a selfless and
noble thing to do, and it really has turned out for
the best, all things considered. But surely you
can understand why I wish to go away.'

'Because you still love him.'

She drew back her hand. 'Yes. And it will tear
me apart to see him go on with his life, knowing it could all have turned out so differently.'

Laurence finished his breakfast and touched
the linen napkin to his lips. 'You can't go to
Italy on your own. But I can't leave town just
yet either.'

'I know, but Angelique will come with me.
You can join me when you are able.'

'The play may run for several months. Are
you willing to stay away that long?'

Victoria picked up her teacup. How could she
tell him that she could happily have stayed away
for ever if it meant never having to face Alistair
again? 'Why don't we see how it goes? We can
write to each other every week, and, in a month's
time, I shall see how I feel. I may love Italy so
much I never want to leave.'

For a time, the patter of the rain on the pave-
ment was the only sound that intruded into

the room. Then, 'Do you think you will ever marry?' Laurence asked.

'I don't know.' It was a question Victoria had asked herself many times. 'I'm not sure I'm all that suited to marriage. I would rather do something useful with my life and I won't be able to do that as some man's wife. Oh, I know you don't agree, but that's because you *are* a man and you see things differently. But I know what avenues are open to me. I am in the enviable position of being able to afford my own establishment and, if I live there alone, I will do so quite happily.'

'So you would be willing to leave London, uncaring that Devlin thought the worst of you,' Laurence said.

'I cannot afford to care. I know how he feels, Laurie. It's best I just accept it and carry on with my life. No doubt by the time I return to London, he will be married or engaged and the matter will be at an end once and for all.'

'And will you be happier for knowing that it is?'

'No, but I shall accept it because it is the only thing I can do.' Victoria didn't look at him as she said, 'That is the way it is. There really is nothing more to be said.'

Alistair was dressing for dinner when his butler arrived with a letter. 'This just came for you, Mr Devlin.'

Alistair didn't look at it. 'Is anyone awaiting a reply?'

'No, sir.'

'Then leave it there. I'll deal with it directly.'

The butler bowed and placed the letter on the dressing table.

Alistair stood by while his valet put the finishing touches on his cravat and then brushed down his jacket. Dinner with his family was always a formal occasion and he knew better than to arrive undressed, especially when he was feeling so out of sorts to begin with. He had been in a foul mood ever since his last conversation with Victoria—a conversation he had handled badly and from which he feared there was little hope of redemption.

And yet he had gone to the soirée hopeful of so much more. Taking Valbourg's words to heart, he had purposely sought Victoria out, intending to apologise for what he had said in the hopes they might be able to move past their differences and start again. He had wanted to see her smile at him the way she had that day at the orphanage, perhaps even to hear her say she cared for him as much as he did her, and then to relive the intimate moments they had shared at the masquerade.

But she had not said or done any of those things. When he had taken her in his arms and led her on to the dance floor, she had remained stiff and unyielding in his embrace, with her eyes averted and her beautiful little chin raised in defiance.

Only once when he had pulled her close and swept her into a turn had her composure deserted her. Her hand had trembled in his, and when he had looked into her face and seen evidence of her confusion, he had rejoiced in the knowledge that she wasn't as unaffected by his nearness as she wanted him to believe. Unfortunately, instead of acting on his instincts and confronting her about her feelings, he had done the worst thing possible.

He had changed the subject. After thanking her for her donation to the orphanage, he had asked her if she really was leaving London—and if she would miss anyone while she was gone.

Stupid, really, since they'd both known who he was asking about.

But again, there had been no warmth in her voice when she had told him, in the most unforgiving of tones, that one must have a reason for missing someone and that she had not been given a reason by anyone. That she had, in fact, been given more reasons *not* to miss anyone.

The harshness of her words had kept him awake long into the night that followed and had caused him any number of sleepless nights since.

But it was the memory of her eyes…and of that fleeting glimpse of remorse…that had buoyed him up and given him hope. If she'd no feelings for him at all, she would not have looked at him that way. She would have regarded him with ambivalence and disdain.

But it was not disdain that had caused her body to tremble in his arms.

It wasn't much, but it was enough to convince Alistair that matters were not as hopeless as they seemed. If he let Victoria walk out of his life without making one last attempt at putting things right, he was a bigger fool than he already believed himself to be…

'Your gloves, sir,' his valet said. 'And I've ordered the carriage brought around.'

Alistair glanced down at his gloves, his mind on something else entirely. 'Thank you, Beech. Don't bother waiting up. I'll go on to my club after I leave my parents.'

'Very good, sir.'

The valet bowed and quietly withdrew. It was only after the door closed behind him that Alistair remembered the letter. His brow furrowed when he saw who it was from and he held it for a moment before breaking the seal and reading it through, first with disbelief, then with a growing sense of surprised pleasure. He read it a second time, then thoughtfully set it back down on the table. *Was it possible…?*

He drew out his watch and flipped it open. It was half past six now and he wasn't expected at his parents until eight. The letter asked that he call before seven—timing that coincided exactly with his own plans. Coincidence or something more?

Alistair drew on his gloves, walked purposefully down the stairs and out to the waiting carriage, and gave the coachman the direction of Green Street.

Victoria glanced at the letter in her hand and felt her pulse begin to race. 'He wishes to call upon me?' She raised startled eyes to her brother's. 'Why?'

'How should I know?' Laurence asked. 'I'm only the messenger.'

Victoria returned her attention to Alistair's letter. The writing was little more than a scrawl, as though he had written it in haste, but the message was very clear.

He wanted to see her. Tonight. There were things that needed to be said. Matters that needed to be discussed. And he was hopeful of a positive resolution.

Victoria glanced briefly at the clock. It was six forty-two. The letter said he would call before seven. She had less than twenty minutes in which to make up her mind. Twenty minutes to decide whether she would take this unexpected opportunity to try to set things right, or accept that it was too late and move on.

She thought of the night he had kissed her in the garden. A night when he had spoken from his heart and when anything had seemed possible…

'What do you think, Laurence?' Victoria said, getting to her feet. 'The blue silk or the lavender?'

She was seated at the pianoforte when Alistair arrived. Having been too distracted to read, Victoria had turned to her music, knowing it would occupy both her hands and her thoughts. But when she heard the knock at precisely seven o'clock, her mind went blank and her fingers fell silent upon the keys.

Behind her, Laurence stood up. 'It's time, dearest.'

Victoria nodded, wishing the butterflies swirling madly in her stomach would go away.

'You look beautiful, by the way,' he whispered as she rose from the bench to stand beside him. 'The lavender was the perfect choice.'

Victoria managed a shaky smile. She had decided on the lavender gown, not because she

knew she looked well in it, but because it reminded her of the flowers that grew so abundantly around their home in Kent, a place where
she had always felt safe and secure. As for the
rest of her appearance, there had not been time
for Angelique to fuss with her hair so Victoria
had gathered it into a simple chignon. She wore
no jewellery and, as pale as her complexion had
been, she was glad she hadn't let Angelique
reach for the rouge pot. Judging by the warmth
in her cheeks now, she doubted there was any
need for enhancement. Alistair had already accused her of behaving like an actress. She didn't
want him thinking she looked like one, too.

'Mr Devlin,' the butler announced formally.

'Thank you, Quince,' Laurence said. 'Good
evening, Mr Devlin.'

'Bretton.' Alistair advanced slowly into the
room. 'Miss Bretton.'

'Mr Devlin,' Victoria said, the sound of his
voice causing her pulse to quicken. She raised
her eyes to his. 'Won't you sit down?'

'Thank you, but I prefer to stand.'

'As you wish.' Her voice was calm, but her
insides were quaking. He didn't seem angry. If
anything, he seemed uncertain and perhaps a
touch apprehensive. 'To what do we owe the
pleasure of your call?'

A faint smile appeared on his lips. 'I thought

you would be the one to tell me. I am here at your request.'

'My request?' Victoria's eyes flickered briefly to her brother's. 'There must be some mistake. Your letter said you wished to see me.'

'*My* letter?'

'Yes. The one I received not more than twenty minutes ago. One in which you said you wished to pay a call on me this evening.'

Alistair's dark brows drew together in confusion. 'I sent you no letter, Miss Bretton. I am here, in part, because I received a letter from *you* asking me to call between the hours of half past six and seven. In it, you gave me reason to believe this would be a private interview.'

'And it will be, Mr Devlin,' Laurence said calmly. 'Once I've said what I brought you both to this room to hear.'

'*You* brought us here?' Victoria stared at her brother in bewilderment. '*You* sent the letter?'

'Yes. And the one to Mr Devlin, signed with your name.'

'Really?' In an instant, Alistair's expression changed, his smile vanishing, his eyes turning hard as stone. 'How interesting. It would seem I have been treated to yet another display of your family's formidable talents, Miss Bretton. You'll forgive me if I don't stay—'

'Wait!' Laurence interrupted. 'Hear me out,

Devlin. For my sister's sake, if not for my own. She had nothing to do with this deceit.'

'Then you admit it *is* a deceit,' Alistair said harshly.

'Of course, but I was damned if I was going to let the two of you go your own separate ways without making at least some attempt to clear up this wretched misunderstanding.'

'Laurence, you are meddling in matters that don't concern you,' Victoria said, mortified that her brother would interfere in such a way.

'On the contrary, I am meddling in something that concerns me deeply and, contrary to what you might like to believe, it has *everything* to do with me. You see, Mr Devlin, my sister *was* telling you the truth when she told you she was Valentine Lawe a few weeks ago,' Laurence said. 'She did write those four plays. Every last word of them. Without any assistance or input from me.'

'Then why did you claim the role when Sir Michael asked Miss Bretton the question?' Alistair shot back.

'Because at that point, she had too much to lose by telling the truth. We all did,' Laurence admitted. 'My father and uncle had both been heard to deny the rumour in public—'

'As had you.'

'Yes,' Laurence said, not attempting to deny

it. 'And because I was afraid of what would happen to our family's reputation if Victoria told Sir Michael the truth, I decided to do something about it. That's why I said I was Valentine Lawe when Sir Michael asked the question. *And* why I didn't allow Victoria an opportunity to contradict me. I was determined there wouldn't be a shadow of doubt in Sir Michael's mind when he left the house that day.'

'I see.' Alistair let the silence stretch long before saying, 'Am I to assume that, with the exception of your sister, you had your family's approval to this bizarre plan?'

Victoria winced at the harshness of his tone, but Laurence merely shook his head. 'I didn't have a plan, Mr Devlin. How could I when none of us knew Sir Michael Loftus was going to turn up on our doorstep asking questions? You saw what happened when Victoria walked in. Did her reaction of shock look planned to you?'

Victoria held her breath as Alistair's dark gaze found hers. It was impossible to tell what he was thinking. She knew he was angry and he had every right to be. Her brother, whatever good intentions he might have had, had brought both of them to this meeting under false pretences. Clearly, Alistair believed she had written him a letter, just as she believed he had written one to her. And if *she* had harboured the hope, even for a moment, that his reasons for wishing to see her had anything to do with putting matters right between them, wasn't it possible that he had come with exactly the same thought in mind?

'Mr Devlin, you have been told…a number of different stories by various members of my family,' Victoria said, knowing it was time for her to take charge. 'And I'm sure that at times it has been difficult to know who really is telling the truth. But *because* you are a man to whom the truth matters, I want there to be honesty between us. I told you I was Valentine Lawe because it was the truth. And I had planned on telling you much earlier than I did. The day after the masquerade, in fact. But then I came down with that dreadful cold and was scarcely able to get out of bed, and before I had recovered enough to venture out, the news broke and we were all thrown into a state of confusion and panic.'

'Miss Bretton—'

'No, let me finish,' Victoria said, aware she had to get it all out before he offered a reply. 'As soon as the news became public, I wanted to tell you the truth, but my uncle felt the best way to handle it was by denying it. He knew what validating the rumour would do to my reputation in society…to my family's standing in society… and he didn't want that to happen.'

'So you went along with it,' Alistair said.

'Yes. At the time, I thought it was the path of least resistance,' Victoria admitted. 'Especially when my father added his agreement—'

'As I did mine,' Laurence said.

'Indeed, everyone seemed to feel it was the right thing to do. And for a while I thought they must be right,' Victoria said. 'But as time passed and I came to feel worse and worse about the lie I was perpetuating, I *knew* it wasn't the right thing. Neither was deceiving you. I hated that most of all. You defended me to your family and friends. You believed something of me that wasn't true, and for that reason, I knew I *had* to be the one who told you the truth. So I did,' Victoria said quietly. 'And I know you believed me because I saw how angry you were.'

'And yet, nothing changed,' Alistair reminded her. 'Your family didn't correct the falsehood.'

'No, because the longer we perpetuated the lie, the harder it became to deny. All of our reputations were on the line. My mother and father's, my sister's, my aunt's and uncle's. Even Laurence's. We all stood to lose a great deal and so we kept silent.'

'But you were going to tell Sir Michael the truth that afternoon in the drawing room,' Alistair said. 'I know you were. I saw it on your face.'

'Yes, because even though it would have damaged our family's name, I truly wanted the pretence to be over,' Victoria said. 'I wanted to stop lying to everyone. I knew it would be difficult, but I thought it was the right thing to do.'

'Obviously, your brother did not,' Alistair said narrowly.

'No. Like my uncle, he believed it best to perpetuate the myth,' Victoria said. 'So he concocted, in that moment, the perfect solution to the problem. He became Valentine Lawe. He knew there would be no shame in *his* claiming to be a playwright and, by doing so, he would clear all of our names. But he did so without our knowledge or agreement. You must have seen how shocked my father and I were. We never expected Laurence to step forwards and make such an outlandish claim.'

'Because your brother is not the actor,' Alistair said.

'No. At least, we never *thought* he was. I admit we've all been caught a bit off guard by how well he's taken to the role,' Victoria said. 'But he did what he did out of love, Mr Devlin. Not for his own benefit.'

'Yet you cannot deny that his life has changed drastically as a result of what he said,' Alistair pointed out. 'He is now the famous playwright. I doubt he can walk down the street without people coming up to him and telling him how much they enjoy his plays. Lovely young ladies vie for his favours and literary pundits hang on his every word.'

'I do not look for anyone's praise, Mr Devlin,' Laurence said. His voice was quiet, but Victoria heard an undertone of anger creeping in. 'It is Victoria to whom the accolades should be going and she is denied that by virtue of her silence. That is why I pass along every comment I receive. I want her to know what people are saying about her work and how much they enjoy her plays. I don't flatter myself that I possess even a fraction of her talent. And I regret that all this has led to there likely being no more Valentine Lawe plays in the future.'

'No more plays?' The remark clearly took Alistair by surprise. 'Why should there not be any more?'

'I leave that for her to explain,' Laurence said, heading for the door. 'I think I've said enough for one evening.'

'Yes, I rather think you have,' Alistair said without smiling.

The remark was made with such condescension that Victoria actually cringed. Dear Lord, if she'd ever needed proof that his opinion of her was no better, she had just been given it. Even Laurence looked a little crestfallen as he went out and closed the door behind him.

Victoria kept her gaze fixed on the fireplace.

Better that than be forced to look at Alistair and see again the disillusionment in his eyes. 'Please say what you must and then leave, Mr Devlin,' she said in a voice so low the words were almost inaudible. 'I regret that you were brought here under false pretences, but if nothing else, at least now you know the truth about Valentine Lawe.'

'Are you so sure there *is* nothing else, Miss Bretton?'

'Your tone makes it abundantly clear there is not.' Victoria felt tears burn in her eyes. 'I can see how angry you are. I cannot imagine what you think of me.'

'What I think…' he said, walking towards her, 'is that you are impulsive, outspoken, rash and guilty of flouting convention at every turn. It is your passion for writing that has brought you to this point and no doubt your passion for writing that will continue to plague you. However…'

Victoria slowly looked up. 'However?'

'I also find you generous, intelligent, loyal and courageous…to say nothing of talented in the extreme and beautiful beyond all. And I know,' he added gently, 'that for someone as honest as you to go through what you have would be enough to give anyone nightmares. It certainly would me.'

'Then...you understand what I have been trying to say?'

'I do more than understand it. I have *lived* it. Why do you think I've been so secretive about my involvement with the orphanage?'

Victoria frowned. 'Because you did not wish to be praised for your work?'

'I would not have been praised,' Alistair said. 'Apart from Isabelle, very few others would have approved of what I was doing. My parents certainly would not.'

'But you told me they supported your charitable efforts.'

'They support the idea of my providing for those less fortunate, but strictly from a distance. They would never have approved of my being so closely involved with the people I wish to help,' Alistair said. 'They would be horrified to know that I spent time with street urchins and those whom society would just as soon turn their backs on as lift a finger to help. Especially if they knew it was inspired by what happened to Helena.'

'But surely that makes the cause even more noble,' Victoria whispered. 'You are so very worthy of admiration.'

'As are you. You have a gift, Miss Bretton. A gift for writing plays that entertain thousands of people. If you were a man, you would be celebrated for your talent, as your brother is being celebrated now. You must not think any the less of yourself for having done what you did.'

'But you were angry with me when I told you the truth.'

'Yes, because in my arrogance I saw only that you had not been completely honest with me,' Alistair admitted. 'And having believed you to be everything I admired in a woman, it shook me. But one of the other things I've come to admire about you is your passion for something beyond fashion and society. You have an imagination— something very few women possess. And you were going along very nicely, writing your plays and seeing them performed, until I came on the scene and inadvertently forced things out into the open. You didn't have to tell anyone the truth because no one really *needed* to know. And you had made your mother a promise that you would not.'

'That doesn't take away from the fact that she would have preferred I *not* do it,' Victoria acknowledged ruefully.

'No, but an inclination like that cannot be denied. What was it your brother said? That the ideas spring like water from a well and cannot be stopped by wish or inclination? I'm sure he must have heard that from you. And believe it or not, I *do* understand impulses like that,' Alistair said. 'A doctor can no more turn away from his desire to heal the sick than an explorer can resist going off to discover new worlds. God knows, there are few of us talented enough to follow our dreams, let alone who have the drive and dedication necessary to see it through. You *have* that talent and the courage to make it happen. Your success as Valentine Lawe is more than adequate proof of that.'

'But it has cost me…so much,' Victoria said, for while she heard his words of praise, she heard nothing of affection. 'I saw how angry you were when you found out my brother had tricked you into coming here. And though it is pointless to wish things different, I would if it meant I could change your opinion of me.'

'My darling girl, my opinion of you doesn't need to change. I love you!'

Victoria gasped. 'You *do*?'

'Of course. That's what I wanted to tell you the night of Lady Morgan's soirée. It's the reason I came here tonight.'

'But…I thought you came because of Laurence's letter.'

'I let you think that's why I came, but I had planned on coming here before the letter arrived. I had no intention of letting you leave London without telling you how much I loved you. *That's* why I was so angry when I found out your brother had sent the letter. I thought *you* had sent it,' he told her. 'I thought it meant you were as anxious to clear up this misunderstanding as I was. So when I learned you hadn't written the letter, I realised nothing had changed, that your feelings for me were no different. And I saw all my hopes for the future turn into dust. That's why I was so disappointed. I thought I'd lost you for ever.' He took a step closer and reached for her hands. 'Surely you must have suspected how I felt about you?'

'I didn't,' Victoria whispered. 'I'd hoped… desperately hoped that you cared for me, but everything was so twisted up in lies—'

'I know, and that's why I came,' he murmured, pressing a kiss to her temple. 'And it's why I'm not leaving here until you tell me you love me and say that you will be my wife.'

Victoria closed her eyes as his arms slipped around her and drew her close. 'I love you, Alistair. And there is nothing I want more than to be your wife. But…what are we going to do about Valentine Lawe?'

'Must we do something about him?'

'We cannot allow Laurence to continue in this charade.'

'Why not?' Alistair nuzzled the unexpectedly sensitive area just beneath her left earlobe. 'He seems to be enjoying it.'

'But he has never even written a play,' Victoria murmured, determined to settle the issue before his kisses rendered her totally insensible. 'What will people say when he doesn't produce any more?'

'And I ask again, why should there not be any more plays?' Alistair reluctantly raised his head. 'You're not really going to stop writing, are you?'

'Well, yes, I thought that's what you would want. Especially if I am to be your wife.'

'Do you expect me to give up my involvement with the orphanage?'

'Of course not, but it is hardly the same thing.'

'It is to me. I don't want you to give up any part of yourself, darling,' Alistair whispered, pressing his lips against the softness of her hair. 'Unless you *wish* to stop writing. But you said yourself, you have been writing for a long time and you love what you do.'

'Yes, and at one time I thought it was all that mattered. But then I fell in love and realised I had to make a choice, so I chose to be with you.'

'And your brother chose to be Valentine Lawe, so why should we change anything else?' Alistair said. 'Laurence's stepping into the role is the perfect solution for all of us. It allows him to enjoy a standing in society he never had before and allows you to write your plays and have someone else act as your public face.'

'Then...you would be willing to see this continue?' Victoria asked. 'Even though by letting society believe Laurence is Valentine Lawe, we are perpetuating the deceit.'

'My darling girl, anything that allows us to be together is acceptable as far as I'm concerned,' he said. 'I want you to be happy as my wife.'

'I will be, as long as you love me.'

'You need have no fear on that account. But perhaps one day when you are old and grey and in need of a diversion you will publish your memoirs and tell everyone that you were, indeed, the famous playwright Valentine Lawe and that I was a party to the fraud.'

'I couldn't!'

'Of course you could. It does an old lady good to have a hint of scandal in her life. Just think how they will seek you out for all the wicked details.'

She started to laugh and, resting her forehead against his, said, 'Oh, Alistair. You have no idea how happy you've made me.'

'On the contrary, I'm the one who's been made happy and you're the one who's done it. You risked a great deal by telling me the truth, love. You put me in a position of being able to expose you and your family for everything you've done. If that's not proof of your love and integrity, I don't know what is.'

Victoria's mouth twisted. 'I'd like to say my

confession was motivated by the most noble of motives, but the truth is, I wasn't able to sleep for worrying about this.'

'And that, dear girl, is all I need to hear. If you hadn't suffered a moment's guilt, it would have meant your conscience was clear and that you could live with the lie.'

'I'm not sure I know what to say,' she said.

Alistair smiled and, trailing a finger down her throat in a manner that made her shiver, said, 'How do you think Valentine Lawe would bring this scene to a close?'

'I know how he would *like* to bring it to a close,' Victoria said with a low, throaty laugh. 'But I doubt it would survive the censor's pen.'

'Then I suggest we act it out. And I expect you to be very convincing in your part.'

'Darling man, when it comes to loving you,' Victoria said, drawing his head down to hers, 'I find there is absolutely no need for me to act at all!'

* * * * *

Author's Note

The Licensing Act of 1737 introduced the heavy hand of censorship to the British theatre. It was initiated by Robert Walpole, one of the period's most influential and powerful men, and its main purpose was to prevent satirists of the day from lampooning politicians—Walpole in particular—and from presenting anything felt to be subversive or distasteful to the British public. As such, it required that a Lord Chamberlain and his 'Examiners of Plays' approve every play prior to its first public performance. Any content deemed to be insulting, derogatory, inflammatory or controversial was removed.

The Act also restricted the production of serious dramatic works to Drury Lane and Covent Garden, two theatres already in possession of royal sanctions. Theatres that did not hold this distinction—like the fictitious Gryphon—resorted to producing melodramas, ballad operas and burlesques, which relied heavily on musical interludes, facial gestures and body movements, and either eliminated or restricted the use of spoken dialogue altogether.

The scope of the Licensing Act caused a resurgence in the works of William Shakespeare, given that plays written before 1737 were not subject to censorship and could be performed without permission from authority, but it also fostered a deep distrust of government officials by both playwrights and the public alike. As a result, many successful playwrights turned their hand to writing novels, which were not affected by the same strict rules. Surprisingly, the Act remained in effect until 1968, when it came up against mounting pressure from influential anti-censorship groups.

I have taken a certain amount of artistic licence with regard to the content of Victoria Bretton's plays. I tend to think her remarks about members of society and the clergy would probably have been 'red lined' by the Examiners, but for the sake of the story, I wanted there to be some 'controversial elements' in her work. And while it is true that a number of women were successful in writing plays in and around the Regency, it was still not a recommended occupation for young ladies. Oh, how far we've come!

So you think you can write?

It's your turn!

Mills & Boon® and Harlequin® have joined forces in a global search for new authors and now it's time for YOU to vote on the best stories.

It is our biggest contest ever—the prize is to be published by the world's leader in romance fiction.

And the most important judge of what makes a great new story?

YOU—our reader.

Read first chapters and story synopses for all our entries at
www.soyouthinkyoucanwrite.com

**Vote now at
www.soyouthinkyoucanwrite.com!**

HARLEQUIN®
entertain, enrich, inspire™

MILLS & BOON

SYTYCW

A sneaky peek at next month...

HISTORICAL

IGNITE YOUR IMAGINATION, STEP INTO THE PAST...

My wish list for next month's titles...

In stores from 2nd November 2012:

❏ How to Sin Successfully – Bronwyn Scott

❏ Hattie Wilkinson Meets Her Match – Michelle Styles

❏ The Captain's Kidnapped Beauty – Mary Nichols

❏ The Admiral's Penniless Bride – Carla Kelly

❏ Return of the Border Warrior – Blythe Gifford

❏ Unclaimed Bride – Lauri Robinson

Available at WHSmith, Tesco, Asda, Eason, Amazon and Apple

Just can't wait?